BLOOD ON THE MOON

JIM TULLY

BLOOD ON THE MOON

BY JIM TULLY

INTRODUCTION BY
PAUL J. BAUER & MARK DAWIDZIAK

COMMONWEALTH BOOK COMPANY
ST. MARTIN, OHIO

THESE

WIND-WHIPT SHAMROCKS

TO PLACE UPON THE GRAVES

OF OLD HUGHIE TULLY

PEDDLER OF

LACES AND LINENS

IN THE SOUTH

BEFORE THE CIVIL WAR

WHO WALKS AGAIN

THE ROADS OF EARTH

IN MY IMAGINATION

AND

THE BEAUTIFUL

N. D.

WHO HAD THE FAITH OF A WOMAN

AND THE COURAGE OF A SNOB

"*In most books, the I, or first person, is omitted: in this it will be retained; that, in respect to egotism, is the main difference. We commonly do not remember that it is, after all, the first person that is speaking. I should not talk so much about myself if there were anybody else whom I knew so well. . . .*

Moreover, I, on my side, require of every writer, first or last, a simple and sincere account of his own life, and not merely what he has heard of other men's lives; some such account as he would send his kindred from a distant land; for if he has lived sincerely, it must have been in a different land to me."

—THOREAU

CONTENTS

BOOK TWO

INTRODUCTION

Paul J. Bauer and Mark Dawidziak

Jim Tully (June 3, 1886–June 22, 1947) was an American writer who won critical acclaim and commercial success in the 1920s and '30s. His rags-to-riches career may qualify him as the greatest long shot in American literature. Born near St. Marys, Ohio, to an Irish immigrant ditch-digger and his wife, Tully enjoyed a relatively happy but impoverished childhood until the death of his mother in 1892. When the Tully family could no longer care for Jim after the death of Bridget Tully, he was sent to St. Joseph's Orphanage in Cincinnati for six years. The nuns taught him to read and write but life at the orphanage left him overwhelmed with sadness and an abiding sense that he was truly alone in the world. After six years, although still a child, he became too old for the orphanage and was dismissed. He left with what little formal education he would receive. He also left with a sense of alienation that would haunt him for the rest of his life. He hopped a train and what further education he acquired came in the hobo camps, boxcars, railroad yards, and public libraries scattered across the country. Finally, weary of the road, he arrived in Kent, Ohio, where he worked as a chainmaker, professional boxer, and tree surgeon. He also began to write, mostly poetry, which was published in the area newspapers. If St. Marys, Ohio, set the stage for Jim Tully's youth, Kent, Ohio, is where he matured into a writer.

Tully moved to Hollywood in 1912, where he began writing in earnest. His literary career took two distinct paths. He became one of the first independent reporters to cover Hollywood. As a free-lancer, he was not constrained by the studios and wrote about Hollywood celebrities (including Charlie Chaplin, for whom he had worked) in ways that they did not always find agreeable. For these pieces, rather tame by current standards, he became known as the most-feared man in Hollywood—a title he relished. Less lucrative, but closer to his heart, were the dark novels he wrote about his life on the road and the American underclass. He also wrote an affectionate memoir of his childhood with his extended Irish family, as well as novels about prostitution, boxing, Hollywood, and a travel book. While some of the more graphic books ran afoul of the censors, they were also embraced by critics, including H. L. Mencken, George Jean Nathan, and Rupert Hughes. Tully, Hughes wrote, "has fathered the school of hard-boiled writing so zealously cultivated by Ernest Hemingway and lesser luminaries."

Blood on the Moon (1931) is Tully's fifth and final book in what he called his Underworld Edition—a series of autobiographical books focusing on different aspects of his childhood and youth. The first of these, *Beggars of Life* (1924), chronicles Tully's life on the road, criss-crossing the country as a road kid or young hobo. ("I was a road-kid," Tully notes in the foreword to *Blood on the Moon*, "and not in the strict sense of the word, a hobo. The latter is a migratory worker.") The second volume of the Underworld Edition, *Circus Parade*

(1927), is also set in Tully's road years but from a period when he worked for a traveling circus. Tully's collection of circus freaks and carnies burnished his growing reputation as a hard-boiled writer. *Shanty Irish* (1928) was a departure from the grittiness of his road books. Rather, *Shanty Irish*, although not without its dark passages, is largely an affectionate memoir of his childhood surrounded by his Irish immigrant family in rural western Ohio. The fourth book of the cycle, *Shadows of Men* (1930), recalls the grifters, yeggs, and criminals of his road years. *Blood on the Moon* is a look back at the events of his life that made him, indeed compelled him to become a writer. It is worth noting that Tully dedicated *Blood on the Moon* to the two people most responsible for setting him on the path to writing: his grandfather Hugh Tully, whose stories and tall tales told in a musical, lilting Irish accent captured Tully's childhood imagination, and Nellie Dingley ("N.D." in the dedication), a librarian in Kent, Ohio, who pushed and challenged Tully to write like his hero, Jack London.

There were of course others along Tully's path to writing. His father, also Jim Tully, was an itinerant ditch digger who passed the time between jobs reading novels. Jim's sister Virginia looked after Jim following the death of their mother, Bridget Tully, and kept the young boy supplied with magazines that both satisfied young Jim's innate curiosity about the world and instilled in him a love for the written word. Such encouragement from family and friends is necessary but not sufficient in the making of a great writer. There must be something deep inside, something gnawing, something begging for expression. Tully reckons with this bone-deep force in *Blood on the Moon*.

Aging out of the orphanage but still a child, Jim was sent to work on a farm run by a cruel overseer named Solomon Boroff. Tully recalls in *Blood on the Moon* that "Neither on Boroff's farm, nor in any other circumstance in which life was to place me, was I ever to be a complete part of my surroundings." This sense of alienation, of being a perpetual outsider, was to become a major theme in Tully's writing.

As for the book's title, Tully leaves the explanation to Old Hughie. "It was me that said to thim at yere birth, me bye, 'He's born at the time of blood on the moon. Go aisy in yere judgment of him. For it's blood on the moon that manes throuble, an' thim that are born whin the moon is rid niver have pace till thiy die—an' thin thiy go to hill.'" Old Hughie's prediction that his grandson would never have peace would prove eerily prophetic. And to his son, Jim's father, Hughie says of his grandson, "He's the one bird from our tray that may be worth a damn … There was blood on the moon, me son, the night he was born, blood on the moon; I saw it reflicted in the water of the Forty Acre Pond as I drove here to the birth. It run red all over the idge like the blood of a sthabbed to dith shape."

As the concluding book in the series, Tully looks back at subjects from the previous four Underworld books. There are hobo stories that would have fit well in *Beggars of Life*, there are Hughie Tully's stories that could have come from *Shanty Irish*, the Great Slavinsky would have been at home in *Circus Parade*, and there are grifters who could have plied their trade in *Shadows of Men*. There's also the brutal description of the 1906 World Lightweight title fight between Joe Gans and Battling Nelson. The fight went an incredible 42 rounds in 100 degree heat and Tully's description is as tough and vicious as anything that would later appear in Tully's classic boxing novel, *The Bruiser*. And in the chapter "Ladies in the Parlor," Tully describes the women who work in a brothel with sympathy but without romanticizing them. They are not hookers-with-a-heart-of-gold but women struggling to survive in a broken world. The women he describes are not made of cardboard but of flesh and blood. He would later write about their lives in his widely banned novel, *Ladies in the Parlor*. *Blood* is not just the story of where Tully has been but a map of where, as a writer, he will go.

For his part, Tully told one interviewer that *Blood on the Moon* is about "men who dangled from ropes who might have been publishers or writers had they had less nerve and more caution—of girls of the underworld as though they were club women without inhibitions." Tully had witnessed the cold hand of fate too many times in his life to dismiss it as a force in shaping the world. The line between an outsider and society was, in Tully's experience, drawn by fate. Fate might have resigned Tully to life in a small, Ohio town. Fate might have left him, like so many other hoboes, buried in an unmarked grave near a set of railroad tracks. Fate might have left him as just one more punch drunk ex-boxer. Fate might have left him swallowed up by factory life. Fate might have undermined his struggle, against all odds, to write. Jim Tully, however, was simply incapable of bending to fate. An integral part of that process for Tully was recognizing, with remarkable candor and clarity, how all of those forces and experiences had shaped him.

Tully is interested in telling the reader not just how he became a writer but why. In the foreword to *Blood on the Moon*, Tully writes, "I have written of the period of social adjustment, and of the people who, before and after, curdled their dreams with mine. With it, I bid farewell forever, I hope, to that life, the winds of which equally twisted and strengthened me for the sadder years ahead." If he doesn't give a voice to these grifters, prostitutes, hobos, and yeggs, then who? And, in doing so, he found his voice as a writer—a voice unlike any other America has produced. What was it in his remarkable life that compelled him to write? The answer is in the pages of *Blood on the Moon*.

"**B**LOOD ON THE MOON" IS the last of a series of five volumes which I began six years ago with the hope that they would be grouped through the coming years and known as the Underworld Edition.

The first book, "Beggars of Life," was given the misleading title of "A Hobo Autobiography" by the publishers. It was intended as a compilation of dramatic episodes in the life of a youthful vagabond, which I was for seven years.

I was a road-kid, and not in the strict sense of the word, a hobo. The latter is a migratory worker.

The road-kid is more cunning and daring. With the yegg, of whom he is often an understudy, he is the most relentless and ruthless species of the roving vagabonds of America.

If not whipped too completely by early environment, a road-kid may later succeed in some calling, which, if not higher, at least has greater financial rewards.

Among pugilists, Jack Dempsey, Kid McCoy, and Stanley Ketchell were road-kids. Others develop as yeggs, and some as ministers of the Gospel. A few become writers — Jack London, Josiah Flynt, and myself.

The names of many road-kids may be found in the records of men who dangled through the traps of gallows.

In "Circus Parade" was described a series of none too happy and often ironical incidents with a circus. Chosen by the Literary Guild and banned in Boston, it aroused the ire of circus owners and their sycophants who stand with the ghost of their smug and benign dead leader, P. T. Barnum, in the front rank of American quacks and hypocrites.

After writing "Circus Parade," I was attacked by paid press agents and others interested in morals for money. One press agent succeeded in having an article accepted by an unsuspecting editor of a literary journal. About such matters I am as impersonal as doom. It is mentioned here as social phenomena.

In "Shanty Irish" was depicted the background of a road-kid who became articulate. Down the avenue of years my grandfather, who dominates the book, has been very real to me. I can still hear, on quiet nights, the whisky rattling down his bony throat. That he talked a great deal was natural, of course, being Irish. He was a sad old man with a broken dream in his head and a fear of death in his heart.

The fourth book of the series, "Shadows of Men," contains the tribulations, vagaries, and hallucinations of men in jail.

While I am immune to the ink-stained bullets of the moral Social Soldiers who carry Truth as a mask, I have thought it best to change names and situations in "Blood on the Moon" to keep them from shooting at those who are my friends.

And, it may be of no importance, the incidents in the book have all been lived. Life, and its pitiful objects, interest me more than literature. Every human is a continued story — whether his existence be narrow as a prison cell, or broad as Balzac's.

To those critics, however kind, who contend that I am a novelist trying to find myself, I will here answer for

the first and only time. If I have not been able to in-
vent a new medium in my picaresque books, I have at
least been strong enough not to conform to one that is
outworn.

I did not study the people in these books as an en-
tomologist does a bug on a pin. I was of them. I am
still of them. I can taste the bitterness of their lives in
the bread I eat today.

In "Blood on the Moon," I have written of the period
which led to social adjustment, and of the people who,
before and after, curdled their dreams with mine. With
it, I bid farewell forever, I hope, to that life, the winds
of which equally twisted and strengthened me for the
sadder years ahead.

BOOK ONE

LIMBO

A S ONE OF THE CHILDREN who put blueing in the vessel of Holy Water at the chapel door, I chanted Latin with serious face while nuns and orphans placed dots of blue on their foreheads. Sister Felicity, an old half-blind nun put her entire wrinkled hand in the water and smeared her nose blue.

The children were made to sit in silence until some one confessed. As the guilty one generally remained silent after such sins, we long before evolved a method of confessing by turns.

It was my turn to confess anyhow; so I took the blame for what the Sister Superior called a crime against God.

My fellow confessor was a German boy whose head was shaped like a pear.

The nuns felt that no woman had strength to inflict the proper punishment. We knew that it was much easier to be whipped by the priest than by the nuns. He was more tender hearted, less vicious.

It was decided that the priest should whip us.

Father Schmidt was a round-faced man, as German as my companion in crime.

We were sent to his study. It was full of books, the odor of cigar smoke, and crucifixes.

He drank a cup of hot water as we entered. Then he went to a small china vessel with a crucifix attached.

It contained his private Holy Water. He dipped his fingers in the water, looked at them closely as if to see that they were not blue, then crossed himself. As his hand touched his forehead, I saw his eyes smile through his half opened fingers.

We stood like convicted soldiers at attention. The priest dallied about the room in the manner of one who dreaded the work of executioner. His black gown fitted him tightly. His stomach projected round as a large watermelon. His cassock shone where he had rubbed his belly.

He seated himself in a red leather chair and lit a cigar, the pleasant aroma of which is still in my brain.

A puff of smoke curled over the room. He rubbed his double chin and asked,

"Are you boys sorry?"

"Yes, Father," we answered suddenly.

"Aren't you ashamed?" He looked at his cigar and crossed his legs.

Like a pistol shot, we answered, "Yes, Father."

"Will you ever do it again?"

Louder and quicker, "No, Father."

He rose, crossed to the window, took a strap which lay upon the sill and placed it across his knee after he had seated himself.

"What would you boys think if Jesus were in this room and asked you why you had tried to change the color of His Holy Water?"

"We wouldn't know what to think, Father." My German conspirator tried to say the words with me.

"And you are both really and truly sorry?"

"*Very* truly sorry, Father," we said together.

"Was it fair for dear Sister Felicity to get blueing in her eyes?" he asked.

"No, Father," we emphatically admitted.

He held the cigar between the two fingers of his left hand, and stroked the strap with his right. Taking a puff at the cigar he looked at the strap and said, "An open confession is good for the soul."

The German boy said quickly, "Yes, Father."

I kicked his ankle.

"I have decided," he puffed swiftly, rose again, walked up and down the room, then stood looking out of the window, the strap dangling behind him. His head was buried in a cloud of smoke. He turned, walked toward us, his red round face almost stern.

"I have decided," he went to the vessel of Holy Water and crossed himself again.

"I have decided not to punish you boys with a strap."

A volley of smoke went the wrong way. He coughed.

"I make it a rule when boys are deeply and truly sorry, not to be too severe." He put the kindest arm in the world around me.

I was his favorite.

My memory had enabled me to write his sermon the day after hearing it. The idea originated in the brain of Sister Mary Edward who wanted to learn whether or not the children paid attention while the priest talked.

Mistaking a natural gift for piety, Father Schmidt insisted that I was destined to become a priest like himself.

He presented me with an ivory rosary. There was a glass imbedded in the cross at the end into which one could look and see a priest serving Holy Communion.

I was very proud of the gift. It did not long remain in my possession. A more pious child stole it from me.

My guilt hurt him deeply. He said pityingly,

"And you, Jimmy, my altar boy. Together we have stood before His Divine Presence. You have seen me drink His precious blood. You learned to speak Latin in this room. How could you have done such a thing?"

"Father — I didn't know — I just thought they were blue marbles. I *didn't know*."

"Very well, very well," he held me to him.

"I am going to ask a promise of you," he said slowly. "You have betrayed our Savior unknowingly. But surely He understands. He was once a boy like you. He was such a boy, my dear children, that even animals loved Him. Once, when they were looking for Him everywhere and He had no place to go, He entered a cave and slept the night away. The soldiers came to the entrance of the cave and wondered if He might not be inside. In the night, a spider wove a big web across the entrance. 'No,' said the leader, 'if He were inside, this web would be broken.' And they went on their way and left the Child Jesus sleep in peace."

He puffed his cigar.

"And you boys desecrate His Holy Water."

He watched a ring of smoke.

"Now again — aren't you very sorry?"

"Yes, Father."

He studied a moment.

"You must go direct to the chapel and ask His forgiveness. Remain there one hour — on your knees. Say nothing about the whipping to Sister Superior. That will be held in abeyance."

We hurried to the chapel and knelt in the last pew.

*

One Sunday, for the first time in four years, I was called to the orphanage parlor. A visitor was announced.

I hurried, with beating heart, to the Sister Superior.

With brain in a furore, I was taken to the parlor door by that old lady, and pushed inside with the words, "Here he is."

Standing in the middle of the room was my grandfather. His sharp old eyes went up and down my body.

"Do ye know me, lad?" he asked.

"Yes — you're Granddad."

He led me to a varnished bench near a window.

"It's a divil of a time I had gittin' here. Yere sister give me the money. I thought the trip would niver ind. It's been near to fifty year since I traveled so far. It moost be a thousand miles."

It was less than one hundred and fifty.

He rubbed his beard while I told him of my life at the orphanage.

His heavy mouth twitched.

"It's so tired yere old Granddad is from the long long journey, I can't kape me face sthraight —"

"Why don't you take me away from here, Granddad?"

"Be patient, me bye, ye'll be lavin' soon. The praest in Saint Marys got a letter from here sayin' they may have to sind ye to the Reform School if no one took ye away — so I came these manys the miles to fix things up to git ye away.

"Before ye came in, the Sister Superior says to me, ye've been here so long, says she, thiy moost make room for ither orphans that're bein' born ivery minute. I'll talk to the payple at home and they'll come and git ye by nixt Sunday sure. For, after all, ye shouldn't be kipt in jail foriver because yere mother died."

"Granddad," I said, "I'll wait till next Sunday and if no one comes, I'll run away again."

The old man watched me closely. His head was bent to one side. His faded yellow celluloid collar was out of place.

"I'd take ye now," he said, "but I've nary enough money to git home on mesilf."

I watched him as he moved toward the door.

"I want to go too, Granddad."

The old man turned, his voice soft as plush.

"Me bye, don't make it hard for yere old Granddad. God knows I'd sind ye home an' stay here if they'd kape me, but I can't pass for a nun an' I'm too rough for a praest."

He stood, legs wide apart, muscles taut, as though ready to deliver a blow.

"But on this you kin depind, yere grandfather, Old Hughie Tully, will sind some one after ye nixt week, or come himself if he has to crawl."

I walked with him in the hallway.

"And now, me bye, a wake from to-day ye'll have yere fraydom."

His right hand trembled on my head.

The door opened. His shoulders filled it for a second. He was gone.

With tear blurred eyes, I leaned against the wall.

Faint steps were heard.

The Mother Superior asked, "What are you doing here?"

"Nothing," I answered, and hurried on.

*

A week before I had received Holy Communion and Confirmation — two sacraments in the Catholic church.

The body of Christ in the form of a wafer is represented by Communion.

When one receives Confirmation he is confirmed in the faith of Saint Peter, to whom, in my childhood I was told that Christ said, "Upon this rock I shall build my Church, and the gates of Hell shall not prevail against it."

The name of a patron saint of the Church is taken by the child who is confirmed. The saint is to stand as a rock upon which the child may lean through the years when the clouds of doubt hang low.

I long wavered between the names of Napoleon and Alexander the Great as Patron Saints.

I decided upon Alexander for fear that Archbishop Elder would discover that Napoleon had not been a saint.

When the Archbishop tapped me on the cheek and pronounced the name of Alexander in Latin, Father Schmidt looked at me with smiling eyes and passed, with his venerable superior, to the next boy.

Each Saturday we were marched to our bath. A wide zinc trough encircled the room. We stood knee deep in the water, holding with both hands the towel about the middle of our nude bodies.

At a given signal we would throw the towel from us and hurriedly sit in the water. The nuns, to avoid the unholy sight, would turn their heads.

For five years we stood at our meals. When it became known that we were to have seats at the table we carried the news joyously from one to another. "We're goin' to have seats, we're goin' to have seats, goody, goody, we're goin' to have seats," were the only words that could be heard.

We hurried, exultant, to the dining room where the Sister Superior stood with several men.

"Children," she said, "you must say many Hail Marys and Our Fathers for the good benefactors here who furnished the lovely benches upon which you are about to sit."

Bedbugs were a constant menace in the orphanage. Each Saturday a group of boys were detailed to catch them. The boy who caught a given number first was allowed to go and play.

Sister Benedictine, an aged nun, counted each boy's catch. She sat near a vessel, holding a rawhide whip in her hand. Her brass rimmed glasses perched perilously before her half blind eyes.

She was stooped nearly double. Her chin was thin

and pointed as her nose. She would lash her whip without warning. We called her "The Witch."

The beds were ancient as the tides. They were painted a dull red. The paint had never properly dried. We discovered that if a tiny portion of the paint were removed and properly shaped, it would pass for a bedbug in the eyes of Sister Benedictine.

One after another, at proper intervals, we would march toward the old nun, a piece of paint on the end of a pin, and exclaim, "Another bug, Sister." She would look at it to make sure it was not an eagle, and tell us to drop it in the vessel of water for captured bugs. We kept our secret. Our ability as bug catchers spread about the orphanage.

The bugs multiplied until one night a noise was heard. The old nun later told the Sister Superior that something attempted to carry her out the window. She thought it was a group of older bugs.

The secret was discovered and the mighty hunters were all put to bed for three days on a diet of bread and water.

The Sister Superior took Sister Benedictine off bug duty. She was so humiliated at the disgrace that she rapidly went into a decline.

She never forgave us.

The boys were kept on one side of the building, the girls on the other. We knew who the girls were by name but were never allowed to talk to them. An older boy was caught hugging one of the girls. He was sent to the

Reform School and held up to the rest of us as an example of sin.

Sister Mary Edward was the most intelligent nun in the orphanage. She was quick, wiry, and red-headed, her eyes narrow, alert, and brown.

Quick tempered and vindictive, she taught me for three years. Always near the head of my class, we were staunch friends in the school room. Her mind was lightning quick. Impatient of slow minds, she spent much time in whipping the more stolid among the children.

The grades in the institution were higher according to age than in other schools over the city. We had nine months of intensive schooling. Sister Mary Edward taught the highest grade. I went into her room at eight years of age, and alternated from the Sixth to the Ninth Reader and Algebra. Two other red-headed children remained with me in the same class all this time. With our red-headed teacher, we attracted the attention of Archbishop Elder, who told us, on his yearly visit to our room, that Jesus and Mary Magdalene had hair like ours. I did not realize at the time that it made no difference.

Archbishop Elder was the ruler of our immediate Catholic universe. He was very old and heavily wrinkled. He had a kind, beaming, and bright face like Pope Leo XIII.

He would be followed through the building by many priests and nuns. Christ was a living man to him. He walked with Him each day.

Across the decades I can hear the saintly old man's voice. I can see his stooped shoulders straighten at the mention of His name.

"He is your friend, children. He is here in this room with you. He weeps when you weep, and is glad when you are glad."

Outside the school room, Sister Mary Edward whipped me often.

One day as many of us worked in the dormitory, we discovered her in back of the high linen curtains of her bed, with a young baker who was studying to be a priest.

Immediately we spread the news of our discovery about the orphanage. We had seen nothing. But our gossip at last subdued the ruthless woman.

She did not punish me again.

Each morning of the year we rose at five. To awaken us the nuns used two pieces of thick lumber hinged together, and hollow in the center.

The nuns' shoes were of soft leather. Their steps could not be heard a few feet away.

Many of them were aged wisps of women. Yellow skin on bones, they were hideous in their black habits and black dresses. The brass form of Christ on a black crucifix dangled from the end of a rosary at their right knee. Each time they took a step, the crucifix with its brass figure went forward.

Sister Superior Alfonso once lost Christ from her cross. I found Him on the dormitory floor. His face was downward. There were little holes in His hands where the nails had worked loose. I traded Him to another boy for two agate marbles. He returned Him to Sister Alfonso who promised the boy that she would pray for him the coming Sunday.

Purgatory and Limbo were places which haunted my imagination.

Limbo was a vast ditch into which went the souls of Protestants and babies who had the bad luck to die without baptism.

Thousands of hearses rumbled over the country roads with the souls of Protestants. They would stop at Limbo.

The drivers of the hearses were priests, without cassocks. Their suits were black and trim. Their faces, hard set, were sharper than knives. They would dump the souls in the ditch. They rattled, in falling, like pans.

Owls flew far down in the ditch. The souls wriggled below under the great lights of their eyes.

Day and night they peered unceasingly among the souls of the Protestants.

Many hundred of years before it had been discovered that a Catholic soul had been placed in the ditch by mistake. God sent the owls to carry it to purgatory where it remained until the slime of Limbo was burned away.

A moon, miles wide, hung above the center of the ditch. It swung back and forth like the pendulum of the old clock in my mother's kitchen. Trees, high and wide, grew upon the moon. Around them were gathered Protestant preachers who chopped at them forever and ever. As soon as the trees started to fall, the preachers would run. As they looked upward, the trees bounced back into position again and all the chips which they had been cutting for hundreds of years were once again in their places.

The preachers began chopping again, while the lights from the eyes of the owls made the axes gleam.

Then the screeches of owls mingled with the laughter of wriggling souls.

At the far end of Limbo was a little church. An owl was stationed in a tree, eternally gazing at its golden cross. The light from its powerful eyes made it visible for a million miles.

The owl was the soul of Martin Luther, condemned forever to gaze at the cross of the True Church which he had denied. He sat on a weathered branch through the aeons of eternity. His feathers were torn from centuries of flaming storms.

Myriads of other birds of many shapes and colors flew below Martin Luther's soul. They eternally tried to sing, but were only able to croak like crows at the owl above them.

Other birds, carrying morsels of food in their beaks, flew within a few feet of the owl who, starving always, could not leave his branch.

Each evening, at dusk, a storm lashed over the ditch. Drops of flame dashed against the naked writhing souls of the Protestants and made them explode like bladders touched with red hot nails.

Flashes of fire, larger than eggs, and falling swifter than light would follow across the chasm.

The storm beaten wings of Martin Luther would burn to a crisp.

His eyes would dilate. He would whirl on his branch and shriek like an eagle. His wings would grow large and become singed with fire. Wrinkling his face in pain he would turn his eyes to the Cross.

THE COW THAT MILKED BLOOD

IT WAS A DULL AND DEAD
December day. A bitter wind whirled the heavily falling snow. Dismal as the day, I trudged toward my new
home.

My thinly clad body ached with the cold. Six months
before I had left the orphanage. Two weeks was the
longest I had remained under one roof during that time.

At last, an insane farmer named Boroff told my father
that he would give me a home and a horse and buggy
if I remained with him until I was twenty-one. With a
cigar box under my arm which contained poems torn
from newspapers, I neared his home.

My heart was heavy.

Boroff came into the house. His faded overalls hung

over his felt boots. A yellow yarn cap, pulled over his head, made it look like a huge egg. With deep set insane eyes, a body large and tall, and a mouth, the corners of which nearly touched his ears, he stood near the kitchen stove, while the snow melted on his shoulders.

His wife, short and hatchet-faced, with black hair sparse on a square head, and broad flat breast, followed him.

Their daughter, Ivy, replica of her mother, after opening the door, went, without a word, upstairs.

"Come on," Boroff said.

He showed me how to water and feed the animals. When we came to the wood, half buried in snow, he snapped instructions where to place it in an outhouse.

A cracked dinner bell rang.

We sat at a table of boiled beans, fat pork, biscuits, and coffee.

Ivy, hollow cheeked, consumptive, beautiful in a dying way, sat next to me. Neither the farmer nor his wife could read or write. They were first cousins. Mrs. Boroff was one of fourteen children, mostly dead of consumption. Her husband had sixteen living brothers and sisters, all more or less insane. Only the youngest could read and write.

The owner of my new home was a liar, a cheat, and a near murderer. He had once cut a gash in a neighbor's head with a large corn-knife.

My life with him was a long agony.

I shocked wheat barefooted. The stubble tore my feet and ankles.

My father was in the same county during the eighteen months I stayed at Boroff's. I saw him once.

He came one winter night to discuss with Boroff the question of buying me underwear for the second winter.

Financing a vast corporation was never given more consideration by two men.

As my father rose to go, he held a bowl pipe in his hand. In the fifties, an awkward man, and near-sighted, he stepped on the cat.

It meowed as my sire jumped. His shoulder hit the gilt-framed chromo of one of Boroff's mad ancestors.

"The cat's talkin' Irish," my father said, lighting his pipe.

As he reached the door, "You get the clothes, Sol, and I'll send you the money."

Boroff said, "All right."

I went to bed happy. The wind threw sleet against the attic window while I dreamed of warm clothes the next day.

My father did not send the money. Boroff did not buy the clothes.

I half froze, again, through that winter.

In desperation I stole a suit of Ivy's underwear. In trying to make them fit my more muscular legs, I ripped them open at the seams. I wrapped strings about them. The strings broke.

I wrapped newspapers about them. They rattled as I walked.

At last spring came.

The Boroff cat brought an unwelcome brood to the farm. We did not discover them until they frisked about.

Boroff put them in a sack and sent me to drown them in Blue Creek.

I started away with the kittens. When I reached the bank of the stream, I lost heart for their murder. I turned them loose and threw the sack in the water.

When I returned, Boroff asked, "Did you drown them cats?"

"Yes, sir," I replied, as we began to saw wood in a corner of the barnyard.

Soon the six kittens trailed back.

Boroff stared.

"I thought you drowned them cats," he yelled.

"I did," I lied, "I put them in the water. They clawed their way out of the sack."

Ivy pleaded for their lives as Boroff chased them with an ax.

They remained on the farm.

More than anything else at Boroff's, I hated to husk corn. From early morning until late at night, I would take the corn stalks from the shocks, place them on the ground, and peel the husks from the corn. A weak sun would melt the frozen mud between the rows of stubble as I worked.

It was lonely work. Boroff would talk constantly to every one else — to me, never.

Each fall and spring, the wild geese flew over the farm. They formed a wedge. If one fell back from the lead another took its place. High up and silent as air, they flew swiftly.

I never grew tired of watching them, going North or South according to the season.

One late March day, I counted eleven flying low toward Kentucky. Like specters, they slid through the slate gray weather.

Bright and warm the sun shone the next day. An immense silver and blue cloud, torn at the edges, dropped so low it seemed to hang by hooks from the sky. It suddenly scurried across the sun and trailed a shadow behind it larger than Boroff's farm.

It scattered in white specks in the blue immensity. Buzzards spiraled in circles miles wide and made me forget the routine of the farm.

At times I rebelled until my head ached.

A loneliness took possession of me. I discarded at once the faith in which my mother died. I had been the youngest child ever to receive Communion at the institution. During three months of rigid instruction in Catechism and Bible History I had not failed to answer a question asked by priest or nun so much as the changing of a word.

Neither on Boroff's farm, nor in any other circumstance in which life was to place me, was I ever to be a complete part of my surroundings.

One October day while Boroff and his family were in Ohio City I went with Dan Borland to hear William McKinley speak at Van Wert.

He was the President of the United States.

Borland was a soldier in the Civil War. So was McKinley.

The soldiers were allowed to stand close to the great man.

His presence dwarfed me. His face, broad as a huge eagle's, haunted me for weeks. His well dressed and well shaped body fascinated me.

When he had finished speaking, the ex-soldiers marched in single file to shake hands with him. I followed Mr. Borland.

McKinley's hand was soft and warm. He looked at me kindly.

I have often wondered what, if anything, was in his mind at that moment. He had been a boy on an Ohio farm. But he did not seem to me like one who had ever husked corn.

I rode home with Dan Borland. We were silent nearly all the way.

I wondered how McKinley got away from the farm.

That night I stayed at Dan Borland's house.

Dogs barked and owls hooted. Still thinking of William McKinley, I fell asleep.

Borland lived a half mile from Boroff where the road

took a sharp turn into another township. The lower part of his house was made of logs, the upper of rough pine boards.

He had taught a country school after the Civil War. He was not a successful farmer. Though he had been settled on his eighty acres for more than thirty years, there was a heavy mortgage upon it. Books and magazines were scattered about his house. Each night in summer or winter he read a long time before going to bed. He took more interest in the affairs of the nation than he did in his own farm.

His goatee, once red, was now yellow. His upper lip was bare, his hair plentiful. His nose was so broad he could only make his spectacles fit on the end of it. He had a large map of the United States in his attic. On rainy days he would trace the course of rivers in the South.

Sam Brooks, a Negro farmer, lived a mile beyond. He, too, had been in the Civil War.

A Northern soldier, Borland admired Robert E. Lee.

One night he explained to the Negro why Lee was a greater general than Grant.

When he had finished the Negro said, "But Mistah Grant won."

Said Borland, "A man can lose and still be great."

It was a drizzling November night. Boroff and his brood were at a revival meeting. The mud was deep in the road. Borland pulled his goatee and glanced at the black night through the window.

Stella, his step-daughter entered. A gust of wind followed her, and made the flame dance in the lamp.

Borland did not attend church. Neither did he worship the God of the ignorant countryside. He lived among his neighbors, peaceful and respected. He never became angry.

Borland's second wife was many years younger. Stella was said to have been born without a legal father.

Borland enjoyed the girl's company and helped her during the long winter nights with her lessons. Clarke Good, her teacher, once gave her the task of writing a composition on Gray's Elegy.

With Stella, I talked it all over with Borland.

He read the poem aloud and explained its beauty to us. With his spectacles on the end of his nose and Mc-Guffey's Fifth Reader spread on his overalled knee, his voice droned the words —

> *"The curfew tolls the knell of parting day,*
> *The lowing herd wind slowly o'er the lea,*
> *The plowman homeward plods his weary way,*
> *And leaves the world to darkness and to me.*

*

> *"Now fades the glimmering landscape on the sight,*
> *And all the air a solemn stillness holds,*
> *Save where the beetle wheels his droning flight,*
> *And drowsy tinklings lull the distant folds."*

*

His voice went lower as he read:

"For them no more the blazing hearth shall burn,
Or busy housewife ply her evening care;
No children run to lisp their sire's return,
Or climb his knees the envied kiss to share."

Late that night I labored over the composition with Borland, while Stella huddled, asleep, in a carpet chair.

The teacher praised the composition, while we kept the secret with Stella.

Borland's farm was a forest when he settled there. The first year he only cleared an acre. After three decades twenty-five acres was still in woods. Blue Creek ran through his forest. Ferns, higher than a man's head, grew along its banks.

A lane, down which the cows and horses strolled, led from the barnyard to the woods.

On Saturday night the horses were turned loose to wander in the woods or remain in their stalls.

Borland would allow no horse that worked through the week to be driven on Sunday.

He loved trees and allowed forest specimens to stand in his cornfields. The shade which they cast ruined the corn for a hundred yards around. Rabbits and squirrels were a menace to his fields. He allowed no hunting on his farm.

He once said as we watched the sun die behind his woods, "Well, that is all arranged for us."

I think of his words when I see the sun go down.

*

Boroff attended every denomination of Protestant church for miles around.

Though converted each winter at revival meetings for many years, no change was ever made in his tiger heart. He was one of those men, numerous in the world, who took the Bible seriously.

As he could not read, I often went through whole chapters for him.

He would clap his hands at the wailings of Jeremiah and sniffle at the plight of Job.

One song had the words —

> *"There is room enough, room enough,—*
> *Room enough in Heaven for us all —*
> *Oh, don't stay away —"*

Boroff had been told by a young farmer that the song had been written by a man in Van Wert, in honor of himself, Sol Boroff.

His eyes would become narrower still as he screeched —

> *"Room enough, room enough, room*
> *Enough in Heaven for Sol —*
> *Oh, don't stay away."*

Riding along the country roads, the young people of the farms would often sing parodies of popular hymns. On cold nights the bob-sleds would glide over the snow-covered grounds, while voices cut the crisp air with —

> *"Oh, Beaulah land, oh, Beaulah land,*
> *'Tis on the highest mount I stand,*
> *And when I come to view my corn*
> *I think I'll never sell my farm.*
>
> *Jesus, my awl to heaven has gone*
> *Here is the stump I laid it on —*
> *Oh, Beaulah land, oh, Beaulah land,*
> *And when I come to pet my mules*
> *I think that city folks are fools —"*

A sacred song, common over the country-side still goes through my brain.

> *"At the cross, at the cross,*
> *Where I first saw the light,*
> *And the burden of my heart rolled away,*
> *It was there by faith,*
> *I received my sight.*
> *And now I am happy all the day.*
>
> *Alas and did my Savior bleed,*
> *And did my Savior die —*
> *Why did He give that sacred life*
> *For such a worm as I?"*

Sam Brooks, the Negro farmer, had no religion. Upon all occasions he wore a newly washed pair of faded overalls. His body was black, round and quick of movement. Like Dan Borland, he wore a goatee. Si Long, a cross-eyed white man, lived with Sam Brooks.

His house, made of hickory logs, was in the center of a hickory grove. Eliza, his wife, was so fat, she moved slowly. Her tongue was never still during the day.

She agreed with all that she heard, saying, "Yes suh, yes suh," to everything.

Si Long was treated with good natured raillery by all.

He proved all things by the Bible, a copy of which he carried with him to funerals, picnics and threshings. His hair, unruly, stood straight up. Excitable in a religious argument, the farmers teased him without mercy.

Sam Brooks and Eliza were welcome everywhere. With his habit of continual laughter and Eliza's way of saying "Yes suh, yes suh," they broke down the social barriers which would have been raised against other colored people.

All of Sam's furniture was made of hickory wood.

Pictures of the presidents from Lincoln to McKinley were tacked to his walls. A picture of Frederick Douglas had been torn across the f .ce. Sam had patched it with a piece cut from the Van Wert *Republican* and the black face of the Civil War Negro made it look half white in the sunlight.

In rain or shine, Sam sang snatches of song —

> *"My fatheh was a fahmeh man —*
> *Washed his face in a fryin' pan,*
> *Combed his haith wit' a wagon wheel —*
> *And died wit' a febah in his heel."*

> *"Oh de robin sat on a swingin' limb,*
> *He winks at me and I winks at him —*
> *So I picks up a rock an' throw at his chin,*
> *An' he yells, 'Niggeh, don't yo do dat agin.'"*

"My masteh had a great big house.
Eighty stories high,
An' ebery room in dat dere house
Was filled wit' chicken pie."

Sam had the fear that he would die of heart trouble. He wore a brass ring on his smallest finger to ward it off.

Eliza wore a rabbit's foot around her neck. She believed it would draw the poison out of Sam's heart each night and be carried away by other rabbits.

I was never tired of watching the birds in the air.

The hens would cackle and the roosters crow when a chicken hawk was barely in sight.

Allie Boroff raised dozens of chickens each spring. When the hens took their broods over the farm, the hawk, according to Allie, would make a noise like a small chicken lost and in distress. The mother hen would leave its brood and search for it, clucking wildly.

The hawk would then swoop down and carry a chick away in its claws.

Boroff rented eighty acres of land "on shares."

Hardly strong enough to guide the plow, I would follow it all day. The horses knew their way about the field so well that I seldom had to drive them. From dawn to dusk I would turn the packed earth into new furrows. I would then break the ground into small particles with a harrow, and later make it smooth as a paved road with a roller which was shaped like an immense round tree with a seat fastened upon it. I would then mark the ground for corn by driving across the field with four heavy pieces of timber fastened a few feet apart. These made the corn rows. After each day's marking, the corn was planted. The next day I marked again. Otherwise the rain might wash the marks away.

A few grains of corn at a time were dropped into the ground.

In a short time thousands of tiny green spots could be seen across the fields. I was soon busy hoeing the weeds from the corn.

Allie Boroff had a turkey hen that was nesting. She could not find the spot where it was depositing the eggs. Morning after morning, she followed the turkey which always eluded her.

Early one Sunday she rose, and, dressed in a new red calico dress which a relative had sent her from Ohio City, went in search of the nest. On her way to the Blue Creek, she crossed a meadow owned by a farmer named Lytle. This would have been of no importance on this bright morning except that — unknown to Allie — in this meadow was a bull.

He beheld Allie trudging along in search of her turkey. He snorted and Allie ran. She reached a barbed wire fence but a few feet ahead of the animal. In her haste to allow the bull to have full possession of the meadow, she left large pieces of her new red dress on the fence.

The bull charged at the red pieces of calico and got its neck caught between two barbed wires.

In its effort to get away, it tore the fence posts from the ground and died with its throat cut.

As no one knew that Allie owned a red dress, Farmer Lytle never learned how his bull happened to die.

A staunch Methodist, he spread the story about the township that the Catholics in Van Wert had tied red rags to the fence to tease the bull.

The revival meetings were held late one spring at the Asbury Grove Methodist Church.

Boroff was now a member of the United Brethren Church five miles away. It was so warm that the windows of the church were open. When the visiting members of other churches arose to testify to the goodness of God, among the last was Boroff.

He talked for a long time near a window which looked out upon a grove, and gave the history of his many conversions. "This time I'm saved for life, no more evil, no more sin. I'm washed, sweet smellin', and clean in the eyes of God."

From outside came the noise of a pole cat. Boroff's clothes became damp. A dreadful odor filled the church. The windows were hastily put down. The odor remained.

Church was dismissed.

Outside a voice yelled,

"You may be sweet smellin' in the eyes of God, Sol, but you can't fool that pole cat."

Allie and Ivy rode home with Mr. Lytle. I disappeared until morning.

After the last yearly conversion of her father, Ivy went to the Mourners' Bench.

In front of the pulpit, it was about a foot high. Sinners knelt before it night after night until they worked themselves into a spasm which they thought was religion.

Irreverent rustics often bet money on how long it would require certain of their neighbors to receive the Light.

Ivy, her thin shoulders drooped over the bench, remained in the same position night after night for more than a week.

Boroff, the preacher, and a dozen others, exhortea, shouted, demanded that God come to Ivy.

The girl remained immovable.

I was not allowed to talk to her during her period of search for spiritual guidance.

Boroff walked about the farm with a strained expression on his mad face. Allie prayed for hours in the kitchen with Ivy.

On Sunday afternoon the preacher called a spiritual meeting.

The sun shone over the desolate country and melted the snow on the green roof of the white painted pine church.

Many children besides Ivy were at the Mourners' Bench. An added effort was to be made to save them.

All but Ivy went down the aisle to the Mourners' Bench with the smiling faces of those who like to attract attention.

Ivy was stern; her mouth drawn. Her eyes stared, vacant.

The other children were converted early. They shouted and laughed, then gathered about Ivy.

As the lighted lamps were lit in the church, she jumped to her feet, sobbing hysterically. Clapping her hands, she shrieked,

"I'm washed in the blood — in the blood of the Lamb."

All in the church took up her words —

> *"In the bloo — ud — in the bloo — ud —*
> *In the precious bloo — ud of the Lamb."*

Soon there was silence.

Ivy had fainted.

She was in bed for weeks.

*

Ivy had once been guilty of sin with me. Her mother sent us to Mrs. Bill Carey's for four dozen thoroughbred Rhode Island Red eggs to place under her hens.

We broke the eggs on the way home and replaced them with those belonging to Mrs. Boroff.

She put them under her hens. The chickens were the colors of the rainbow. Not a Rhode Island Red was among them.

Mrs. Boroff quit speaking to Mrs. Carey.

Boroff traded horses constantly.

I would become attached to a team and pet them in the barn.

He would trade them off. I watched them leave with tears. For want of something to love, I quickly became attached to the new team.

I went to the barn early one winter morning and saw a little colt lying at the haunches of its mother. It was not yet dry.

Boroff told me I could have the colt. I believed him.

I spent every spare hour with it.

The colt, a deep roan, with two white legs and a white spot between its eyes, has trotted through my head all these years.

Without my knowing it, Boroff traded the colt and its mother for a team of mules. He got a red cow to boot. He sent me after the cow.

It was eight miles away.

As I trotted in the wagon tracks, the dust of the road felt warm to my bare feet.

The cow ran nearly all the way to Boroff's. Only by a miracle it turned in at his barnyard gate.

I followed it, exhausted, and was told that my colt had been traded and was gone.

I could not talk for a minute.

Then I broke.

Boroff laughed.

That night the cow milked blood. Allie Boroff screamed.

Scared, the cow kicked her off the stool.

Boroff interfered. The cow ran out of the barn and squeezed him against the door. His face wrinkled in pain. He clutched his groin. Then, cursing, he ran toward me.

"You made her milk blood," he screamed.

I grabbed a pitch fork and stood, ready to push it through his heart. He came, rushing on. My eyes were fixed on his heart. When I was about to shove the prongs into him, he snorted like a bull and collapsed.

"Help pick him up," his wife screamed.

"I'll pin him there." I stood over him with the fork, ready to push it downward.

Ivy threw her arms about me.

"Jim, Jim," she screamed.

I came to my senses and looked at the writhing man.

The cow ran in a mad circle about the barnyard. It kept getting nearer and nearer.

"Where's my colt?"

"I'll get it back for you," Boroff answered weakly.

The three of us dragged him into the house.

The doctor came, then the preacher.

Boroff moaned in bed. His groin swelled like a squash.

The doctor drove away in his surrey.

The preacher prayed. His teeth were yellow-stained. The left side of his face was swollen with a quid of tobacco.

He rubbed Boroff's forehead. Together they called on God for mercy.

Boroff was out of bed in four weeks.

I did all the work on the farm while he was injured.

The bleak countryside soon bloomed with spring. The sun thawed the frozen mud. It packed, turned yellow and hard.

Nearly eighteen months with Boroff, he did not talk once except to give a command.

Since the bad treatment accorded him by the cow and myself, he paid no attention to either of us.

I did not eat with the rest of the family.

I left one Monday morning, my cigar box under my arm.

I had a few pigeons that lived in a small house under the barn gable. I watched them for a few minutes, as they huddled together in the door while a chicken hawk sailed overhead.

A little girl named Effie Freund often visited Ivy. The first of a long series of unfortunate women who became attached to me, she lived a mile away.

She was the daughter of a poor farmer, who, through her intercession, had arranged with another farmer to give me a home should I leave Boroff.

All the Boroffs were gone. I took my time about leaving.

I watered the stock and poured milk for the cats.

The house was very quiet. Only the clock made noise. As I went to the door a mad Boroff ancestor stared at me. Then I walked through door and gate forever.

Once before, during the first few months at Boroff's, I had left. I went south in the direction of St. Marys. Night overtook me and I slept in a haystack.

Boroff and Ivy overtook me. She coaxed and I returned.

I now lingered on a bridge that spanned a ditch at the cross-roads and watched my pigeons huddled in fear of the hawk.

Effie came down the road on the way to her brother's house. He lived north, near the Paulding county line.

She was beautiful to me, with a blue checked gingham apron over a red checked calico dress.

We loitered on the bridge. She went north and I went east. As I watched her skipping along the road, a mood of sadness overwhelmed me.

I never saw her again.

I only stayed a week at my new home. The woman was a chronic invalid. Her husband was wealthy. He had a large house, painted white and green. His lightning rods dazzled in the sun.

They had adopted a half-Indian boy five years before. The woman became deeply attached to him.

One morning she went to call him. His window was open. He was gone.

She never got over the loss. As I was not the kind of a boy to make her forget, I moved on to another farmer who needed some one to drive a team while he attended his harvest.

He paid me ten dollars a month and my board. I was to stay a month — till the harvest was over.

His team was large. I could not reach their backs with

the curry comb. He curried and put the harness on them for me.

A road was being piked from Lima to Fort Wayne. I guided the team to the stone quarry and under immense containers of crushed stone. Men opened slides. The wagon was filled. When I came to where the stone was to be placed on the road, men unloaded the wagon.

I hardly left the wagon seat from early morning until late at night. The team walked, always.

When my month was up, the farmer thought it best if he remained with the threshing machine a while longer and I drive the team.

I remained another month.

One Saturday, a circus came to Van Wert. Everybody went, including me. I spent nearly all my wages. There was a young woman in tights who told fortunes and sold photographs of herself.

I returned to the farm with a dozen photographs of the young woman, and a deck of cards which were transparent and, if turned swiftly, showed a man and woman in lascivious positions.

I worked faithfully after that. Seated on the wagon, I would dream of the lovely fortune teller.

Often, there came to me a feeling of revenge toward Boroff.

It would pass quickly and again sweep over me. One day I saw the colt. With its head over the meadow fence, it whinnied at me.

It was growing large. The thought came to me to steal

it. Then I remembered the thirteen years my uncle had served in the penitentiary for being a horse thief. So I watched it gallop over the meadow, head held high, tail erect.

When my second month was up, the farmer paid me. I left for Saint Marys.

BLOOD ON THE MOON

MY GRANDFATHER WAS dozing alone by a window into which a streak of sunlight entered.

He had aged in two years. His beard was white. His eyes had saddened.

He moved his immense body with an effort.

"So it's home ye are from where ye started," said he. "And sure if I were ye it's no longer I'd be stayin' here than to face the west in the mornin'. All the world I'd give, with a silver fince around it, if I was young as ye."

I rattled money in my pocket.

"God of the unjust, is it money ye have?" he asked.

"Yes, Granddad."

"How did ye git it?"

"I drove team."

He rose in his cot, "An' me lyin' here sick — why, shame on me, Hughie." His tone became flattering.

"Ah, me bye, yere the good lad. It was only ye that would come to yere old granddad at sich a time, whin whisky was scarce as honest lawyers."

I showed him the money.

"Tin whole dollars — I knew always that ye'd come to something — why, whin ye was three years old ye said to me — 'Do ye like stars, Grandpa'— and I said, 'Yis, me son, do ye?' And ye said, 'Yis, it's me that's goin' to find one some day.' I knew then that ye were a bye after me own heart. It's ye and me that will go to Coffee's bar and dhrink to oursilves. Payple will nivir distress ye, me lad, if ye sthay to yersilf, an' don't put yersilf in thire place — and if ye don't let 'em touch ye, they'll niver stip on yere toes. So we'll dhrink alone.

"Have ye bin to confission lately?" he asked me.

"No, Granddad, I've been with the Protestants."

"Well, ye should go before ye git older. Thire's not much sin to confiss at yere age, though. But thire was with me. Whin I was a young fellow of eighteen, I wint to the praest an' told him I'd seduced a virgin at the other ind of the County Dinegal.

" 'How many times,' said the praest —"

" 'An' sure, Father,' says I, 'it's not me that's come to brag but to confiss —,' and we both laughed —"

He stumbled —"I'm gittin' old —it's misrible I am,

me lad, an' sick unto the dith with a heart that cannot die."

In middle life my grandfather was over six feet tall. Even in old age he was handsome. His body was thick and solid as a tree. No face in all the years has remained so granite and eagle-like in my memory. His eyes were laughing and shrewd. His mouth, around which was a close cropped iron gray beard, could shut like a trap. Before his smile, men melted. The stingiest man bought drinks. In repose, there was defiance in his face. His mouth and eyes could look cruel. His nose would be considered Roman.

When drunk, he often bragged of his ancestry. He had a large worn book of ancient Irish heraldry which contained many coats of arms. What he considered his own was among them. He knew considerable of Roman history and that Cicero was called Tully. Though he could not trace his ancestry beyond his grandfather who was a bog walking peasant, he claimed to be descended from Cicero.

He fumbled for his clothes. Shaggy as a bear, and as powerful, the muscles in his aged legs were as hard and twisted as new made ropes. His massive chest was covered with black-gray hair. The muscles across his belly were like the gulleys in a washboard.

"Grandmother could wash clothes on your belly, Granddad," I smiled.

His fingers rattled down the muscles. "Ah yis — that's the throuble with me — iverbody washes thire clothes on me belly — and they wrinch thim in me own heart's blood — but whire in the hill is me shoe? One would think that a shoe would sthay whire ye put it." He found it under the bed. "Now, how the hill did it iver git thire — ye know, me lad — this is a damned nuisance, a man dressin' and undressin' ivery time he turns around. A tiger don't do that and it looks bitter than us. I could go down the strate naked as God on a rainy day and feel all the bitter for it."

He led me out of the door.

"Let's see the money ye have," he asked.

I showed it to him.

"I'll take the dollars for it wouldn't look right fer a boy yere age to be buyin' dhrinks fer an old man."

He handed me a dollar. "Ye might be naydin this," he said.

"It was me that said to thim at yere birth, me bye, 'He's born at the time of blood on the moon. Go aisy in yere judgment of him. For it's blood on the moon that manes throuble, an' thim that are born whin the moon is rid niver have pace till thiy die — an' thin thiy go to hill.'

" 'Will he live?' asks yere sister.

" 'Yis, me dear, sorry am I to say that he will, fer the Lord couldn't use him as an angel. With his hair red as murder, he'd sit the stars on fire. An',' says I to her further, 'and ye must remimber — the children of the poor niver die.'

"Your father looked dolefully at me.

" 'He's the one bird from our tray that may be worth a damn,' I says to him. 'And aven he may have no place to rist his fate whin he dies. There was blood on the moon, me son, the night he was born, blood on the moon; I saw it reflicted in the water of the Forty Acre Pond as I drove here to the birth. It run red all over the idge, like the blood of a sthabbed to dith shape. Ah, me son, could we only live to watch him. He'll carry us far or strangle to dith in the tryin'. It's me that belaves in what the stars and the moon say. Min will git out from the shadow of thire own invy to look at him on his way to the gallows.'

" 'Do you think they'll hang him?' says yere father.

" 'Well,' I says, 'he *may escape* the rope. He has a good nick. But if he don't, indade, it's no dishgrace. Thire's many a good man that's wint swimmin' to dith in the air.'

" 'But I'd like him to be somethin' respectful like,' says yere father.

" 'And why would ye?' says I. 'Did I iver ask it of ye? Throw him on the ash hape and he'll come a lily. Wrap him in vilvit and he'll die of the pimples.' "

In a rusty, once black suit, too tight for his huge body, he walked as ponderously as if he stepped on worlds.

The fingers of his powerful hands curved and touched the heavily calloused palms. For fifty years they had been twisted about the handle of a shovel.

He is as real now as on that long ago day.

The misery of the past two years suddenly hit me between the eyes. The tears came.

The old man held me to him.

"Thire, thire," he said, "a woman may pass along the strate any minute — an' niver let a woman see ye cryin'—"

He swallowed, "Ye'll niver catch a whale with tears." He looked straight ahead, and held his lower lip with his large teeth.

"Things are niver so bad as ye think. If ye weren't here ye'd be somewhire ilse, and if ye weren't somewhire ilse, ye'd be dead, and if ye were dead, ye'd be in hill, which may be as bad as this."

A sparrow pecked at manure on the street.

"As saucy as if it was havin' bread at the Last Supper — that's the way to be, me bye — the more sparrow ye have in yere soul, the bitter off ye'll be.

"It's the likes o' me and ye that's born fer better times than atin' our hearts out here in the bogs of Ohio — the discindents of Irish kings — it's a long time ago and they've come a long way —"

He sang solemnly,

> *"Me father was a gintleman*
> *And came of royal payple —"*

as we turned into the saloon.

"Have ye seen John Crasby lately?" he asked the bartender.

"He was in here this mornin' for an eye opener; he's workin' to-day," was the reply.

"Me God,— it'll sthorm before night."

Grandfather laid my money on the bar. A quart of whisky was placed before him. He filled a glass quickly and drained it at once.

"Give the bye a dhrink —," he said.

"What'll it be, son,— a pop?"

"Give him beer," said my grandfather. "Pop's a whoor's drink."

He suddenly felt his breast,

"Glory be to Almighty God, I've lost me nicktie," he shouted. "It was one of thim damned things that fastened on a button, and now it's gone."

We looked about on the floor.

"The wind blew the damned thing off, I giss — what in the divil would a man's tie be doin' in this place?"

"Well, it looks better without, Granddad," I said.

"Indade, it'll have to — I'll be losin' me shirt nixt. It was a nicktie yere father give me last Christmas — no son worth his salt would buy his father sich a rag for a nicktie; now I'll go blaytin' back home like a shape that's lost its tail, with the wind blowin' through me hind whiskers — may God in His mercy pity an old fool that thries to be a dude — it's a shovel they should give me for a cane — me that can throw a hunk of dirt over the roof of a church — now a silly old buck with no nicktie."

"But I wouldn't worry about it, Hughie," said the bartender.

"Indade, I've got to. What would payple think of Old Hughie Tully walkin' the strates of Saint Marys with no nicktie on? Who in hill iver started wearin' thim first anyhow?"

A voice in the rear said, "Here it is, Hughie."

He grabbed it suddenly and tried to adjust it. A frenzied expression came over his face.

"I've lost the button. Lor in Hiven forgive me. Damn the luck! If anither man iver gives me a piece of foolery for a Christmas prisint, I'll jerk the threads out of it a piece at a time and hang him to the rafter of the nearest Protestant church — I will — so help me Jaysus, I will."

Smiling, I watched him.

"Is it yere old Granddad ye'd laugh at. Me, that's in his dotage an' showin' ye the world like the good grandfather I am."

"No, Grandpa, I was just glad to see you find it."

"Indade — God, Himself, would be glad to see me find it — if He had to wear one of the damned things."

"But God would be glad to see you without a necktie, Hughie," said the bartender.

The old man smiled.

"Ah, me lad, ye know how to beguile an old man. Yere smart as the nettle in the meadows of Mayo."

He paused, "But I'm afraid he wouldn't. There's something of the rapscallion in the old blood of me — indade, I could tell ye the tale of a woman.

"In me piddlin' days I could walk forty mile a day with enough lace and linen on me back to make a pair of pants for Queen Victoria. The wimen would stand silly in their doors as I passed by. The cows would moo in the meadows like I was a bull.

"One time a farmer in Georgia had a cow go wild with the longin' for a mate. What to do he didn't know. So I walked into the field and the cow, seein' me, became quiet as a turtle in love. I had to snake away in the night to kape it from followin' me. An' ivery year whin I passed through with me pack on me back, the cow would hear me comin' a hundred miles away. No one kin till me since that a cow can't love a man. Miny women do."

He looked about.

Behind him, fastened to the wall, was a calendar upon which was the advertisement of a Catholic undertaker.

It contained the picture of Jesus, Mary, and Joseph.

The old man looked at it and swallowed more whisky.

"The face of the Boy, Jaysus, looks like a pie," he said.

The bartender looked shocked.

Old Hughie looked away, "But I should be more riverint." He pondered, then looked at the picture again. "But it does look like a pie."

He put his elbows on the bar.

"It brings me back me early days in Dinegal. It's the roads of Ireland that go runnin' through me heart in me old age. And thire's miny a sad spot on a road that's very long —"

The old man rubbed his forehead as we left the saloon.

"I'd be glad to die to-night if I could be dhrunk in me grave all me life long. It would be grand — with things rollin' through me head and me lyin' thire still as a miser's hand whin the colliction plate goes by.

"Bein' dhrunk is like bein' young, ye niver git enough of it.

"Whin I was young so long an' long ago, a piddler in the South, it was I who picked up with a young fellow who had a litter of recommendation froom the mayor of the payple in Nashville sayin' they saw with thiy're own eyes that he was a man who made the dead to rise. He had bin a piddler of laces an' linens like meself before he took to raisin' hill an' the dead.

"He was a man who rode on a mule with a palm leaf tied to its tail an' he had a moostache, the inds of which wint sthraight up in the air. He swore he could cause rain by ticklin' the clouds with the inds, and though I niver saw him do it, I belave thire was somethin' to his belafe, for niver was thire a day in Tennessee whin we took to the road with our packs that it didn't rain enough to drown a whale. Aich of us had to git boots big as boats, and it made our packs witter than the diapers of Irish babies durin' High Mass, if sich a thing is possible.

"Bein' a piddler, I knew he was an honest man, for

I think that piddlers and min like Jaysus who walk about roads kin raise the dead. If they can't, thire'd be no sins in walkin' about roads, or at laest he knew a lot of piddlers, for did he not say, 'Take up yer pack an' go the other way'— for thire's no bigger noosance than a followin' piddler —

"But we got to a little town an' down we wint to the noospaper an' me frind put some words in it which said that in two wakes from the day at hand he'd raise all thim that had the good fortune to have died in the past tin years, an' he begged all the rilitives to have wagons an' buggies to take thim home at once. He asked for miny blankets, too, for, as he said, that aven the warm air in Tinnisay would be cold to thim that were dead, an' that he did not want the catastrophe of the dead catchin' thire dith of cold before he got thim used to bein' out o' thire graves.

"He started his words in the paper with, 'Jaysus said — Lazarus, rise —', an' thin he sat back an' said,— 'I'll show ye a game, Hughie, that'll make ye money faster'n a mint,' an' he did nothin' but smoke an' dhrink brandy the whole day and night long.

" 'Min niver knows their powers, Hughie, till thiy tap the unknowable — fer that which ye don't know is not as simple as that which ye do. Aven in me piddlin' day, Hughie, ye know that I was a man of books, an', thirefore, a mind that could not be moved aven if the stars fill — fer if things were not so thiy would not be in books — now these payple rid of Jaysus risin' a man, an' how do thiy know I'm not Jaysus — ?'

" 'How kin ye say that, Barney?' I asked —'knowin' of the cotton ye sold fer silk, an' the wire nettin' ye sold fer lace.'

" 'Aisy,' says he, 'aven a piddler kin see the Light, an' thiy'll be glad to know I made a man o' mesilf — for a man may rise froom the bid of murder an' all, an' all, but niver in the history of the world before was it given a piddler to become a saint an' raise the dead — knowin' good froom avil, Hughie, an' how to mix thim both is the greatest problem a Christian has to face, an' indade I'd dispair if it weren't fer hilp froom on High.'

"A few days wint by an' Barney kipt puttin' bigger things in the paper —

" 'The dead will again walk the earth'— says he — wit' a picture of himself lookin' like Jaysus, 'Yere dead wile covort arm in arm with ye in sivin more days — "Thise dead shall rise again," says our first great Dead Riser — do ye not see the tombstones pushin' upward — yere blissid dead are gettin' riddy to come forth — thiy are not dead but slaypin' an' slaypin' shall thiy rise — an' once the dead come back thiy know the secrets of livin' hearts — all of the livin' have thought of the dead thiy know; thiy yield not and nayther do thiy iver forgive — an' the wind from their little finger brings dith to thim by whom thiy were injured. Such power has been given me by Jaysus if I would not abuse it — an' so only do I make the dead to rise in those rare places whire all are pure of heart —

" 'That'll fetch thim, Hughie,' says he —'Are ye not sorry to be but a poor piddler in the prisence of one with sich sublime thoughts?'

" 'If thire's a sublime thought in yere head it would choke a pig,' says I.

" 'What do ye mane, Hughie?' says he.

" 'I was spakin' of the pig,' says I.

" 'If ye knew payple bitter, Hughie, you'd lose yere pack as I did. It's a sthrange world whin Irish meddy larks kin chant the doldrums of thire little minds to eagles like me,' says he.

" 'It is,' says I.

" 'Watch the payple, says he.

"And that afternoon, lo an' behold, a young woman comes up the stairs,

" 'Is it all the dead ye raise?' said she.

" 'It is,' says he.

" 'Oh, God —' she fell to sobbin'—'It's me own husband ye'll bring back.

" 'Can't ye lit the poor man rist in his grave,' says she, 'he'd be disturbed to come back now. It was sure I mint him no harm an' I cried at his funeral like a good girl, as my mother always said it looked will if a girl cried at the funeral of her happily departed —

" 'An' if he came back now he'd find me happily not married to my lover, and he might kill us both —'

" 'Yis, me dear and loyal young lady, I'm afeared he

would. In fact I heard him talkin' to a worm in his grave last night, an' thiy were both laughin' as though thire hearts would break —

" ' "Won't ye be glad," says he to the worm, "whin I kill the unfaithful wife an' the betrayer of her home?"

" 'An the worm chortled till its sides ached an' says, "Yis, yis, it's time I was havin' fresh mate." '

"The woman nearly swooned.

" 'Is thire no way I kin privint sich a catastrophe?' pleads she.

" 'Money talks in both worlds,' says he.

" 'How much would it cost to kape him whire he is?' says she.

" 'That is no matter,' says he.

" 'It will be two thousand dollars — surely that is little money as ye are young, an' dith is long.'

" 'And can I be sure he'll niver rise?' says she, fingerin' the money.

" 'Indade ye kin,' says he.

"She handed him the money and vanished —'Have mercy on the dead,' says she.

" 'And on the livin', says he, foldin' the wrinkles out of the money.

"Then an angry man rushed in, holdin' a sack full o' money —

" 'Violators o' the law o' God an' man,' says he — 'me own mother-in-law has been dead nine years an' eleven months — and near the ten years,' says he —

" 'But,' says Barney. the piddler that was, 'I kin

aisily make it ilivin or forty years to raise so charmin'
a lady froom the dead —'

" 'It was her dyin' request to rest in her grave undis-
turbed,' says the man.

" 'Dyin' requests mean no more to me than livin' requests — it's up she'll come in her night shirt, an' it's
home she'll go at once.'

" 'Is thire no way to lit the poor woman slape on?'
says he. 'Ye see she's very old.'

" 'For a consideration,' says Barney.

" 'How much?' says the man.

" 'Mothers-in-law come high,' says he. 'Pace is chape
at any price. Will fifty thousand to kape her dead for
eighty years be too much?'

" 'That will be all right,' says the man. 'I'm fifty now,
and I'll be in hell by then.' He threw the money and hurried out of the room.

" 'Money is a fearful avil,' says Barney, 'but fer
kaypin' graves full it has no equal.'

"On the day the dead were to rise, a storm came and
broke some stones. An' whin the sun came out, Barney
marched to the grave yard, followed by thousands of
payple, beggin' him to let the dead rist.

"The mayor come up with a hundred min carryin'
bags of gold, an' behind him all the citizens shouted —
an' the mayor says, 'Take this gold away as our tooken
of estheem an' faith in yere powers. We know ye kin
raise the dead; we have seen it. But we are at pace here,
and God is with us. Bein' lookin' as we are, iver onward

and upward, we find that we cannot go back. The eternal march of progress bids us go on and on, facing ever onward to the golden dawn of the future. Thirefore we want our dead to rist in pace. But take this medal and this gold as a tooken of our faith and estheem, for we doubly know that ye are one who can make the dead to rise. More — we have seen.'

"Barney took the gold an' give me the medal.

" 'It was the son-in-law o' the dead mither-in-law who was the spaych makin' mayor,' says I to Barney.

" 'Sure, did ye think I knew it not — how long will ye be contint to be a piddler, Hughie, associatin' with a man like me?'

"Too sad was I to answer."

His mood changed. Slowly, his heavy feet dragged. He looked neither to right nor left. He covered his lower lip with his large teeth. It was his habit when his mind was puzzled.

"Niver be a dhrunkard, me bye, unless ye have a lot of money; and thin, payple will jist think ye're a man about town. It's not me that will worry what ye will do — payple do or thiy don't — excipt me — I rayched out me hand and thiy gave me a shovel while the man nixt to me, with no whit more brains and more nerve, got wilth beyond the drames of a fool — who is it kin say the Old Hughie Tully was baurn to dig thire ditches."

He hiccoughed.

"The only mistake I iver made was whin I took the shovel. Now, belave it, me bye, belave it till ye die —

niver work with yere hands, aven if ye stharve. Between stharvin' and workin' with yere hands, thire's no difference."

His feet dragged.

"Of courshe — it was I who made another mishtake. Yere grandmither's a good an' nohble woman, but I shoulda lit me dead brither marry her.

"Sure and I know it's not wise to buy a cow whin milk's so chape." He looked at me kindly. "It's not I that's agin women. They have thire place in the world, though I can't think whire it is. Water at different wells tastes iver the best, aven whin yere dry."

The house was empty when we returned.

"Say nothin' to thim — thiy'll not know yere old granddad's bin out of the cot."

He threw his coat on the floor and his battered hat on a chair.

"Thank ye, me bye — slape kin now come to me mad old head.

"Ye were iver kind to yere old granddad — it was ye that iver give me the solace of a laugh —

"Yis indade, it was ye that always knew what ye wanted. Whin jist a tot I asked ye what ye liked bist — the sun or the moon — and ye said, 'the sun in the daytime, Grandpa, and the moon at night'— ye see — most people want it different and are always braggin' — tellin' how wise thiy are and how great — no one iver heard me say that I was the mightiest ditch-digger of all time, that's for thim to say that knows; it's more modest am I. Impty wagons iver make the most noise.

"It was the fool at the insane asylum who says to me grandfather —

" 'Where ye goin' wit' that load of manure?'

" 'I'm goin' down here to put it on me strawberries,' says me grandfather.

" 'Glory be to Almighty God,' says the man with no brain, 'I use sugar and cream on me own, an' thiy kape me in here'."

A few heavy chuckles, and soon he was sound asleep.

THE DEAD COMPLAIN

THE MAIN STREET OF THE town was a mile away from the little yellow house in which old Hughie and my grandmother lived. It was about six feet above the edge of the street. The embankment was covered with yellow grass. At one corner, beneath a small grape arbor, was Old Hughie's chair. He would sit there by the hour, his hands clenched to the arm of the chair as if they were strapped. It gave him a view of a street which disappeared into the country and was known as the Saint Marys Pike.

When with some one, he talked constantly. Alone, he would remain motionless as an Irishman in bronze.

Often, for several days at a time he would make no effort to join other men.

I once said to him, "A penny for your thoughts, Grandpa."

"Thiy're not worth it," he grunted. "What has an old man got to think about — he's jist the wind blowin' grass over graves, and soon he'll die and another old man will blow the grass over his grave, and the birds will scatter wades — it's all a miss if ye can't belave in Hiven."

His hands gripped tighter the arms of the chair. His head nodded slowly.

"I'd do anything or be anything if I didn't have to die. It'll be so cold in the grave." He shuddered, and raised his voice. "And so lonesome — nobody to talk to, no wimen in the night, no dhrink when the throat is dry, no frind whin the heart is sad — indade, I don't want to die." He looked pensive. "Rather would I live foriver. It's a little pace I'm getting now — with no wimen tuggin' at me heartstrings and burnin' me up in- side. I kin look at thim now as I look at the quails that hop along the idges of Saint Marys Pike. In me younger days I burned up fer wantin' of thim; and, aven whin I thried to pray, it was still I wanted thim. Thire's things ye can't down with a prayer, and wimen's ligs niver stay togither when they should." He bit his lower lip.

"Ye see, me bye, we're of the Dinegal brade; and it was iver they like wimen. Thire's not a praest among thim. We boast and we quarrel an' we're vain as par- rots in a new green cage. We're nobody's fools, but niver do we pursurvere in anything, excipt to dig a ditch to git a dhrink by. We're brave as all dumb min and our timpers are hot as fire. We have the way with us of sayin' what we don't mane and hurtin' the hearts of ithers, and thin we're sly as foxes and we wape without feeling and sneer whin the back is turned — indade, it's no man who knows the Irish bitter than me. Thiy're rascals in thire souls, and if thiy saw the truth comin' down the road, thiy'd run to the praest and drown it with Holy Water from the nearest ditch. Ah, yis — indade, I hate to die."

"But you'll live to be a hundred, Grandpa."

"Indade, and I'll not — I'll soon be matin' with God and I shall say to Him —'Ruler of the Thunder and the Wave, here's Old Hughie Tully. I wasn't all I should be, Lord, down in the Dismal Valley whire I lift me carcass. I couldn't help the poor, Lord, excipt to make a little joke — but I was a big enough man, Lord, to do without miny things, an' aven yere own great Silf is no whit bigger than the things ye can do without. I only ask ye, Lord to put me some place close whire I kin hear the birds fly over me grave, and kape the snakes froom crawlin' across it. That's not much, me Lord, fer an old man, bint with the labor of the world. I dug yere ditches, Lord, all through Ohio until ye could see the water in thim ripplin' over a pin. It's me, Lord, that's bin so tired whin the long day come to an ind that I made the earth shake under me heavy fate'."

"But, Grandpa, yere not dead yet," I said.

"But it's will, me bye, to practice what yere goin' to

say to Him before ye die. For thim that have done it till me thire's a great confusion comes whin the last breath goes, and some stand before the Great Prisince while thire bids are still warm. They till me at sich a time one shivers with the cold and stutters whin he should be talkin' fast. So I want me spaych riddy, for bein' what I am, there'll be much to explain — and maybe it'll be a trifle hard for aven God to understand."

"But suppose there is no God, Grandpa?"

"Well — it doosent matter; I'll have me spaych riddy anyhow."

"But if there is one, do you think He'll understand?"

"He wouldn't be God if He didn't," replied my grandfather. "No man could git far sittin' in judgment on me unliss he understhood. Thire'd be little use to be God unliss ye can understhand. It's a bizness fer a God, is understhandin'— fer if He couldn't understhand, he wouldn't know what to do and He'd lit the Hivens fall — and that would niver do. Suppose I was diggin' a ditch and the moon fell in it. I'd be damned good and mad, I would. Suppose a cloud fill in yere uncle Tom Lawler's barnyard and washed a cow away — it's a hill of a God that can't juggle a few worlds in His hands without litten' 'em slip."

"I know, Grandpa, but why does He let things go on the way He does — people quarreling and murdering — why in the orphanage —,"

He stopped me.

"Why don't ye look at it this way and give the Man

a chance — ye niver saw a father in yere life who could watch six children all the time, did ye? If thiy are byes, thiy are gittin' girls in throuble; and if thiy are girls, thiy are gittin' in throuble thimsilves. Now God has billions of us; besides the animals and the snakes, and the Protestants, and the birds — and twinty million niggers, and a lot of English. How in the hill He doos as will as He doos is more than iver the brain of me kin figger — to run Ireland, alone, whin I was a bye was a job fer a thousand Gods — an' if anybody iver yilled 'Hurrah fer England,' ye'd nade a thousand more. No, me bye, it's not will to complain. Thire's only one mistake He iver made and that was allowin' dith to come into the world."

"But, Grandpa, if nobody died, the world would soon be so full nobody could move."

My grandfather laughed louder than usual.

"It's not a thinkin' mind ye have. We'd sind the overflow to Ireland and they'd git to fightin' and die soon enough."

My grandfather's eyes never seemed old. They twinkled, always, when he talked of the Irish.

"Yere great-grandfather, me bye, me own father, and may the winds of eternity fan his red hot soul — he hated to die — and I do think he'd have lived foriver if thire had been no lightnin' — it sthruck him one day, thinkin' he was the oak he was. But he didn't turn to doost like other min, sadly born of wimen. He turned into rock. And thiy use the big body of him now to kape the waves froom washin' over Dinegal.

"And whin the moon is out ye kin see him standin' thire — as much alive as ye or me, excipt the heart of him bates in anither world than ours, but the waves touch him not; thiy kape away froom him like the thruth does a lawyer, and ivery night, a little before the dawn comes and the crows begin to wake, he puts his hand to his eyes and sthares across the ocean lookin' for me that was his son who hides froom the sight of him, ashamed that the blood of his blood and the bone of his bone should be a dhroolin' and dhrinkin' man with a throubled brain in his head.

"And, of course, it's a blissing that the dead kin only know the good of thire childern after they are gone. An understhandin' God takes care of that — gintle as dith is to the old, it wouldn't be no use in dyin' if thiy could see too much whin thiy are no more. All min, and proud am I to say it, are not like him that was yere great-grandfather, for whin thiy die, niver no more will thiy hear the jay thrushes whistlin' in the rain.

"All in all, dith is a sad thing.

"It's not good fer min an' proper fer wimen. Thiy are like roses and should die early, the very moost beautiful at thirty, so long and no longer.

"A woman's like a paych — no good whin her skin gits wrinkled — and all that she learns doos her no good, and by dyin' early she laves room for the younger ones to soothe the sad and broken hearts of the min they lave behind.

"God knows bist and it's not me that would be attimptin' to run His world fer Him — but if I was, indade, thire'd be many's the funeral of old wimen.

"And before many years some bright young man will invint a grave ye kin see out of ivery Sunday, and then a man will not nade to lose touch with the world. He kin kape on livin' like a Repooblican and no one will know he's dead.

"In the winter a man could have a stove in the grave whin the undertaker came to bury his hands in yere pockets for all the money ye have in the world to pay for yere pine coffin fixed up with chape plush like a cigar box in silk.

"It was over in Paulding that the young invintor got a contraption workin'— he had his usual throubles with the payple thire. Of course it had to have a flame, and a Jew pawnbroker, dead forty-one years, complained that thire was lard in the wick and the smill of it kept him from braythin' aisy in his grave — for it was in his crade that the Lord said 'thou shalt have not the lard of a hog before thee'— and a Methodist objected because the thing run on Sunday — he said that one should kape sich a day holy aven in the wormy halls of dith — so to plaze the Jew and the fool, the young invintor changed the machine — and thin a Seventh Day Adventist complained because the damned machine worked on Monday — for that was really the sivinth day on which the Lord risted froom his labor of makin' the world — fer if a man makes the world in seven days he's damned good and well in nade of a rist — so he shut the machine down that day — thin the Catholics objicted because it run on Friday — it bein' the day the Lord died — and Saturday the Episipalians complained about the noise — for thire should be none, they said, on the day before the Lord was gittin' riddy to rise froom His grave — he nayded time to think things over — so the young invintor worked and changed — and thin the Chamber of Commerce brought out a motion that he was makin' the dead too comfortable, and sint telegrams to one of the dead prisidints thin livin', and Congress voted for the machines in the Sinate; thin the undertakers hild one of thire convintions to learn how to bist rob the livin' fer the dead, and thiy made a motion that the heat made the coffins fall apart a day too soon, and the doctors took up the burnin' question on the ground that the dead did not want to lave thire graves to be dissicted because it was cold outside. . . .

"The man who made the most noise over the new invintion was one I knew viry well. He complained of the heat in the grave, claimin' it was warm enough as it was —

"A lady sang in a Mithidist choir in Dilphs and he got her in throuble, and to make matteis worse, he married her. That night as they wint to bid, as usual, togither, a head poked itsilf in the window, sayin'— 'For shuttin' the gates o' romance foriver to a kind lady, I condimn ye to die — for the laest a lady who sings kin hope for is the variety, and she's bitter off with a change in min —.' With the head lavin' the window, the man died — and his soul begun to smoke right away — min came for the miny's the mile around to git it out of the house before it caught the house afire.

"Down the chimney roared the voice of the head —

" 'Hell's a waitin' for him, min, and ye cannot save a soul or body that burns in bid — it will flame the house down —' so we rushed to the roof and tore it off — but his soul, bein' ragged, caught on a shingle at the idge, and the house begun to burn. In a minute, the lightnin' sthruck and it rained; but the house was burned in ashes away — and now whin the man's voice was heard above the other complainers, the young invintor in the dispiration of genius said, 'To hill with all ye slaypy bastards, fold yere mantels of dith around ye and snore in yere bones through all eternity — for I have but learned that the only way ye kin do things for the dead is to let thim be dead, and the only way ye kin do things fer the livin' is to let thim die — ye kin all go to hill in a rubber tired buggy and ask the divil not to laugh at ye fer bein' the damned fools ye are'— and with that, he was gone —

"Since thin, the invintors do little about dith."

He sighed.

"But if a man has to die, which so far as I'm aware, one must, it's bist to die in pace of soul, for not aven me would want to make a bad imprission on God.

"It was me own great-grandfather that the praest came to whin he was dyin',

" 'Forgive yere inimies,' said the praest.

" 'I have no inimies,' was the answer of me grand-father.

" 'What!' shouts the praest, 'a wild man like you and no inimies.'

" 'No, Father,' pious said me grandfather, 'I've killed thim all.'

" 'But is thire no one good act in yere saintly life?' says the praest.

" 'Yis, Father, thire is, but it's not braggin' a man should do on his dith bid.'

" 'But tell us the act,' says the holy man, 'that I may till yere illigitimate children.'

"Me own great-grandfather got tired of all this blather. Like me, he was modest and said but little, as one should whin he sees the Great Prisince coming down the road with a coffin on His back and a shovel in His hand.

" 'Ah will,' says me great-grandfather now that is gone, 'if ye must know, and bein' a praest ye kin till no one but thim that will listen — I killed an English-man in a moment of joke.'

"The praest laughed till the shingles shook on the roof, then he poked me dyin' grandfather in the ribs — and the old man sat in the bid and laughed till he nearly died.

"And the praest poked him agin — and says, 'Me

good man, yere over modest. I was wonderin' why ye were dyin' paceful as a saint — that is not a sin — but a command from God —'

"And laughin' agin till it stopped the clock, me grandfather gave up the ghost, unwillin'— and forty years thereafter the angels dropped turnips on his grave."

TO JOIN THE NAVY

A ROW OF DILAPIDATED
saloons were along the railroad.

I would sit on a chair in front of the Jaycox saloon in
the manner of my grandfather, and watch the freight
trains go in and out of Saint Marys.

I observed how brakemen and hoboes got on and off
moving trains, and early absorbed the lingo and out-
look of vagabonds.

With several other boys, I decided to beat my way to
Lima.

At Buckland, half way, we were put off the train a
few hundred feet from a long trestle. The other lads
caught the train again. It would soon be on the trestle.

Not running with the train, I grabbed at an iron ladder suddenly. My hands slipped.

My body began to twist under the wheels. With instant thought, I lurched away from the train.

The heel of my shoe caught under the edge of a wheel. Dazed with pain, I rolled down the embankment.

My companions rode across the trestle, got off, and hurried back to me. The leather was cut from my swollen heel. I limped for days.

My fare was paid the eleven miles home.

As general utility boy at the livery stable, I would deliver horses to different homes and walk back to the stable.

Often I would take young women for drives over the county.

Two young women, the daughters of leading Irish Catholics, once called for a rig and driver to go to Lima. At four that afternoon, I stopped in front of their house.

One girl, with red rimmed eyes, carried a handbag. The other, wearing a cloak, held her arm.

The team trotted away. There was a long silence in the rear seat.

When we reached Glynwood, the girls asked me to stop the team at the cemetery, while they walked and wept among the graves.

My own mother and her parents were buried not a hundred feet from where I sat.

As the team jogged on, the girl in the heavy cloak sobbed.

The other girl said, "There, there, don't cry." Her voice became lower. "You'll be married in Chicago and not come home for several years. No one will ever know."

The train came to Lima at dusk.

The sister who had carried the handbag returned to me.

The girl was married in Chicago.

The baby was born. It will soon be a priest.

*

I OFTEN took traveling salesmen to nearby towns and returned with them late at night. I enjoyed the talk of the salesmen. It expanded my world.

The "shooter" for the Standard Oil Company boarded his team at the stable. His wagon, loaded with nitro-glycerine, a highly dangerous explosive, was kept in a vacant lot.

He often required a driver to accompany him when he shot an oil well. The regular employees did not care for such dangerous work. The task often fell to me. I accepted with no qualms and bumped along the road with enough nitro-glycerine to blow up a Senator.

The shooter would place a "go-devil" in the well. Filled with explosives, it was shaped like a torpedo with a cap at one end. It would go swiftly into the drilled earth for thousands of feet.

A rumbling of the earth would follow after the "go-devil" reached the bottom. Rocks, earth, and oil gushed upward.

The well would be put under control immediately if not a "gusher," and within a few hours if it were.

The oil shooter had been a sailor in his early days. About forty-five, he was silent and stern.

He had married a dollar whore out of Rabbit Town, the small Saint Marys underworld that bordered the Lake Erie and Western tracks. He was an aristocrat among oil workers. Other women would not associate with his wife. If it ever concerned him, he was never heard to say a word.

My job was principally to guard the team and wagon. In order that I could see how he worked, he would allow me to unhitch the team and tie it in a secluded place some distance from the wagon.

On a journey to Montezuma, he suddenly became talkative and told me the different places in the world he had seen as a sailor.

Upon our return to Saint Marys, he gave me three dollars. I decided to join the navy.

The nearest recruiting office was in Chicago, over two hundred miles away.

I went to Lima and waited in the railroad yards for a freight train bound for Chicago.

With what the hoboes call "beginner's luck," I reached the large city about as easily as if I had paid my fare.

I walked down State Street and stared at the buildings until I came to the Recruiting Office in the Masonic Temple. From the windows could be seen the blue beauty of Lake Michigan.

A ship, far out on the lake, could still be seen.

"On its way to Duluth," said a boy, "I wish I was on her."

Taken in to a large room, my clothes taken from me, I stood nude before the physicians.

Soon I was passed to the Chief Examining Surgeon with a report.

"This is too bad," he said, "how old are you?"

"Eighteen," I lied.

He smiled.

"Why do you want to join the Navy?" he asked.

I told him why with swift words, and finished —"It will be a home and by the time four years are up I'll be a man."

"This is a shame — you are too young and too short — a perfect body, strong as an ox." He pinched my arm.

A tall red-whiskered man of about sixty, with a kind gleam in his eyes, he walked to the large window and gazed over the lake. His left hand was held under his right arm pit. The right hand stroked his beard. Seemingly oblivious of my presence, he stood in the same position for some minutes.

He turned quickly, put me on the scales again, measured my height. "Eighty-five pounds — four feet eleven." He shook his head.

"It can't be done, my boy, I'm very sorry —" He pressed a long thumb against my cheek. "Open your mouth again." He looked at the left side of my mouth.

"Perfect teeth — chew your food more on the left side," he suggested —"they'll rot if you don't use them." He tapped my chin. "Have you a toothbrush?"

"No."

"You must use one," he said.

I did, years later.

He looked at a tooth that projected out of place in my lower jaw. "Have it pulled out some day."

"I will."

"I'd make a new rule to have you in the navy." His words were kind. Tears came to my eyes. He pressed a button. An assistant came.

The Chief Examining Surgeon left the room for a minute. Returning, he said, "Good-by, my boy."

An assistant took me away.

Youths who had passed the examination talked of Newport News, where they were going.

With a heavy heart, I walked for miles to the railroad yards.

While waiting for a freight, I reached for my small knife.

A five dollar bill was in the pocket.

*

I REACHED home in two days.

Still dazed over my failure to join the navy, I went to my grandfather. He consoled me.

"The viry idea of thim not wantin' ye in the navy!

Ye should be thankful. It's only wimen that joins the navy. The good counthries have no sich things. Look at Ireland and Sweden. Nobody worth the salt on a turnip iver fought on water. Whire in the hill kin ye pick up a brick on the ocean?"

Not knowing, I did not answer.

For a long time that night I watched the muddy water of the canal which ran in front of the livery barn.

A sleepless night passed in the hay mow. I heard the engine of the midnight freight whistle as it climbed the hill into the town.

The next day I went toward the little cottage in which my grandfather lived.

I watched him from across the street.

He was sitting, as of old, his face toward the Saint Marys Pike. His hands gripped the arms of his chair. His shaggy head was on his breast. His eyes were closed.

I did not awaken him.

WHITHER THOU GOEST

For seven years I wandered in and out of Chicago, the hub of the hobo wheel. I early learned the worst too young, and became wise in many things not worth knowing.

It was a haven for youthful brigands, potential murderers, pickpockets, pimps, hoodlums and gutter snipes of all varieties. There was little honor and no tolerance among us. We had all the ignorance of our poverty stricken ancestors, combined with new cunning. A few could be trusted during the first few months of this environment. After that, never.

The law made war upon us. We hated its representatives in return. We thought, that no policeman could be trusted. We hated lawyers and other hypocritical parasites. At one institution we were given a bed and a morning and evening meal for a dollar a week. This place was full of bedbugs, cockroaches, misery and the smell of soft soap. The minute we would get enough money to live elsewhere, if only for a week, we would leave the place. We lived always at high tension, in terms of newspaper headlines. The latest murder held our interest. Bandits were our heroes, and lads who died on the gallows our martyrs. We mistrusted each other, and rightly.

In all that miserable mess, only one youth was of high quality. He knew that his companions were sneak thieves. Like myself he would share in loot. Though it was part of our life, it was also our code not to tell our greater enemies, the police, the doings of the frayed citizens of that world of which we were a part.

One who comes out of such a world might well feel his neck in the night and be amazed that a rope is not there. If he is beyond it he can chant no platitudes. If he still has an eye left for beauty he can but wonder at the miracle. He will, however, if he is intelligent, respect environment as a strong social force.

If he realizes as he grows older, that people in so-called higher phases of life have as little honesty and less courage, but more veneer and pretense than the boys with whom he prowled through youth, he will be thankful for the fear which keeps them all from each other's throats, and come more to understand why a policeman has an important place in the scheme of things.

*

HE came from the Ozarks to be a janitor at the News-boys' Home. His beard hung in a long string. The lower lids of his rheumy eyes were turned down and showed red. Water continually slid off them. His mouth, partly open, made his long face seem longer.

A gentle, whimpering, weak old man, he was out of place among the young wolves of the street who lived at the Home. Hardly able to do his work, he dragged his ancient legs around, his feet scraping the floor.

He had only been at the Home a week.

We often helped him make the beds and set the long oil-cloth covered table in the dining room.

It was in the cellar of the building. Gas jets hung from the center. The roar of street cars could be distinctly heard. They shook the table.

One winter morning four of us sat dejected and penniless along the wall of the dining room. All the work was done.

Old man Lockert had gone to his four by six room upstairs.

The janitor, and other flunkies ate at a table in the corner of the room.

A white headed boy crawled under the table, rose with a leather wallet in his hand, glanced quickly at us and started to leave the room. We pounced upon him.

The wallet was taken from him. He began to cry.

"Shut up," another lad snarled, "if you cry you get nothin'."

He ripped the rubber bands from the wallet and

pulled out dozens of ten and twenty dollar bills. Then he threw the wallet on the floor.

"Pick that up," snapped another boy.

Whitey picked up the torn and empty wallet.

"We'll divide four ways," said the boy with the pocket book. I edged in, ready to fight for my share.

He counted the money, nearly five hundred dollars.

I took my share with Dan Perkins and walked out of the building.

Whitey and Syracuse Tommy followed us.

Four days later we met Whitey.

"Where's Syracuse Tommy?"

"He ducked with my share," Whitey answered.

"How did that happen?" I asked.

"He got me to leave it with his friend on Sixteenth Street till the trouble blows over."

He began to cry.

"I did like he told me an' when I came back for my share he'd been there before and took it all."

"The dirty little crook," said Dan Perkins.

We each gave Whitey five dollars.

That night we scrambled into the dining room. The matron stood at the end of the table with old man Lockert. He had been crying.

When we were seated she said quietly, "Boys, Mr. Lockert has lost his money — his life's savings which he intended to put in the bank to-day. If any of you find it will you please return it to him?"

Every boy in the room answered "Yes" and began eating.

The matron led old man Lockert to his seat at the table in the corner.

He sat with wrinkled bloodless hands on the edge of the table and stared straight ahead.

I felt sorry for him later — not then.

The money was spent with the whores.

*

Jim Radell was out of a reform school. He had been yegg, pimp, and all around desperado from boyhood. He was about twenty-three and had never begged. Times were hard with him and he wished to go from Chicago to Pittsburgh. I volunteered to take him on the brake beams.

He was burly, with a big head, strong features, a hooked nose, and sharp eyes.

No one knew his right name.

Boroff lived on the Erie Railroad over which we would journey to Pittsburgh.

I begged money on the streets and kept Radell supplied.

When we reached Ohio City, I told Radell my mission.

"Do you need any help?" he asked.

I asked him to walk along.

Radell waited at the gate. I walked to the door.

Boroff met me.

His hair was deep gray. His shoulders stooped.

All hatred had gone from him. He showed me pictures of Allie and Ivy, both dead of consumption, lying in their coffins.

Their hands were folded, their faces sharp.

"Well," said he as I started to leave, "you'll soon be a man. Purty soon you'd have a horse and buggy."

"That's right," I returned, "I'd forgot about that."

He walked with me to the gate.

"Did he give you any money?" asked Radell.

"Gee, I forgot."

I ran back. Boroff was not yet in the house.

"Could you let me have twenty dollars?"

He peeled the money from a roll.

I hurried back to Radell.

*

NEAR the jungles at Youngstown was a boy much younger than myself. He wanted to see the world, and after stealing ten dollars from his mother, was waiting for a freight to carry him away.

Night was a few hours off when I approached with Radell.

The boy was lonely and wavering. Our presence loosened his tongue. We learned of the stolen money.

"Have you got it all with you?" I asked.

"Every bit," he replied.

"That's fine," I said while Radell hummed a tune of the Road.

The lad's eyes twinkled and the dimples showed in his chubby face.

Radell called me aside, and said mockingly, "We can't let this boy go out on the road this way. Suppose some hobo gets him for a punk. They like fat boys like him. We'd be doing us all a favor if we taught him a lesson early."

I thought for a minute,

"I have a plan."

We returned to the boy.

"Would you like me to cook a nice mulligan?" I asked.

The boy was delighted.

"All right — come on." The boy walked with us to the deserted jungle.

"Now you gather wood for the fire and put it all in a pile here."

We walked a few steps.

"Better let me have the ten dollars for grub," I suggested.

He handed me the money.

I hurried away with Radell.

He was gathering wood diligently as far as we could see him.

That was many years ago. He may be there yet.

We did not return.

Riding between two coke cars, we reached Pittsburgh in a heavy rain.

Radell immediately made contacts with old friends. I soon discovered that they were nearly all wanted by the police, and remained away from them during the day. I walked miles through the suburbs and read for hours in the Public Library.

At night, if accosted by the police, it was easier to convince them that I worked during the day.

One night I came near to becoming a robber.

Falling in with Eddie Wilds and another youth, we decided to get money by robbery. I had lived on stolen money, but had not directly stolen. There was in me, whether good sense or fear, or an inherited force beyond my control, something that kept me out of jail except for the minor offenses of vagrancy.

We walked about the dark streets for what seemed hours looking for our prey. Eddie carried a gun, the other youth, a blackjack. I was the look-out.

Had we immediately seen a man who looked prosperous, the course of my whole life might have been changed.

Through my mind raced many thoughts.

Suppose I was caught and my sister heard of it. The shame might kill her.

I did not moralize. All Reform School boys and other jail birds I knew, had lost something.

Finally we came to a badly lighted street corner and talked.

"I'm going back, fellows," I said. "None of this for me."

"Are you losin' your nerve?" asked Eddie.

"Call it that if you want to."

"Stick along," pleaded the other boy, "Some one'll pass soon. It won't take long.

"Not for me — I'll see you later."

I walked back to the room which I shared with Radell.

"What's the matter," he asked.

"Nothing — it's safer bein' just a hobo."

He lay propped on his elbow, his heavy nude shoulders denting the pillows.

"I guess you're right," he said.

Not long afterward Eddie came in. He had a silver watch and twelve dollars.

"Slim beat it — I gave him fifteen and kept the watch."

"Let's see the turnip," said Radell.

Eddie handed him the watch.

"It belonged to some Bohunk. I'll bet you can't hock it for three bucks."

"I'll carry it then," returned Eddie.

"You'd be a damned fool if you did. It'd be a dead give-away if you got picked up by the cops." Radell rolled over, "I'd throw the damn turnip away — it's not worth the having."

"Would you like to have it, Jim?" asked Eddie.

"Not me."

"Let's go and scoff," suggested Eddie. "Come on — get your lazy carcass out of bed."

"Better leave the gun here," said Radell.

Eddie put it in a bureau drawer.

Within two weeks Eddie Wilds was shot through the heart by a citizen who refused to be robbed. The other lad was captured.

He was sentenced to twelve years in the Western Penitentiary. Given three months off each year for good behavior, he served nine years.

Upon his release, I helped him.

"What became of Radell?" I asked.

"Didn't you hear?"

"No."

"He's doin' it all in — Shot two cops to death —"

"Life."

"You said it — doin' it all — he was a good guy too —"

"None better."

"Funny, ain't it, there bein' somethin' kinky in Radell? He was smart — an' he'd of made good at anything. Women were crazy about him. Now a guy like me — it makes no difference. I ain't never had a chance —"

Jack lit a cigarette.

He is now doing fifteen years — solid — no time off for good behavior.

*

SHE came into the morgue where Eddie Wilds was lying on a slab.

"I wanta touch him, please," she said to the keeper of the dead, "I told him I would. You see we was goin' to be married."

She was known as Bedelia.

We would chant at her the words of a popular song —

> *"Bedelia — I'd like to steal ya —*
> *Bedelia — I love you so —"*

Bedelia was about sixteen.

She had been the plaything of boys and men from the time she was twelve.

Then she met Eddie.

They were both undersized and shriveled, their faces pinched from early malnutrition.

"Listen," Eddie said, "you're goin' to be my girl, an' if I ketch you cheatin' I'm goin' to beat holy hell outta you — git me?"

"I do. I'll be good. I want somebody to care what I do."

We laughed at their devotion.

They walked down Smithfield Street, hand in hand.

Bedelia had well-shaped legs. Her shoulders sagged and her eyes, very sad, bulged from her head.

"Why don't you git Eddie to quit robbin' people?" she asked me.

"I've told him it was dangerous, but he said he had to eat."

"I could feed him," she said, "I'm slingin' hash now."
She tried to straighten her shoulders, "But he's too proud
and I wish he wasn't."

The keeper of the dead saw no harm in allowing
Bedelia to pat Eddie's forehead.

She moaned a few times.

He walked through his dormitory of the dead until he
heard a shriek.

He turned in time to see Bedelia half fallen, clinging
to Eddie.

A bottle fell to the cement floor.

The keeper ran toward her,

"Put me on a slab the side o' him — I told him if he
ever went I'd go too —"

Her mouth, drooling, searched for his tight lips.

The keeper pulled her away — dead.

I DRIFTED INTO A MINNESOTA town with a young grifter.

A county fair was advertised.

A canvas covered wagon, drawn by two jaded horses, turned the corner on Main Street.

On the side of the canvas was printed

"UNCLE COFFEE SAM'S COFFEE

IS

THE BEST IN THE WEST"

A few people passed. Church bells tolled. Heat waves, heavy as mirages, moved slowly.

I followed the team which stumbled in a cloud of vivid yellow dust while a man inside the wagon played a fiddle and sang,

"Matilda went fishing —
Matilda caught bawss
Matilda fell in
Clear up to her awss

Now the warning, young maidens
Wherever you roam —
Keep your pretty legs crossed
And stay right at home."

An old lady in a black straw bonnet which covered her ears, and a heavy black silk waist, heard the voice, dropped her prayer book, looked in scorn at the slowly moving wagon, picked up her manual of devotion, and hurried on.

The bow scraped the fiddle and the voice continued —

"Come, all you young ramblers
From over the land,
And teach the young maiden
To love a good man —"

Fiddle and voice became quiet. To avoid the dust I lingered far behind. The wagon turned again on an unpaved road, down which could be seen the pine grandstand of the county Fair Grounds.

It turned in at the entrance to the Grounds and was lost to view.

We walked toward the Fair Grounds.

My companion's manner was careless and confident. His eyes, bright blue, gave his girlish face the expression of innocence.

He traveled over the Middle West from early spring until late fall as a grifter.

Each week he obtained several dozen rings which were marked "14 karat-gold shell." He would scratch off the last two words and explain to rustics that the ring was a gift from his dead mother. The scratched place was where the jeweler had engraved his initials at her request. He deeply regretted selling the ring. He would ask the rustic for his name and address, promising to send twice the amount asked as soon as he reached home. They nearly always insisted on buying the ring outright. As he found men eager to profit by his supposed misfortune, he sold many rings.

Once a road-kid, he would not pay railroad fare. Instead, he carried differently colored pieces of paste board. They looked like the hat checks used by conductors of passenger trains. He knew which color indicated his destination. He would cut holes in the paper that resembled those made by the conductor, and ride free.

If he happened to have no paste board, he stole the hat check of a passenger going far enough.

An imitation gold watch was always on his person. Inside the rear lid was engraved, "Warranted 25 years. Solid gold. Adjusted five positions."

He carried several such watches in his valise. They cost eleven dollars a dozen.

Each time he looked at the watch, he bragged of its value if any one was within hearing.

"Let's walk over to Coffee Sam's," suggested my com-rade. He motioned toward the wagon I had seen. A man wrapped the American flag about the post of his pine stand as we approached.

"Hello there, Buddy," he greeted my companion.

Around sixty, Coffee Sam was hatless, and bald headed. The top of his head was red as his face.

"Thought I lost you over in Stillwater," he smiled.

The young fellow placed his valise on the counter.

"Not me, mate. I had a soft touch over there and got held up for a day. Would you like a nice fourteen-karat gold ring for some of your grub?"

The red-skinned man laughed. "Not me — I'm not like these yaps, lookin' for somethin' for nothin'. But if you're strapped, I'll feed you." He looked at me. "Who's the kid — some runaway?"

"Quit foolin'— he don't look like no runaway — wanta flatter him," said the lad with the valise.

Smiling, Coffee Sam said, "All I got's stuff I brought on the wagon — this bread's harder'n a wedding stick, but you fellows got good teeth."

"Not for wedding sticks," laughed the youth.

In a few minutes we were seated on the shady side of Coffee Sam's lunch stand.

"I been travelin' twenty-four hours to get here. Matilda ain't got up yit — she's still hittin' the hay in the wagon," he said.

A lull came. Matilda snored loudly.

Coffee Sam trembled.

"Father in Heaven, I thought it was an earthquake. Do they have them in this state? I'm 'fraid as hell of them. Ever been through one?" He looked at my companion.

"I'll say I have — it don't sound like a biscuit shooter snorin' though."

He shook condensed milk into a large tin cup of coffee, and swallowed, sputtering, "This stuff would wash the dirt out of a dago section hand's ear."

"Well I don't claim that," laughed Coffee Sam, "but I'm puttin' it up in cans next year an' advertisin' it in the big magazines — I'm gettin' damned good and tired o' workin' for a livin'."

Coffee Sam smiled.

"It's come day, go day with you kids, ain't it? I don't know what's comin' o' the world. You little devils know more about sin than the devil did when he was chucked out of Heaven."

"Sure, the devil was a chump. I coulda sold him a ring any day. He even got throwed out of Heaven where everybody was a sap."

A noise was heard.

"That's Matildy gittin' up," sighed Coffee Sam, "She's performin' her mornin' absolutions. They hain't no house big enough for a woman an' a man, an' I live wit' an itchbay in a wagon. They sure oughta let me in Heaven. I'm sap enough."

"You'll never make it sellin' the kinda coffee you do.

If St. Peter ever drunk a cup of that stuff it'd give him the diabetes."

"Don't make fun," advised Coffee Sam. "Who knows the kind of coffee he drunk? There was no decent canned cream in them days. Now a bum like you kin have luxuries our dear Savyure couldn't never knew."

Coffee Sam wiped a cup.

"But I'm kiddin' on the square," said the youth.

"So was He, an' you'd of tried to sell Him a ring."

The youth pondered for a second.

"It mighta been good luck for Him at that. He could always unload it. Them apostles were all saps. They didn't know whether they was comin' or goin', afoot or a horseback. They were always fishin' or somethin', an' you never saw a fisherman that had any sense. What the hell guy in his right mind kin sit on his hind end all week and feed worms to things in the water?"

Coffee Sam heard another noise in the wagon.

"Well, I kin think o' worse things to do," he concluded.

"Well, think again," snapped the grifter as Matilda looked over the scene, swollen-eyed and cross. A pair of Coffee Sam's shoes, unfastened, were on her feet.

"Gimme a cup o' that hot java?" Her words were a snarl. Coffee Sam handed her a steaming tin cup of liquid, which she took without a word. She looked about, saw a seat under a tree, and walked, her shoes nearly falling off at each step, toward it.

Coffee Sam rubbed his sweating bald head; then shook

it slowly, "They're all alike, a lot of itchbays." As if to translate his lingo, he added —, "bitches, every one."

A spotted cur jumped out of the wagon.

"Come here, you ugly man's dog," said Coffee Sam.

The dog yelped in joy, while Coffee Sam sang,

> *"There was a jolly bachelor*
> *Who died at ninety-eight.*
> *And by his will, the old boy left*
> *The whole of his estate*
> *To women who had answered, 'No'*
> *When he asked them to wed —*
> *Oh, he was very thankful for*
> *The happy life he'd led."*

A LEADER OF SONG

UNCLE COFFEE SAM WORE A faded Grand Army of the Republic uniform. His voice could be heard far over the Fair Grounds as he shouted to passersby the merits of his coffee and food.

He had been making the rounds of the same fairs for years and could call many people by name.

He had a different woman with him each season. "They're like socks, you gotta change 'em often," he used to say.

His dog, Spot, would wander over the grounds. Sam petted him each time he returned from his wanderings.

On a brass tag attached to his collar were the words,

> *"I'm an old bird dog and I belong*
> *To Uncle Coffee Sam —*
> *And if I get lost, he'll pay the freight*
> *And he won't give a damn."*

An address in Saint Paul was scratched below.

Sam gave his permanent address to all his customers.

A placard tacked to a post near a large coffee urn read —

> *"Old soldiers welcome, either side*
> *Four years of blood and four years of tears*
> *Let us be friends in our declining years."*

Tobacco stained and senile veterans of the Civil War loitered near his stand.

He was cheerful and carefree with me.

"Stay around as long as you want to, Son — you can always get grub and coffee, and you won't roll off the ground if you want to sleep. If you hang around with that other kid you'll get pinched, and then where'll you be? You've got to watch them kinky kids. If the police pick you up, you can tell 'em you're workin' for me."

I helped him wash the granite cups and plates during rush hours.

One night when the grounds were deserted, an old ferris wheel owner stopped at the tent.

Matilda disappeared with money that day. Coffee Sam finished his daily denouncement of women and asked me,

"Have you seen that young grifter?"

"Not to-day," I answered.

"Do you reckon he put her up to stealin' that money?"

"It's hard to tell."

"Well, somebody did. She hasn't brains enough to

think of it herself." The owner of the ferris wheel said, "Forgit your troubles, Uncle; have you any coffee?"

"Sure thing." He went to an urn and filled three cups with the black concoction.

"Where'd you learn to make coffee so good?" asked the ferris wheel owner.

"In the army," was the reply.

"Which army?"

"Which army?" Coffee snorted. "Which army do you suppose? Why, the Union Army — do I look like a Rebel?"

"No — not exactly." The ferris wheel owner grinned. "I had a brother that served."

"So did I — two of them," said Coffee Sam. "Zeke had charge of General Sherman's horses." He asked quickly, "Ever see Sherman?" "Nope."

"I have," said Coffee Sam proudly. "He was the quickest movin' man I ever did see."

The owner of the ferris wheel sipped coffee. I watched Coffee Sam.

"He moved like a streak of lightning."

"That's movin' fast," said the ferris wheel owner.

"Yes sir — ee —" emphasized Coffee Sam. "Without old Razor Lip Sherman we'd be fighting yet. It was Bill Sherman that won the war. His brains were all up in his head."

Coffee Sam's manner became more serious.

"I was a sharpshooter all through the War. You wouldn't think to see me now that I could knock a squirrel's eye out two hundred yards away. If they'd of had a gun that shot far enough I could of nipped a button off the pants of the Man in the Moon. I plinged so many of the Johnny Rebs in Tennessee they thought it was hailin' bullets, and they put a rock over old Andy Jackson's grave so he wouldn't get up and start shootin'.

"They captured me the last year and sent me to Andersonville.

"I escaped and caught up with Sherman's army on its march to the sea.

"The Rebels began to send the Yanks away hundreds at a time to other prisons. There must of been fifty thousand of us when I was there. The stockade wasn't any bigger'n thirty acres."

Coffee Sam whistled.

"Fifteen hundred men to the acre. We were packed like sardines, and darn near as naked — no clothes but our underwear, and barefooted as just born Nigger babies.

"The whole prison was excited when we heard that Sherman was coming to free us.

" 'Soldier for soldier,' old Razor Lip Bill said, 'I'll shoot every Rebel in Georgia. When I get through this march a crow'll starve to death a mile behind us.

" 'I didn't start the war, but by God I'm goin' to end it,' says he, and if he hadn't done what he did in Georgia the war'd of dragged on till the North gave up and allowed the South to take their Niggers and separate."

Coffee Sam rubbed his bald head.

"Any how when they give the order that if Sherman got within seven miles of Andersonville to shoot us all like rats, I tunneled under the stockade."

I could hear the coffee simmering. Spot barked at a slice of moon.

Coffee Sam listened.

"I think sometimes Spot's part bloodhound," he said half to himself.

"He do sound that way," returned the ferris wheel owner.

"He makes me think of the bloodhounds at Andersonville. They used to bay all night and the only way you could get away from them if you escaped was to climb a tree. If you didn't they'd tear you to pieces. And if a Yank prisoner got wounded by a dog, he got no doctor when they took him back in the stockade."

Coffee Sam looked at the ferris wheel owner. "It was tougher in Andersonville than runnin' a ferris wheel in the winter.

"We had no wood in the stockade, and no way to cook our grub. Some kind of mush that tied our guts in knots was thrown to us once a day and we fought over it like dogs.

"At first there was some pine trees but they were cut down. 'No shade for a God damned Yankee,' says Captain Wirz. I'll bet he needs shade where he is now — they popped his neck after the war."

I could hear the knuckles crack in Coffee Sam's hands as he opened and closed them.

"A lot of prisoners tried to escape over the stockade by making a rope out of old blankets. They were betrayed by other prisoners, and afterward a deadline was made about twenty feet from the stockade. If a prisoner put his hand over the deadline, he was liable to be shot by one of the guards who were on little platforms above the stockade and overlooking the whole prison.

"It was a hundred and ten in the shade, and no shade. We dug holes in the ground to get out of the heat. Many a sick prisoner died in these holes, and the priest had to crawl in after them.

"The least thing that happened inside, the guards shot their muskets into us. I've seen many an innocent fellow get shot.

"And only one doctor for thousands of men. A splinter in your hand would cause gangrene. I've seen them rot till they could be cut off with scissors.

"One poor young devil from Indiana was so filthy for so long that another prisoner, to tease him, told him that we were all to have a bath and our wounds dressed and fresh clean clothes in the morning. The next day came, and nothing else. He got shot when he went crazy and tried to climb over the wall. His mouth drooled blood, and his eyes rolled like loose glass marbles in his head.

"I don't think he was much older than myself. It was hard to tell age there, with the mud and the lice and the blood.

"He studied a few months to be a doctor when the war broke out.'

"He came to Andersonville a week after me. His hair was yellow then, and in two months there was patches of gray all through it.

"They dragged him to the shack they called the hospital. It had no floor and if a man died in the morning he laid there till night, with a million green flies buzzing around him. You could smell the place so far away that even the farmers had to move. Every bit of filth stayed right inside.

"That winter was the coldest ever seen in Georgia. We burrowed into the ground to keep warm. Blood from our cracked feet oozed on the frozen ground. The guards told us to write home for blankets and flannels, that we'd be allowed to keep them. Our women sent us all we asked for. But the damned guards took them.

"One man went crazy thinking of food. He would sit by the hour imagining he was home with his family and keep saying, 'Have some more fried chicken, Eddie —and more biscuits and gravy, Mary.' We breathed easier when he croaked.

"There was an Irish kid," he looked keenly at me. "His hair was red like yours, and freckles ran across his nose. He'd only been in this country a little while when he joined up in the winter of '63. From the north of Ireland, too, a Protestant kid, I remember.

"He had a sore on his foot, big as an egg an' full of gangrene. The sun burned it in the day, the fever at night.

"The priest's name was Father Hanlon, I think. He

forgot about whether the lad was Catholic or not. He just knew he was a kid in trouble.

"He took off his own socks and gave them to him. He tried to give him his shoes, but the lad couldn't wear them.

"When he started for Savannah to get medicine for the kid's foot, he says, 'You'll be a good brave boy until I come back. Pain's hard to endure — but our loving Christ endured it. The nails tore through His hands and made holes as big as the one in your foot.'

"But little Flaherty moaned in the night and raved in the day.

" 'Father Hanlon, Father Hanlon, Father — God have mercy — me foot is burnin' off — Rather would I be dead, oh, Holy God — rather would I be dead — mother, mother, father, mother, Ireland.—Father Hanlon — Father Hanlon — God have mercy.'

"Sore foot and all, he dashed across the deadline — 'Shoot me! Shoot me! — Turn me soul loose with your bullets —'

"I wasn't over thirty feet from him.

"Two bullets turned him clear around. He stretched his arms out, and the blood turned his hair redder still.

"Father Hanlon came the next day with the medicine.

" 'So the boy's gone home," he said to Captain Crail. 'I'll write and tell his mother.' 'Yes, do,' says the Captain, 'she'll be proud to know.'

"Father Hanlon was tall, and his face was thin, and his eyes sad and kind of gray. He'd close the eyes of the dead and write to their families, and he'd cry a little as he looked about among us.

"I can swear that I saw his shoulders droop a foot while I was there. His eyes got more hollow and sad. There were no preachers among us at all. When he walked among us we stood at attention like he was Razor Lip Sherman. If there's no heaven anywhere, which I don't know, they ought to build one for men like him. But of course he'd be sad there. His heaven was in helpin' others down here in hell.

"In the freezing weather some kind Southern people sent us some clothes.

"General Winder threw the clothes out and yelled till he was purple that the whole damn country was turning Yankee.

"When we were dying a hundred a day, Old Winder yelled, 'The God-damn Yanks ain't dyin' fast enough.'

"Winder looked like those pictures of Kentucky colonels you see on whisky bottles. He had long white hair, and a mouth that sneered at the corners.

"One time he took some visitors to the cemetery where three thousand northern soldiers were buried that month. He waved his hand over the graves and bragged that he was doing more for the South than a dozen regiments.

"It rained every day for a solid month. The swamp around the stockade was a foot thick with the maggots from men who'd died to make niggers free. They flew like a lot of bullets loaded with gangrene, and they stung like bees when they bit us.

"I've seen the scurvy make many a poor devil's teeth fall out. Their gums would swell till they stuck outside their lips."

Coffee Sam breathed deeply, and looked at the gauge on the largest coffee urn. He closed his eyes and rubbed them for at least a dozen seconds.

He continued slowly,

"There was one captain in the prison from New York State. He used to sit alone by the hour. Was a big fellow. Even Andersonville could not make him thin. His name was Crail.

"He'd been captain of a colored regiment. The guards hated him more than us. 'Damned Nigger commander,' they used to call him." Coffee Sam gulped, "But he was a man if there ever was one.

"He never whimpered, never even got his lips out of place. His mouth was sharp like General Sherman's.

"When we scrambled for grub like starving wolves, Captain Crail, as hungry as any of us, stood back.

"After a while, men made way for him. His face was square and large; his eyes were small and soft black. They didn't seem to belong with his jaw.

"You can get some idea the kind of a man the Captain was when I tell you that at first one man going there could carry a pail. Later it took two men to carry it. Then they got so weak they could only carry a half pail between them.

"But Crail never changed. Insults from the guards left his face the same. He walked so stiff he couldn't have bent his back even if Razor Lip Sherman passed by.

"The guards watched him closer than any one else.

"He told me one time about his wife and little girl. He'd been married right after he got out of West Point. They lived in a little town near Syracuse.

" 'They're very beautiful,' he said, 'very beautiful.' His eyes were as stern as ever, 'Are you married?' he says to me.

" 'No,' I admitted, 'a sharpshooter don't want no wife.'

"I might as well of said nothing. He paid no attention.

" 'You will never be happy until you are,' he says. 'My two are very beautiful, very beautiful.'

"I never saw him change but once. That was when we heard that Sherman was coming. He was another man then, a great leader.

"He organized the whole prison and got thousands of men to singin'—

> 'John Brown's body lies a moldering in the grave
> But his soul goes marching on —'

"If I live to be older than God, I never expect to hear anything like those fifty thousand men, ragged as scarecrows, barefooted, in their drawers, their hair matted with mud, singin' like men gone crazy. Jesus Christ — what a scene!

"They called out extra guards. We paid no attention."

Coffee Sam was no longer a vendor of brown water — but a soldier before whom marched the intrepid ghosts of golden and glorious and mighty vanished days. In his eyes were flames. In his heart the gift of words.

"Those poor broken devils were something grand to see. Too weak to carry a pail of water, they sang till they God-damn near cracked the clouds.

"It made me love them, and makes me tingle around the heart even yet — made me feel that maybe in spite of everything there was something of Christ in men.

"Those voices," Coffee Sam wiped his eyes, "are most of them quiet now. But they sang like fiends then,— loud enough to shake the stars —

> *'Mine eyes have seen the glory*
> *Of the coming of the Lord;*
> *He is trampling out the vintage*
> *Where the grapes of wrath are stored;*
> *He has loosed the fateful lightning*
> *Of His terrible swift sword*
> *His truth is marching on.'*

"Captain Crail's shirt was torn far down. The hair on his chest, thick and black as burned grass, went up and down like a wave.

> *'I have seen him in the watch-fires*
> *Of a hundred circling camps;*
> *They have builded Him an altar*
> *In the evening dews and damps;*
> *I can read His righteous sentence*
> *By the dim and flaring lamps*
> *His day is marching on.'*

"You could hear Crail's voice above all the rest when he came to the line —

> *'Let the hero, born of woman,*
> *Crush the serpent with his heel —'*

"At the last, he held his long arm high and waved it slowly, till everybody sang low —

> *'In the beauty of the lilies*
> *Christ was born across the sea,—*
> *With a glory in His bosom*
> *That transfigures you and me:*
> *As He died to make men holy*
> *Let us die to make men free*
> *While God is marching on.'*

"For a moment, Crail stood, frozen in my brain forever.

"Both arms reached up as if they would grab the moon. His fists closed big as mallets.

" 'Over again,' he shouted. 'Over, and over, and over, and over, and over once again'— You should have heard those voices — God Almighty, how they roared —

> *'As He died to make men holy*
> *Let us die to make men free,*
> *While God is marching on.'*

"The Negroes broke out of their corral and defied the muskets to swarm around Crail.

"It was hours before they got things quiet."

Spot barked again.

"God-damn that dog," said Coffee Sam, irritated.

"What became of Captain Crail?" I asked.

"I'm comin' to that."

"When five of us planned to escape we went to Captain Crail. He heard our plan.

" 'What do you want me to do?' he asked.

" 'Go with us,' I said. 'You're too good a man to be in here.'

" 'All right,' he says.

"We only had one left handed man and we needed another, for too many right handed fellows made the tunnel go to the left in a kind of circle.

" 'Are you right or left handed, Captain?' I asked.

" 'Either one,' he said.

"It took us weeks to get the tunnel done, hidin' in it in the daytime with old blankets and watchin' so's our our own men inside didn't betray us.

"I never saw Captain Crail get tired. He'd dig with a canteen for hours and we'd carry the dirt away in old boots.

"We drew straws to decide in what order we should crawl out under the stockade. I got first and Crail second. We made the getaway together and before we got a hundred feet away I heard musket shots, and Crail fell.

"I leaned over him for a second.

" 'Hurry — you'll get shot,' he gasped.

"There was no more shootin', just why, I never knew. I've always thought it a scheme of the Johnny Rebs to git Crail. If it was, they never got a better man."

TRUSTING PEOPLE

UNLESS THE WEATHER threatened, Coffee Sam would roll the canvas from above his seat when starting on a journey, "So I can see the stars."

His team never trotted.

"A horse should do what it wants to do. It's hard enough being a horse without somebody whipping you besides."

The Fair closed on Friday night at one county seat and opened at another the following Tuesday. Even if Coffee Sam had to skip a county, the distance he traveled was never over a hundred miles.

During the first two days of the Fair he would make genuine coffee. During the last two, he would mix it heavily with chicory. "When you get the rubes to comin' you can sell 'em anything."

With a half dozen farmers at his counter he would say aloud to himself, "Yes, sir, yes, sir, without the farmer we'd all starve to death. Suppose nobody farmed anything for a year — then where'd we be? I'd hate to tell you."

When they were not around he referred to them as rubes and apple-knockers.

He was rated as wealthy.

Only half his revenue came from the sale of coffee and sandwiches. An adept short change artist, it distressed him to make correct change.

His eyes traveled over the Milky Way.

"Know what makes that white up there?" he asked.

"No," I answered.

"It's buffaloes kickin' up dust across the sky."

I said nothing.

"Do you believe in God or somethin'?" he asked, staring straight ahead.

"I don't know what to believe — do you?"

"Nope — it's all hit or miss — a lot of devils grabbin' each other's tails off."

He clucked at his slow moving horses, and said several minutes later, "If there was a God — Captain Crail wouldn't have been shot."

I made no comment.

"Am I right?" he asked.

"Maybe."

He held the lines loosely in his hands, and clucked at his team. They paid no attention, but dragged their heavy hoofs listlessly over the dusty road.

"When they mustered me out in Washington I went to see Captain Crail's wife." Coffee Sam gripped the lines tighter, "And God — I didn't blame him for likin' marriage. I've never in all my born days seen but one other girl as purty. She was in a joint in Chi—. She was like a porcelain with blood runnin' through it — I mean the Captain's wife — and the other one —

"She had a smile there was nothing like and her hair was the color of a yellow butterfly's wings when the sun's a shinin' on it.

"She lived in a house big as the City Hall in Saint Paul, and when a servant let me in I felt like runnin' away.

"Then she came into the room and I could have cried for Captain Crail in that damned Georgia grave, leavin' a woman like that with her arms empty.

"There was a picture of the Captain and her on the organ. I looked at it.

"'He was that proud and fine lookin' right up to the last,' I says — and I told her what he said about me bein' married.

"'I'm so glad,' she said, 'so proud just to have had him so short a time. He is tangled in my heart forever. There can never be another like him.' She looks at him there in his uniform, handsome as General Lee, and she put her strawberry lips against the glass and says, 'You dear, dear, dear, great rock in a weary land'— she turns quick to me and says, 'It was lovely of you to come here —' 'No, it wasn't ma'am,' I came right back— 'Seein' you is worth the trip.' Then I told her of the time he led us in song. She kept wantin' me to stay for hours and talk just about him.

" 'The little girl's asleep,' she says. 'You really must see her. She has eyes like her father's.'

" 'No, Madam, I'd rather not — one pair of eyes like his is all even a sharpshooter can stand in a lifetime — You just tell her a man came from her father, won't you'— and I hurried away.

*

"ALL that night and the next day and the next night I thought of Captain Crail in his grave — and a woman like that sleepin' alone till I made up my mind there just couldn't be a God, and if there was — he wasn't a white man, or one that ever knew what it was to have a woman like that."

He slapped the lines on his horses' backs.

"I may be wrong, but that's what I decided anyhow."

The team ambled on.

"No sound of crickets along the road, an early winter," said Coffee Sam. "It's a sure sign; they burrow down in the ground an' come up birds in the spring — that's more'n we can do —

"Oh, well —

"If I should die, bury me deep —
Bury me down where the willows weep —
Put my dinkus on my breast —
And tell the chippies I went West.

And if they ask for a man like me —
Tell 'em to look through eterni — tee.
Hoop de oodle de oodle de ay —
A man like me ain't born every day."

He put his collar up.

"The snow birds'll soon be flyin'— where do you hang up in the winter, Kid?"

"Most any place," I replied.

"I was in Chi a month last winter — that's *some town.* There's a joint there over around Custom House Place where the sky's the limit — the girls are purty — one of them I met I'd make coffee for the rest of her life — I'd put her on a chair and look at her an hour each morning before I'd do anything else. She's the only one's as purty as Captain Crail's wife."

He sighed deeply.

"It's hell — a fellow likin' 'em purty as I do — and cartin' haybags around like Matildy — but we can't get everythin' in this world — if you have ham you need eggs, and bread you need butter, and a heart you need a woman."

"What's the girl's name?" I asked.

"Chlorine."

"That's a poison."

"That's what she says she is," Coffee Sam laughed.

He sighed again.

"I'm settin' on this wagon to tell you that better men than me can take worse poison than her though."

"What joint's she in?"

"Gettin' anxious?" he laughed,—"Paddy Croan's — near the Polk Street Station."

We drove on in silence for some distance.

A rig passed.

"I wonder who's in that rig." Coffee Sam looked at me. "You'll never know — neither'll I. That's what makes it all so funny. Like a game you get started playin' and can't quit till you're broke."

There came the moan of autumn wind. The canvas flapped.

"Three more weeks and I crawl for the winter like a cricket."

"Maybe you can see the girl in Chi."

"Not me," said Coffee Sam — "I'm an awful fool, but I don't get my foot in no trap like that. I might of right after the war. Many a woman's gone to bed with a uniform, but not now. She's barroom smart — now if I was your age — I'd take a chance. Suppose you make good — you got what a million dollars can't buy. Boy!! — she's got a leg that'd make a bishop wish he was a priest again."

Coffee Sam started to whistle and broke into rapid song.

> *"I wish I was single agin, agin,*
> *I wish I was single agin—*

Oh, when I was single my money did jingle,
I wish I was single agin.

I married me a wife oh then, oh then,
I married me a wife oh then —
I married me a wife; she's the plague of my life,
I wish I was single agin.

My wife she died oh then, oh then,—
My wife she died oh then,
I married me another, the devil's own mother —
I wish I was single agin.—"

He stopped suddenly —"But I got a better system now — a new one every year — of course they're not so new. I'm too old to pick 'em new, but they've never been used by me, and that's a little help. A guy'd get tired of the Queen of Sheba even if she had silver bubbies.

"I wish I was single agin, agin,
I wish I was single agin,—"

"But that Chlorine, she sticks in my head right along. Old Razor Lip said if he owned hell and Texas, he'd sell his interest in Texas and live in hell. Well, if I owned Heaven and Chlorine, I'd lease Heaven for a County Fair Grounds and live in a shack with Chlorine.

"It's all the bunk anyhow, Kid. None of it's worth the sweat on a cop's ears unless you got a gal like Chlorine. I've seen a lot in my time and the only time I've been happy was when I was nuts on a skirt. Of course you get double crossed and everything, but that's the game — that's what makes it good when you get it."

The team turned on a better road and climbed a hill.

The moon, yellow as the road, and nearly as low, was directly in front of us.

Coffee Sam, his eyes staring at the moon, said, "It's funny, this damned woman business. It's like grub. You've got to have it. You get a belly full and you think you're all fixed up, and you die if you don't get more. It's the same with a woman. You lay up with 'em all night and you get so God damned sick of 'em, you could put a one cent stamp on 'em and send them to hell with no return address on 'em. The next night, by God, you want the itchbays. I'd like to be a eunuch — but then I suppose I'd get a rain check —

> *"I wish I was single agin, agin,*
> *I wish I was single agin."*

*

WHEN the stand was ready at the next county seat, the young grifter approached.

Coffee Sam looked at him closely and asked,

"Did you see anythin' of that damned itchbay of mine?"

The young grifter laughed.

"What the hell do you think I'm doin' — robbin' old ladies' homes — you think because you pick up them worn out skirts that I want 'em. Not me! I like 'em just when they're peekin' out of the shell — did she nip you for much dough?"

"About forty dollars," replied Sam.

"That ain't much," said the grifter. "I thought she took you for some real money."

"All money's real that a woman gets." He took off his blue coat. "A lot of rubes have gotta guzzle a lot of chicory to get me forty bucks back."

"Only about a dollar's worth," returned the grifter.

That night the young fellow asked me to take a walk with him.

In a small hotel, Matilda sat waiting.

"I fixed it up for you," he said. "Just go and tell Sam you find you can't live without him — he'll believe it — they all do — don't tell him you gave me the money — it might make him mad — he thinks all women are crooked anyhow; so you ain't done him no harm."

Matilda returned.

"I just couldn't live without you, Sam," she said. "I never knew no one so kind as you."

Coffee Sam studied a moment.

"I love you, Sam — you kin make the best coffee in all the world. I never had sense enough to know it till I left an' had to drink that hot water other people make and call it coffee."

"Well," said Sam, "I understand, Matildy. "You're like all the other women — you'd never commit a sin if no man was around to tempt you. I understand."

Matilda straightened her slattern body and laid a red wrinkled hand on the counter.

"You're a good man, Sam, and a forgivin' one. I jist couldn't hurt you no more. From here on I want to work with you an' learn how to make coffee. I kin surely learn if I put my mind to it — by spring —"

"Well, *maybe*," Sam looked doubtful. "No woman ever learned how to make coffee yet."

The young grifter appeared.

"Well — glad to see you both."

Coffee Sam smiled.

"Glad to see you, Kid. Sorry I spoke the way I did yesterday."

"Oh, well, no harm done, Sam. Every man makes mistakes where a woman's concerned. Men are always accusin' other men of doing their family chores for them, and it ain't right. I'll tell you, Sam, you look for the worst in people and you get it. When people think I'm honest I just can't sell 'em a ring — Now you try thinkin' right thoughts, Sam, and see how it works."

Matilda's eyes clung, beaten, dog fashion, to the young grifter.

Too young to sense the pity of the situation, the woman's eyes made me feel uneasy.

The young grifter stood at one end of the counter with Coffee Sam. He held a watch in his hand.

"You know, Sam," he said warmly, "I wouldn't hook you. We're on the same side of the fence." He opened the back of the watch. "See here," he pointed, " 'Warranted 25 years. Solid gold. Adjusted. Five positions.' "

He closed the watch. "It's a steal at twenty dollars. I nipped it out of a guy's pocket last night. He looked like a pickpocket himself — or a lawyer."

Sam examined the watch closely. "She does look like a good turnip," he said.

"Sure, it's a good turnip. I wouldn't cheat you. Why you can pawn it for twenty dollars. That shows that it's worth eighty. A Jew'll only give you a fourth of what it's worth."

Sam inspected the watch again.

"If you take it, Sam, I'd want you to let me have it back when I get a little more flush. I wouldn't have to peddle it now, but a Nigger jockey cheated me in a crap game. You know, Sam, if a fellow pawns a watch, they change the works and steal the jewels out of the case and everything. That's why I'd rather leave this with you. I'll see you in Superior and give you thirty dollars for it back."

Without another word, Sam laid twenty dollars on the counter and put the watch in his pocket.

*

THE Grand Army of the Republic held a parade on the last day of the Fair.

Coffee Sam marched with his comrades.

Matilda had charge of the stand.

I returned at dusk.

"Bill's arrested," I confided to her. "The police want fifty dollars to let him go."

Bewildered, she gave me the money.

I hurried away.

TO SEE A WOMAN

COFFEE SAM'S DESCRIPTION of Chlorine remained with me. I thought of her often.

The December sun was hot over California. After winning a hundred and ten dollars in a crap game, I decided to go to Chicago. I could live there all winter on a hundred dollars. Besides, I would take a chance on Chlorine.

As it would not be safe to travel with so much money, I mailed a hundred dollar Post Office Money Order to myself at General Delivery, Chicago. Wrapping the identification slip in a piece of newspaper, I pinned it in an inside shirt pocket.

For thirteen hours I rode under the Golden State Limited to Tucson, Arizona. Pebbles thrown upward by the speed of the roaring train made my face and body raw. Before noon the next day I crawled from underneath and went to the jungle.

It was full of hoboes bound for the sunshine of California.

That night I went under another Limited until I reached El Paso. I was fourteen hours in making the trip, the most of which was through a freezing gale.

The man at the pump house there had been a brakeman before he left one leg under a train.

His job was to keep the large tank full of water for engines bound east.

"Which way you headed, Kid?"

"Chicago."

He whistled.

"You'll freeze your ears off. It's near zero, and gittin' colder right along."

He walked about swiftly with a crutch. "It's near a hundred miles to Dalhart, no gittin' off less you freeze an' fall off once you git on. Your blood's got to keep purty hot."

A tall man approached.

"Which way, 'Bo?"

"East."

"Well, there's the track east — keep a walkin'. I'm the Law."

I walked east about fifty feet and turned into a saloon, not far from the track. The bartender had been looking out the window.

He turned as I entered.

"Cold enough for you, 'Bo?"

"Yeap — give me a shot — and a half pint."

He put the liquor on the bar.

"Who's the tall guy — railroad bull or town clown?" I pointed to him.

"Town clown — why?"

"He just told me to walk out of town."

"The hell he did — on a night like this — a hell of a guy he is."

The tall man entered the saloon.

"What do you mean makin' a man hit the ties this kind of weather?"

The town clown replied,

"He was botherin' Limpy over there."

"You know better'n that — you just want to show your authority — why don't you watch the town and let the railroad people look out for themselves?"

I made for the door as the Limited whistled.

"Are you ridin' to-night, 'Bo?"

"Yeap — I'm on my way."

"My God, you'll freeze your ears off. It's ninety miles to the first stop."

"I can make it if you have the Law here let me alone."

"He'll let you alone all right. Have a drink, Slim."

I hurried to the pump house and wrapped burlap around my shoes.

"It'll freeze right through them," said the one-legged brakeman.

"It's better'n nothing," I returned.

The head light of the engine cut through the frozen mist like a long yellow knife.

To keep the saliva from freezing on my lips, I curled my tongue back.

"For Christ's sake, if you're goin,' wrap this around your ears — you'll lose 'em along the way if you don't."

The one-legged brakeman tied a large handkerchief around my head.

"It's five below, Boy. Good luck."

When the train pulled out, I was underneath.

Neither pebbles nor sand flew upward from the road-bed. They were frozen fast.

I twisted myself into position to get the whisky to my mouth and, loosening the handkerchief slightly, drank sparingly. Too much, I might doze and fall beneath the swiftly grinding wheels.

The wind was sharp as flying razor blades.

I began to count the minutes. In an hour and a half I would be in Dalhart.

My feet were soon heavy and cold as stone. I put the whisky in a coat pocket, wrapped my arms about the rods, and lifted my half frozen feet with an effort.

I lost track of time in the whirling cold.

A prolonged shriek came from the engine whistle. My heart jumped. We were nearing Dalhart. The train slowed for a second and gave two long and two short shrieks. It was for a road crossing.

What seemed an eternity passed. I gulped the last of the whisky. The empty bottle fell noiselessly under the train.

I dared not touch the rods with my bare hands for fear they would stick to the frozen iron.

A numbness tried to control my brain. I could feel the whisky dying. I fought to keep awake. My eyes went half shut and opened as the wheels crashed over a railroad crossing.

A light flashed under the train. I hoped again.

It stopped. I rolled off by instinct.

I fell to the ground and struggled to rise. Unable to call out, I rolled about like a beheaded chicken.

A car knocker came along, inspecting the train.

"Will you help me on my feet, Mister?" I asked.

"Sure, Boy."

He lifted me up.

I fell down at once.

"Gosh — you're froze, Boy."

"Will you help me to a telephone pole? I'll kick my feet till they get warm."

I kicked at the pole with heavy feet and held it with my arms.

The car knocker returned and dragged me to a little all night restaurant a block away.

He stood me erect at the door and cut the burlap from my shoes.

Dragging me inside, he placed me on a chair.

A man ran from behind the counter.

"Git him some java," shouted the car knocker.

I gulped at the hot liquid and burned my throat while he brought me a basin of cold water.

I dipped my hands. They stung as though I grabbed needles.

The car knocker took the handkerchief from around my ears.

"Why you're a white kid, ain't you? I thought you was a Nigger — you're froze blue."

"Sure, I'm Irish."

"The hell you are — I didn't think there was that damn big a fool among 'em, to freeze their ears off on a night like this — God — it's twelve below zero."

At last I could stand alone.

"Will you fix me some ham and eggs and a lot of coffee? I got money."

"Money and no brains," said the car knocker.

"You're right."

The car knocker left, still scolding me, "You damn fool kid."

"Well, I gotta see my mother. She's sick in Chicago."

"Oh, hell, you kids all got sick mothers some place. Why the devil don't you stay home with them!" He slammed the door.

"He's a good guy," said the restaurant fellow. "He's been helpin' hoboes goin' through here eight years, that I know of."

"Well, he saved my life," I said, as the grub was placed in front of me.

"What are you so nuts to git to Chicago about?"

"Just want to get there for Christmas."

I paid him for the meal and twenty-five cents for a bed. I slept till late afternoon, and rode that night through Oklahoma to Liberal, Kansas, where I waited on a heavy grade two miles east of the town. A fast cattle train had to slow up.

I rode it into Hutchison where a switch lamp tender told me there was a wreck on the Southern Pacific twenty miles down the line. I hurried to the Santa Fé tracks a short distance off and parallel.

The California Limited would pull out of Hutchison at eight that night. Chicago was about eight hundred miles away. I would be there in two days, with good luck. I made sure that my identification slip was secure.

Getting my bearings, I went to a restaurant to eat and wait until the train came in.

A rough looking fellow sat next to me at the counter.

He asked the usual, "Which way, 'Bo?" as I laid a five dollar bill on the counter.

Thinking him another hobo, I pocketed the change and told him I was wheeling out on the California Limited.

He looked at a heavy clock on the wall.

"She'll soon be here."

When it came in, he walked with me toward it.

"Where you goin' to ride?" he asked.

"The gunnels, under the observation car."

When the train was about ready to leave he said quietly, "If you don't hand me the change from that five dollars, I'll tell the crew you're ridin', and where."

"That would be tough," I said to gain time and kept on walking slowly toward the end of the train.

"You bet it would. If they pick you up here, it's three months besides."

"That'd be tougher."

"I'll say it would." I looked at him sideways as we walked.

"Don't you think you could find a better graft than holding me up this way? There's a lot of banks and rich people in Hutchison — why don't you stick them up?"

"That's my business," he snarled. "All I've got to say's if you want to ride you kin fork over them four dollars."

The engine whistle sounded twice. The brakes loosened. The train moved.

The front end of the observation car was even with us.

"My God,— look who's comin'," I exclaimed. The man looked.

I cracked him on the jaw.

As he fell, I ducked under the car.

*

I RODE without further mishap into ——, a short ride from Chicago.

The lights glimmered over the steel rails.

Two men stopped me. One held a revolver, the other a blackjack.

The squat man asked,

"What you doin' on railroad property?" He poked the revolver in my side. "Put your hands up." I lifted my hands.

"Frisk him."

The man with the blackjack began to search me.

"You fellows're dicks, ain't you?"

"Why?"

"No yegg would pull a gun on a tramp kid."

"Shut up — we know our business."

They found all my money but a dollar.

"Is that all you got?" one asked.

"Sure — I didn't know I had that much."

They looked at each other.

"Search him again."

The man with the blackjack began to feel over my shirt. When he came to the identification slip, his hand stopped. He ripped the pocket, tore the newspaper, and looked at the stub.

"A hundred dollars, huh — and cheatin' the railroad."

I let my arms sag at the elbows.

"You fellows surely won't take it, will you — it's my stake for the winter."

"The hell we won't take it."

When the man with the revolver turned his eyes, I knocked it away from me with my left. A bullet blazed out of it as I hit him in the groin with my right.

The blackjack fell on my head. I went down and knew no more.

*

THE snow was falling in my face as I regained consciousness. I looked about the yards.

A streak of dawn was appearing in the east. The blood had congealed and matted my hair.

My clothes were soaked with melted snow. My head ached.

Christmas was two days off.

The snow continued to fall heavily.

The roofs of the cars and all objects were covered white.

I felt in my pockets with the hope of finding more money. It was hopeless.

I took the dollar they had failed to find and went to a lodging house. The cheapest bed was fifty cents. I paid it, went to a saloon on the corner and bought two drinks of whisky at ten cents each.

With enough left for breakfast I went to bed. Before falling asleep, I wondered how I could get the money at the Post Office. The word of a tramp would be no good with the government.

The person with the receipt could collect the money.

Learning early on the road to accept the worst and be surprised at the best, I tried to picture the two men.

I could hear factory whistles blowing.

"It's seven o'clock," I thought. "A lot of poor devils have to go to work."

I pushed a window open. The wind flapped the shade.

The noon whistles in nearby factories awakened me.

With my last cent gone for food, I walked, dejected, around the town.

*

A SHRIVELED old man, in a Salvation Army uniform, stood on one of the principal street corners and exhorted for alms as I passed. He held a utensil, shaped like a skillet, in his right hand. Hurrying people dropped money into it. Above him, on a post, in large letters were the words, "Keep the Kettle Boiling."

His coat fit loosely. His red cap crowded his ears. With whining voice and tearful eyes, he pleaded for the poor. Every now and then he looked about pitifully, as if eager for relief. A thought came to me.

Leaving him singing plaintively,

> *"Oh, how I love Jesus —*
> *Because He first loved me,"*

I straggled on to the Salvation Army Headquarters.

A lithograph was on the streaked wall. It represented the figure of a man with a close cropped red beard, clinging to a rock-shaped cross in the middle of a roaring sea.

He wore a red and blue robe much longer than himself.

Beneath, in a scroll, were the words,

> *"Rock of Ages, cleft for me,*
> *Let me hide myself in Thee."*

My arrival was not noted as a noon day meeting was being held.

A long Salvation Army coat hung on a nail in a hallway.

"What's the Major's name in charge here?" I asked a derelict who stared into the grimy and snowy street. "Williams," he answered tersely.

One door led to the hallway. Another to the street.

Taking the coat and cap from the hook, I left quickly.

Putting my torn cap in a pocket, I donned the headgear of the Lord.

The old man's rheumy eyes were glad as I approached.

"Major Williams sent me to relieve you," I said.

Without a word, he handed me the receptacle for the money.

He rubbed his cold hands together.

"They who give in the cause of the Lord shall be thrice blessed," he chattered. "It has been a generous day in His name. Major Williams will be pleased with the work of his humble private soldiers."

He lifted his cap to relieve his ears.

"Peace to you, Brother, and success in the Lord."

He turned in the direction of Salvation Army Headquarters.

Wondering how long it would take him to arrive at Headquarters, I began to sing,

"Blest be the power of Jesus' name."

Two heavy men glared at me.

"City detectives," I thought, and sang heartily while they glared.

My heart beat fast as one started toward me.

He was quite close when a siren screeched.

Traffic stopped. The fire department clangored by.

The crowd followed quickly.

I went in the other direction.

*

THE old man had collected nearly a hundred dollars.

I left at once for Chicago.

WHEN CHLORINE CAME TO Paddy Croan's, I stepped up to her and said, "A man told me, in Minnesota, that you were the most beautiful girl he'd ever seen."

She smiled. "That was nice. Was he blind?"

"No — he told me to give you his regards." I told her of Coffee Sam.

"What a life —, but I'd like it, I think."

She was dark and full of luster. Her eyes were large, vivid and brown. Lithe and graceful, she appeared to be about twenty-five.

"Will you have a drink?" I asked.

She scanned me with concern.

"If you'll let me buy it," she answered.

"I've never cared yet who bought my drinks."

"I care who buys mine," she retorted.

We moved to a table.

"What do you do for a living?" she asked.

"Nothing."

"Don't you ever work?"

"Not if I can help it."

"Suppose everybody felt that way."

"It's all right with me."

An old man approached us.

"Hello, Slavinsky," Chlorine smiled.

"Who's the boy?" he asked.

"How should I know," she sighed.

"May I sit down?" he asked.

"If you like — we're not planning a murder."

She looked at the old man and nodded at me. "The boy here brought a message from a man in Minnesota — he said I was the prettiest woman he'd ever seen — wasn't that nice?"

"Nice — and true. He must have got off easy."

I put money on the table. The girl pushed it toward me.

"I must be going," she said. "I have a heavy date to-night —" she frowned, "God, how I hate it." Then smiling at me, "Stick around, Kid — I'll take a drink on you later."

The old man went to the bar. Chlorine left. I sat at the table alone.

The next day would be Christmas. Two large bowls

containing Tom and Jerrys were on the bar. They were surrounded by dozens of china mugs.

Already the saloon was taking on the merriment of Christmas Eve.

I made sure that the money was intact. I could get a clean room on South State Street for twenty-five cents a night if I paid by the week, in advance. There was a dismal lobby with worn gray linoleum on the floor, and many smooth wooden chairs.

I paid four months rent in advance and had more than sixty dollars left. Second hand clothes and shoes would cost twenty more. I went without an overcoat and bought a woolen sweater instead.

I changed at the hotel.

From there I walked to Paddy Croan's.

The old man who had talked to me before stood at the bar. With him was a good looking mulatto.

"Come here, son," he called. "Have a Tom and Jerry, — this is Christmas Eve."

He turned me toward the good looking Negro. "Joe," he declared, "this boy just came in off the road." He motioned to the bartender.

"We are all brothers this Christmas night — I am the Great Slavinsky," he beamed proudly, "and this is Joe Gans."

"I've read a lot about you," I said to the Negro.

"I hope it wasn't nothin' bad," he grinned.

"And haven't you heard of the Great Slavinsky — the Emperor of Magic?" the old man asked.

"Sure — I've seen you on the stage — you're great."

"A bright boy," the old fellow said to Joe Gans.

"Have another Tom and Jerry?"

The liquor made my body warm and my brain tingle.

I had learned the art of telling a tale in a saloon from my grandfather.

Gans and the old man listened while I told of the Post Office Money Order.

Chlorine entered with a tall man. Her eyes went over me, "My you look different," she said.

"He's telling a story, Paddy," the old man said to the tall man, "It's of the road." I knew it was Paddy Croan.

"Let's sit down," suggested the old man, "Begin over, Boy," he said kindly.

I told it swiftly. When I had finished, Paddy Croan exclaimed, "God damn."

The three men exchanged glances. Chlorine looked at me with wide eyes.

"How long have you been on the road?" she asked.

"About six years."

There was a silence.

"What about the date?" asked the Great Slavinsky, looking at Chlorine.

"I passed it up till eleven. I didn't want to hear a diamond peddler brag all of Christmas Eve. He's coming here."

"Well, it's time for my show," said the Great Slavinsky —"Come, walk over, Joe."

They went out together.

Paddy Croan walked behind the bar and looked at the cash registers. Chlorine remained at the table.

She looked pensively about, then back at me.

"You're a Catholic, aren't you?" she asked.

"I was."

"What do you mean by — *was* — once a Catholic, always a Catholic. The Church never leaves you when you need it."

She pressed a button in the center of the table.

"Make mine very small," she said to the waiter. "And you?"

"I'll take another Tom and Jerry."

"I didn't tell all that story," I said, when the drinks arrived. "I left off the beginning. It was about you."

"Heavens — do tell me."

"I've had you in my head ever since Coffee Sam told me about you. I made up my mind to come and see you,— and here I am."

"What do you think it's going to get you? I'm not a whore."

"If you were, I wouldn't want you," I lied.

"The same old stuff," she said. "Men all talk alike."

"But they don't tramp two thousand miles to see a girl," I returned.

She looked at me as though half convinced.

"I'd like to believe you," she admitted. "After all you're just a kid. You can't be as rotten as older men. You haven't had time.'

"Well — I'm telling the truth. I got stuck on you as soon as Coffee Sam told me about you. I'm not cadgin' money. I've got my room rent paid till the first of May. You can always eat if you have your room rent."

"I know," she volunteered. "I've been there."

She looked at a diamond ring as she spoke.

"A long time ago," I put in.

"A lot less than a hundred years."

"About ninety-five less."

"Maybe," she smiled.

The place became crowded. Waiters rushed to tables with drinks while music came from an elevated platform in the rear.

A fat man came toward us.

"Here comes grief," Chlorine said. "I'll see you here to-morrow night."

The man looked at his watch. "Well, well," he said.

"I've been worried for fear you would be late," Chlorine smiled sweetly at him as she rose. "I'm sorry I was unable to see you sooner."

Paddy Croan watched her as she left.

During the day I loitered about the city, dividing my time between the library and the crowded streets.

I soon became useful to Paddy Croan. I knew how to make drunkards spend money at the bar.

I knew, through long training, how to make the tempo fit the occasion. If a man drank to forget trouble, I too, had trouble. If he were hilarious, I fitted his mood.

Often, I remained with drunken men for several days.

I knew many poems by heart, and made others up to suit the audience.

If the crowd were listless, a catchy tune, a swiftly recited verse, a dramatic tale made them more alert.

With two or three others, whisky before us, a song would be started,—

> *"The old gray mare ain't what she used to be*
> *Ain't what she used to be*
> *The old gray mare ain't what she used to be*
> *Twenty years ago —!*
>
> *Oh, the old gray mare ain't what she used to be*
> *Twenty years ago.*
> *Oh, when she was full of —— and blood —*
> *She'd knock the door knobs off a stud —*
> *Twenty years ago."*

One after another the verses would follow, each one making my drunken companions laugh the louder.

> *"In a cavern in a canyon*
> *Excavatin' for a mine —*
> *Dwelled a miner, forty-niner,*
> *And his daughter, Clementine —*
>
> *Light was she just like a feather,*
> *And her shoes were number nine,*
> *Shoes that fit a Denver copper*
> *Were too small for Clementine.*
>
> *Drivin' ducklin's to the water*
> *Every mornin' far from home*
> *She stubbed her toe upon a splinter*
> *And fell into the ragin' foam.*

> *Up then come from off the water*
> *Little bubbles soft and fine —*
> *But I was never no good swimmer;*
> *So I lost my Clementine —*
>
> *Then the miner, forty-niner,*
> *Soon began to peak and pine;*
> *So we sent him on a halter*
> *For to join his Clementine."*

The audience became noisier. Even Paddy became gay.

Paddy's favorite was "Ostler Joe," the tragic story of another man deceived by a woman, and who bore up bravely under the blow.

It never failed to get an attentive audience. Dynamiters blended their tears with those of the scoop gang. Even the head bartender cried.

I needed several heavy drinks of brandy before being able to recite the poem effectively.

> *"I stood at eve when the sun went down,*
> *On a grave where a woman lies,*
> *Who lured men's souls to the shore of sin*
> *With the light in her wanton eyes,*
> *Who sang the song the siren sang*
> *On treacherous passion's height —*
> *Whose face was fair as a summer day,*
> *And whose heart was black as night."*

After this introduction, there was never an interruption. I resumed:

"Yet a blossom I fain would pluck to-day
From the garden above her dust,
Not the dangerous lily of soulless sin
Nor the blood red rose of lust —
But a sweet white blossom of holy love
That grew in one green spot —
In the arid desert of Phyrne's life
When all was parched and hot."

The story went on for twenty verses. Ostler Joe married a winsome girl. She betrayed him for another and became a great actress while Joe still followed the horses about the barn.

He went to her —

"In his arms death found her lying,
From his arms her spirit fled,
And his tears came down in torrents
As he knelt beside his dead.

Never once his love had faltered
Through her sad and sinful life
And the stone above her ashes
Bears the sacred name of wife."

Then with great feeling, I would recite the second verse over again.

I learned early that such verses always made Paddy Croan feel sad. He once gave me three silver dollars after I had recited "Ostler Joe."

"Don't say it around here any more. I don't want to hear it."

Paddy talked seldom and then in terse sentences.

His face was sharp and purple. His neck was long,

with a heavy lump in the center. His collar turned at the edges as if to give it freedom. More than six feet three inches tall, he weighed two hundred pounds. His jet black hair was turned gray at the temples.

He dressed immaculately in a black suit and black tie. In the winter he wore a heavy fur coat. During the hottest months he carried an expensive light overcoat on his left arm. In his right hand was a heavy cane which came from Ireland. He had a dozen canes of the same wood, but a trifle varied. Each cane was heavily loaded with lead at one end.

He once ejected a miner from his saloon. "You were a damned murderer in Alaska," he said drunkenly to Paddy. He was hit suddenly with the end of a cane and dumped into the street. "If I iver see ye agin, I'll be a murderer here," Paddy shouted.

Croan's Eskimo dog followed him into the saloon and stretched on the bare floor in the corner. Its eyes were always on Paddy.

He would leave the saloon without saying a word to the dog. It followed him.

A porter placed a pad on the floor. The animal pulled it away, scratched at the floor for a second as if to remove the last vestige of softness, and laid down.

Paddy Croan noticed the dog's action and smiled grimly.

The dog died suddenly, people thought, of poison. Paddy did not mention the loss.

People tried to sell him many types of dogs later. He

would have no other. A stray dog once drifted into the saloon.

"Get the damned cur out of here," he yelled.

Paddy never laughed loud but once. It was after he had taught me the trick of shifting money.

During a busy period one laid a five dollar note on the bar and asked for a drink.

The bartender, from force of habit, always looked at the money the second it was laid down. This fixed the denomination in his mind. He then brought the drink, placed the money in the register, and made change.

If, while he was getting the drink, one put a dollar note in place of the five, the bartender, the larger amount fixed in his mind, made change for five dollars. That night when the money was counted in his register, he would be short more than four dollars.

The trick became useful.

One night while Paddy was relieving the head bartender, I worked it on him and then asked him to look in his register. He laughed outright.

Paddy would not allow three people to light a cigar from the same match in his saloon. He would grab the match before it touched the third cigar.

He liked pugilists. Long after they had become demented from punches, he gave them free drinks and money.

He pitied men about to die. "When does so-and-so stretch a rope?" he would ask. He would send a quart of whisky to a man the night before he was to be hung.

He would stand by the hour with the collectors. When the collector treated, Paddy would take whisky, wine, or beer, according to what the man sold. When the collector raised his glass, Paddy would empty the contents of his in the brass trough in full view of all. When Paddy treated he would pour a small glass full of orange juice and drink it.

He would get drunk every two months.

While drunk, he would neither shave, bathe, nor change linen. He would live at a twenty-five cents a night lodging house, with pine-board walls, a pine door, and wire netting for a ceiling. He rented the room on each side of the one which he would occupy for the night.

These rooms were kept locked. A bullet might pierce a thin wall. It would hardly go through two walls.

When going on a two weeks debauch, he would take a thousand dollars with him. No matter how drunk, he would say nothing of himself. He would pick up decrepit vagabonds and watch them get drunk. When they drooled, he would give them a dollar and push them away. His heavy polished cane became greater in contrast as he became more disheveled.

A beggar asked him for a quarter to get a meal.

"If you got grub you'd only get hungry again — don't you know the highest price you can pay for anything is to ask for it —"

"You mean askin' you for it," returned the vagabond.

The answer pleased Croan. He gave him a quarter.

During his debauch, he would cry over the misery of a world into which he fitted so well.

He once kept a darky with him all day. His job was to sing —

"Oh my poor Nellie Gray,
They are taking you away,
And I'll never see my darling any more, any more,—

They are takin' you to Georgiah
For to wear your heart away,
And I'll never see my darling any more —"

When the saloon closed, he gave the darky twenty dollars.

No hand could be placed upon him while drunk. No derelict could get close to his pockets. When going from one saloon to the other with scalawags he circled his cane so that he might walk untouched.

None of the men with whom he associated during his sprees could buy him a drink. Neither would he reveal his identity during a debauch.

His debauch ended, he would walk directly to his saloon and start counting money.

A half sneer would come to his eyes as he looked at himself in the mirror.

A MOTHER VISITS HER DAUGHTER

IN THE MONTHS THAT PASSED I learned much of Chlorine, and of the people who frequented Paddy Croan's. She often expressed surprise and doubt that I had tramped so far to see her.

I might have spent the winter in Chicago had I never heard of her. Of this I was silent.

I had no criminal record, and no enemies about the place. The police, on Paddy's word, did not molest me.

My life, always checkered with solitude, was not unpleasant.

I could go to Grand Opera for fifty cents and into the gallery of any theater for twenty-five. The Art Institute charged admission but two days a week. I spent hours in the building.

Thoughts of my future came; I resolved to write some day. Each resolve melted before the heat of life.

My desire for Chlorine was constantly ignored by her.

She smiled coldly and shuddered,

"If I don't begin I don't have to end. It's enough to make a fellow scream, when you think that every person you see means just that, and nine months with hell at the end of it for some woman. A hundred million people here, three hundred million in China, that many more in India — God — !! How awful — no wonder the priests don't get married."

"Maybe they don't have to."

She looked scornfully at me.

"If all men were decent as priests — but they wouldn't thank me to defend them."

Adultery was the one mortal sin in her opinion. The other girls called her *The Blessed Virgin.*

She had one sister, a nun in California.

When depressed, she threatened to join a convent. "It's peaceful there. No men trying to get the best of you."

She was very vain.

Her presents from men were many.

She had a smattering of knowledge on many subjects.

Her shrewdest affectation was that of being a deeply attentive listener while men talked on the subject most dear to their hearts — themselves.

Chlorine had dozens of novels which had been given to her.

One evening as I talked of what I had read, an idea came to her.

"You read these and tell me what's in them. I'll never get time to read the damn things. I'm too busy living."

"It'll take me a lot of time to read them, Chlorine."

"You've got all the time there is — that's all you have got — but I'll help you with money if that's what you mean."

Chlorine was charming as sin, and cunning as Sicilian murder. She soon chattered of books.

I came upon one about which she was not satisfied to hear me tell.

For hours I read "The Garden of Allah" aloud to her. It was the story of a devout Catholic girl, who married a monk, not knowing that he had broken his vows. The heroine was deeply sexed and emotional. The book was heavy to me then, with the inscrutable weight of life, the haunting feel of the desert.

Chlorine, in a silk kimono, which allowed the outline of white round breasts to show, listened with deep attention. She was unconscious of my glances between paragraphs, but stared at a picture of Christ crucified on a hill, the top of the cross lost in a cloud. Her mind seemed a million miles away.

Dominie, after a great love and greater happiness, was hearing the monk's confession. For twenty years he had been in the monastery.

Her eyes fastened to the Cross. She broke in, "And she was thirty — a virgin — God, what a wedding night."

The girl took the monk back to his vows, to see him never again.

I closed the book. Chlorine still stared at the Cross.

"My God —," she exclaimed, and held me suddenly to her.

The kimono dropped from her breasts. I put my hands upon them.

"Would you have done what she did?" I asked.

Chlorine, still staring, "You're damn right, I'd have done worse — I'd have shot him."

"Why?"

"For taking that happiness from me."

"He brought it to her."

"That was the mortal sin — I'd have shot him."

"Then you'd go to hell."

"I'd take a chance on that — there'd be one man less in the world anyhow, and another one down in hell."

"She was to have a baby, that would of made her happy."

"Oh, hell," she pulled her kimono tightly around her, "that's the worst lie of all — no brat can take the place of a man. When a woman loves a man, he's a baby too, and he's — *everything*."

"Did you ever love one?"

"None of your damned business."

Her form was outlined.

"A baby — so she was to have a baby —"

"That's how you're here."

She looked at me; then at the Cross. "Not me — a dove's my father — I'm like Him up there."

"When'd you get the picture, Chlorine?"

"My brother gave it to me. I like it because the cloud's so near — all they had to do was reach down and unfasten the nails and pull Him right up in the sky. He could ride Heaven on a star."

"Where's your brother?"

"He's —," she stopped, shrugged her shoulders and said, "Oh, never mind," and went to the telephone.

"It's Mink," she sighed. "The poor kid's in trouble again — she's some woman's baby too! — oh, hell —"

"But about your brother, Chlorine."

"He was killed — in Alaska — he was just a kid — we used to play soldier together."

She glanced about the room. Her eyes returned to the agonized Christ.

"I'll tell you something so you won't think you're a matinee idol on a white horse. The reason I took to you was because he was a rover like you. He never stayed anywhere long. You hear about the Irish always fighting — he was five years older than me, and from the time we were babies we never had a quarrel. I never even heard Mother raise her voice to either of us.

"My sister went to a convent when I was fourteen. I can see Mother bidding her good-by yet. Mother was beautiful and didn't have a wrinkle. She always wore black silk dresses with long lace collars and cuffs.

"We all three walked to the depot with sister.

"I cried when I saw the train coming. My brother patted my shoulder. Mother fidgeted with her lace collar.

"Sister got on the train and sat by a window that was open.

"When she had gone we walked with Mother and held her arms.

"She kept saying all the way home —'She's married to God.' We put her to bed and she slept all day.

"We couldn't do anything with Blarney after that. He was such a smooth little devil and flattered all three of us so that we never called him anything but Blarney.

"Lorain was the only one he would ever listen to — and after she left, he was soon gone too.

"I've often thought if mother hadn't had a pension it might have changed him.

"I got a letter from Nome a month after everything had happened. I went up, anyhow, after telling my mother that Blarney had struck it rich. It surely was a damn fool thing to do — but I was a kid and I didn't know what in the hell to do. I bundled Mother up and took her so she could be near Lorain.

"I only thought of one thing — that my mother was not going to know about Blarney if I could help it. I saw what she did when Lorain went away, and that was enough for me.

"My grandmother used to always say when I was a little girl —

'Oh, what a tangled web we weave —
When first we practice to deceive —'

"I learned that after I got to Nome. Except with my brother, I was always pretty much of a liar. I just couldn't be honest with my mother.

"When I got there I had to make the lie good by making Mother think I was sending her money from Blarney.

"So I started to work in a honky tonk. And talk about the lies I had to tell to keep men from raping me!"

Chlorine adjusted her kimono and looked at me as though I doubted. "No man ever got me and none ever will unless I'm damn fool enough to get married."

It seemed to make her feel easier.

"I got out of Nome as quick as I could. But I kept sending Mother money from Blarney and me.

"If you want to know how silly men are, be a hustler in a honky tonk. I came across with nothing but smiles and got presents from all of them.

"When I got to Seattle I went in a five dollar whore house and took every man to the room, and collected the money, and gave the landlady her two and a half and never came across to one man. Not a one ever gave me away, and every one of them believed that if I did come through he would be the man. Talk about women being silly — !

"This went on for a month. One old fellow followed me from Nome. He wanted to marry me there and kept it up in Seattle even worse when I took him to the room and charged him five dollars for a hug and a kiss.

"He must have been seventy. He had gray hair and side-whiskers. He said he'd always swore he'd marry the first woman he couldn't seduce."

Chlorine laughed.

"He was the cockiest and most conceited old bastard that ever lived. I used to tell him he looked like George Washington at Valley Forge and he believed it.

"Well, he bought me a whore house. It was full of paintings of naked women with behinds big as barns. I made them take every one down and put up pictures of women that looked like five dollar whores should look. Not even a Methodist preacher would go to bed with a behind big as Texas.

"I kept sending Mother fifty a week and telling her that Blarney was in the interior of Alaska on a big mine and might not be able to get word to any of us for several years — that he'd left me with enough to send her the money each week, that I was looking out for things in Seattle. I put it on good and heavy. Lorain wrote me letters that made me cry. 'Time is full of mercy,' she said. 'Mother is happy now that I have given myself to God.'

"One Saturday afternoon the door-bell rang and two of the girls came running to me.

" 'There's a woman down here who says she's your mother and wants to see you.' I nearly died right there.

"The graphophone was going, a drunken miner was

playing the piano — the house was noisy as hell. I told the girls to shut off the noise and go to their rooms. So I swallowed my heart all the way down stairs and let my mother in. I took her to my room, while the bell kept ringing and men could be heard coming and going.

"Finally I couldn't stand it any more; so I called the girls in and said to them —'Girls — this is my mother.'

"If a lot of women ever made a fuss over an old lady it was those girls. They carried her on a chip for two days. I think she really wanted to stay and I had to get ready and take her back to Lorain.

"She never knew it was a sporting house. The girls talked of their parents and their work.

"On the way to Lorain she said to me. 'Why, dear, those girls are just too sweet for anything, and so popular. I never saw so many handsome men callers.'

" 'Yes, Mother, they are nice,' I told her. 'I forgot to tell you — it's a branch of the Young Women's Christian Association.'

"Mother was shocked for a minute.

" 'Protestant — dear, dear — why they were as nice as any Catholic girls.'

"I was glad I got out of it as well as I did, but I took good care that as long as she lived I didn't send Mother letters from that address any more."

Chlorine smiled.

"Mother always felt that if you didn't believe a thing, it wasn't so."

Chlorine picked up the book I had read. My mind was busy with something else.

"What about Blarney?" I urged.

She poured two drinks and looked again at the Cross.

"That's another story," she faltered.

THE MARRIED VIRGIN

CHLORINE WAS THE QUEEN of the dynamiters. She could wheedle more money from men than any girl in Custom House Place.

Her beauty was such that her life was a constant battle with men.

She early sensed the craving of men for virginity.

The dynamiters in Paddy Croan's received no salary. They were given fifty per cent of the money for drinks they inveigled men into buying.

There were about forty women in Croan's place. They were in three classes. Twenty were known as dancing girls. Each time these girls danced with a man he paid fifty cents for a drink. The girl was given a check by the bartender which called for twenty-five cents at closing time when she settled with the house.

The second class were faded women with nimble tongues and tired ankles, who had spread their vast share of disappointment in the bedrooms of the world. Spent fires that burned feebly, they gossiped and drank with men who had not enough money to interest the more beautiful and clever class of girls known as dynamiters.

These girls were cold, soft spoken, well-dressed. Too shrewd to be prostitutes, and mercenary as Midas, they turned smiles and flattery into money by fanning lust in the hearts of men who were known in their world as suckers.

Each girl had her own method of getting money from a victim. Sometimes they worked in pairs. Chlorine was known as a lone wolf. She knew by a highly developed intuition whether or not a sucker had money. She was drawn toward this type as if the money was a magnet. Once the victim was in her net, she took her time. He did the talking while she listened attentively. At the proper moment she began to work. As it would not look well to become too familiar in public, the man was wheedled and petted surreptitiously.

The waiter worked with her. He was always in the wrong if the victim complained. Chlorine would send for Croan or the head bartender. The waiter would be transferred. The victim felt that he had been discharged. This would gain his confidence and please his vanity.

When Chlorine worked with a confederate, they began on the sucker with the usual flattery. After he had spent considerable money for wine, Chlorine would leave the table on a pretext.

The other girl would say confidentially, "Chlorine is surely in love with you. I've been with her for a long time and have never seen her take to any man before." The girl would sigh with regret. "But I don't blame her. Look *who* you are."

Chlorine would return to the table.

The girl would say, "Let's have another drink."

Chlorine would call the man by name and say to the girl, "No — John will spend no more money here. He's been nice to me and I've grown fond of him." A sudden thought would come to her. "I'll tell you what I'll do — John's been lovely — I appreciate it and I'll buy all the drinks."

She would call the waiter and write on a piece of paper, saying,

"Take this to the boss and tell him I want a hundred dollars."

The waiter would return with the information that Croan would give her no money until pay day.

Chlorine would go to Croan at once, while the victim watched, as men will, a woman battle for her rights.

An argument followed.

Chlorine would return indignant.

"Is there no way I can get money from him?" she would ask the waiter.

"Not unless you quit your job."

"Well, go and tell him I'm quitting."

The waiter would return with the reply that her contract called for her to work until three.

Chlorine, in deep thought, would say to the victim, "He thinks I'm in love with you and he won't give me any money to spend."

Then, a happy thought, "I'll tell you what let's do — you loan me a hundred till four — then I'll give it back to you and we'll go away from this wretched place."

After Chlorine had the money, the other girl would say to Chlorine, "You know, dear, John wouldn't let a woman buy *him* drinks. They're *men* where he comes from. I can tell in his eyes he was teasing you."

John would buy more wine.

Near closing time, Chlorine would excuse herself. The other girl entertained the sucker by chanting the praises of Chlorine.

Later on, they would go to Croan together and ask for Chlorine.

Croan would look at the victim sternly.

"You should ask me where she is after talking her into quitting. She got her money and went home. She can't work here no more either — falling in love with the customers."

Between the menace of Croan and the treachery of Chlorine, the man who was loved so suddenly by a beautiful woman, hurried from the house of sin.

*

WHEN Chlorine took an interest in a pretty dancing girl, there was, as always, a method in her kindness.

No matter how old, fat, or ridiculous, the men loved to dance.

Chlorine often complained of the infinite patience it required to teach the quickest witted dancing girl how to fleece an old man without being obvious.

She taught the girl to make a mental note when he changed a bill.

While the girl danced with a sucker, Chlorine sat in full view. The girl would look at Chlorine and then at the sucker and say, "Gorgeous, isn't she? You wouldn't believe that I had a sister like that, would you?"

The gentleman, being of the old school, and not one to doubt the word of a lady, believed at once.

The girl would confide, "She never goes out, of course. Her husband is Paddy Croan, the boss." Her voice would become lower. "She doesn't love him. Poor girl. Many men have made love to her, or tried to, rather."

She would circle the gentleman about so his eyes would meet Chlorine's at this moment.

Chlorine would smile at the gentleman.

The dancing girl would say coyly,

"My goodness, she's falling in love with you — I'll shame her when I talk to her."

With feathers in his head and lead in his feet, the gentleman stumbled on.

The girl would say innocently,

"You know, she has a strange story. On her wedding

night, being a pure girl, she loathed her husband so she would not allow him to touch her. She suffers a great deal, but she's Irish like me, and no other man can touch her."

Pressing her breast close to the prancing dynamo, she would confide,

"She's a one-man woman — but she hasn't found *him*." She would hold him closely. "They say there's always the right man in the world that a woman is waiting for." Becoming more languid in his arms, "I certainly wish my sister could find *that man*."

The gentleman would make no comment. He knew he was *that man*.

When the dance ended, the girl would say, "Would you like to meet her?" There was only one answer.

Chlorine would be coy and diffident.

The dancing girl would leave at the proper time.

After a moody silence, Chlorine would ask impetuously,

"Why is it one doesn't often meet a man like you?"

The gentleman would be too modest to answer. He would touch Chlorine's hand. She would withdraw it with a frightened look about.

"Isn't life strange?" Chlorine would ask. "There is so much unhappiness if two people do not blend."

The gentleman would ponder.

Chlorine, knowing men, never departed from the obvious.

"Men who are masterful and strong," she would look away with dreamy and compelling eyes.

Then at the gentleman, propelled by the cosmic urge, "It's hardly fair, do you think?"

The gentleman would agree that it wasn't fair. Just what was not fair, he did not know.

Chlorine, half submissive to his blandishments of love, would say, "But you would *hate me afterward,*" and recoil.

The gentleman's words came quickly.

"Hate you — that could never be — there's a deep mystery in your life. *I know.*"

"How shrewd you are."

The sucker would accept the compliment as though it had been delayed.

Then Chlorine would tell a tale of heartbreak.

"Why, the man is a brute; he doesn't understand you." Chlorine would nod sadly and say again, *"How shrewd you are."*

The by-play would keep up until within a short period of closing time.

She talked of her husband.

"Living with a man under such conditions would be adultery," she confided, "I dare not let him touch me."

After the gentleman pleaded, she would reluctantly accompany him to his suite.

"I'll go if we'll just sit still and talk."

The gentleman would agree.

Some time later, the door would be opened.

Chlorine would suddenly be in complete disarray.

Paddy Croan, ignoring her, would say to the gentle-man,—"Well, well," and brandish a revolver.

He would turn to a man near him.

"Keep the newspaper reporters out of here until we're ready."

Turning to the man, "Look at this woman! Are you a cave man? It will take a great deal of money to get you out of this."

The man with Paddy showed a police badge.

The gentleman always paid.

Men once caught in this trap did not return.

Only one man ever showed up again. He came the next night, kindly as ever. Paddy Croan looked at him suspiciously, and evidently decided that so simple a man would cause no harm.

The man bought many drinks. Paddy called him aside and offered to return the money taken the night before.

"It was just a little joke," said Paddy.

He would have none of the money.

"I take another man's wife, I pay," he said.

Chlorine joined him again. They laughed heartily.

Olaf was beefy, red, and blond. His feet were large and flat, his face puffy. His hands were hard, the fore-arms hairy and muscular.

On the third finger of his left hand was a heavy plain gold ring.

Chlorine looked at it —"For my dead wife — she wore one — so did I."

The girl, knowing that sentimental men, when drinking spend more freely, followed the subject.

Olaf, it seemed, could not be made to believe that there was wrong in the world. Women who stole from men, and men who tried to snare women, were all just having a good time.

"How can they let a man like that run loose?" Chlorine asked Joe Gans.

That bronze mystery looked at Olaf and shrugged his shoulders.

"I don't know."

Olaf was never more happy than when Chlorine was with him. He was morose without her. His capacity for liquor was only equaled by his generosity with money.

Men, while drunk, talk a great deal. Olaf was good natured and talkative about everything, but how or where he had made his money. He told Chlorine that his wife was dead, that she was Swedish, and had lived with him twenty-four years.

He talked of Alaska and Sweden.

If Croan hinted of Alaska, the jovial Swede would say nothing.

THE EMPEROR OF MAGIC

THE MAGNIFICENT SLAVIN-sky, Emperor of Magic, was any age between fifty and a hundred. His hair, long and gray, fell in heavy ringlets on his shoulders. His hat, a wide sombrero, was pushed backward on his head. He carried two heavy gold watches, one in each vest pocket. The vest was striped, black, gray, and green; a heavy chain stretched across it. In the middle dangled a huge crystal of many vivid colors.

His arched eyebrows gave him the expression of continual surprise.

He wore a long bow string tie, the ends of which touched his shoulders.

His pace, when walking, was so swift he nearly trotted.

With his out of the ordinary appearance, and his fast pace, he attracted attention everywhere.

He enjoyed the stares of people.

He did not read a newspaper beyond the front page. He was constantly buying newspapers.

The Great Slavinsky never wanted to be alone. He would talk to the first stranger rather than face such a calamity.

He could remain in his hotel room but a few hours each night. Unable to stay away from people, he would leave the room and talk with clerks, bell boys, or loiterers in the lobby.

His favorite drink was bourbon and gingerale. To keep from being disturbed too often, he would have a quart of bourbon and several pints of gingerale placed on the table before him.

At one point of the Great Slavinsky's career, he made crystal gazing a fad. He had a factory in Wisconsin where crystals were manufactured. They were said to come from India.

When his factory burned, he bought thousands of glass door-knobs and sold them to customers. To further the sales of his crystals, he formed a Crystal Gazers' Guild and sold a great many membership cards with instructions, at five dollars each.

Members of the Guild were told to drop everything they were doing when the sun was at its zenith each day, and gaze into the crystals with sufficient concentration. If they failed to get that which they wanted, it was only because they had failed to concentrate sufficiently. There was another obstacle in the crystal gazer's path. He must also guard against too intense concentration. That would defeat his purpose. All things must be at the proper equilibrium; so taught the Great Slavinsky.

In the Great Slavinsky's later days, he gave up magic to some extent to devote himself to what he termed "the mazes of the mind." Considered the equal of any magician then plying his artful trade, there was too much physical detail and not enough pomposity to suit his aging ego.

Mind reading allowed him to gesticulate in rich robes and to constantly talk to people. By nature a scold, and as irritating with advice as Roosevelt, he was without humor and full of affected affability.

The Great Slavinsky could answer the mightiest question of the universe — if it were on a piece of paper. At each of his mind reading performances, hundreds of questions, written on paper, were heaped on a table in view of his audience. A bridge connected the stage with the center aisle of the theater.

The assistants crossed the bridge, passed the slips of paper to the audience, and waited for the questions to be written.

In collecting the questions the assistants used a velvet silk-lined bag about ten inches in diameter and a foot and a half deep. It had handles at least twenty inches long. The bags had double compartments. The assistant did not touch the paper. The person in the audience put it directly into the bag.

One compartment contained blank slips, the other contained the questions when the assistants returned to the stage. A twist of the handle and the blank slips were ceremoniously dumped upon the table in the full glare of lights.

The assistants hastened from the stage and took the velvet bags with them. They were opened below the stage before an assistant with a telephone mouthpiece so attached that he could talk and handle the slips at the same time.

Everything arranged, he would address his audience:

"Ladies and gentlemen, it is not often in a world of wide wandering that I am called upon to address an audience of such intelligence, vivacity, and sense of wonder as I stand before to-night on this auspicious and momentous occasion.

"Looking across the vistas of your magnificent city to-day, the thought came to me that here was the beginning of another Athens, or Cawnpore of the blessed India memory, in which I meditated so long.

"Now, ladies and gentlemen, there are those in learned repute in citadels of wisdom over the world who claim for me high and unlimited power in the mazes of the mind. Like all men who delve much into the infinite, I am not one to bolster any claim that would challenge your discrimination. After the performance you may each and all draw your own conclusions."

The Great Slavinsky's speech was always timed to the second. The last word was the cue of the operator below stage.

He would speak the first question through the telephone in a low tone.

The Great Slavinsky would walk to the table containing the blank slips, wave a long ivory wand above them and repeat the question.

"Am I going to succeed in the business in which I am starting?"

The Great Slavinsky would gaze into the crystal and answer in funereal tones.

"If you work hard you cannot fail. I see success and long happiness in the nebula of the crystal for you."

The Great Slavinsky would look over the audience. Naturally the American citizen would feel proud of himself and beam with gratitude. Slavinsky's eyes would light upon him. The eyes of the audience would do the same.

The Great Slavinsky would have people "planted" in favored seats about the audience. People who traveled with him, they were unknown to others in the audience.

His next question would read —

"A lady wishes to know if that which is worrying her will turn out all right."

Slavinsky would turn the crystal slowly and for a second gaze into it when turned completely around. Then, holding the crystal in his left hand, he would walk dramatically toward the footlights and point to a woman, young and beautiful.

"Of course, in the divine scheme of the Yogi, my beautiful young lady, everything will be all right. Within due course of time you shall be the happy mother of a seven months old baby."

The woman, in bewildered confusion, would put a handkerchief to her eyes and sob hysterically.

The Great Slavinsky would gaze tenderly at her. The sobs subsided. The audience became tense.

The woman, with deeply resonant voice, would enunciate the words slowly —

"I — am — not — married."

A gasp would come from the self-respecting audience. A woman had been trapped in adultery among them.

The Great Slavinsky would shake his head, "I am sorry, my dear girl, to bring so private a matter to so public a gaze, but I must answer the question which the Divine Power has impelled you to ask."

The woman would rise and leave the audience.

This would happen during the first engagement.

The audience gossiped after leaving the theater. It attracted future audiences.

The Great Slavinsky always made the acquaintance of local mind readers and clairvoyants.

They realized his appearance was excellent propaganda. Such people exchange lists of clients among each other.

The Great Slavinsky made use of names of wealthy clients.

A confederate would get the names of such people two weeks or more in advance of his arrival.

Circulars advertising stocks would be sent to them a few days before Slavinsky reached the town. A percentage of these people would attend one of his performances. They would often ask the value of stock, if it would rise in price, and if it would be wise to buy.

Slavinsky would give emphatic advice to buy all such stock as was possible. He would receive half the money which the client invested.

One law of chance played even against the Great Slavinsky.

A stock which he recommended highly made fortunes for a half dozen men before the Great Slavinsky had completed his engagement. A committee of the Better Business League called upon him. Slavinsky was modest. It was all in a day's work. "Faith with reason can not only move mountains, gentlemen, it can circumvent the very laws from the secret heart of the God of Chance."

They importuned the Great Slavinsky to give a special performance before them. That wily gentleman, after much pleading, and a considerable guarantee, managed to grant them a date six weeks in the future.

Within a short time the members received letters asking them to purchase stocks. They were all saved and re-read on the day when Slavinsky appeared among them.

He recommended their purchase after reading all the questions at once.

The gentlemen of finance who ruled the community listened intently while the Great Slavinsky said — :

"In a toiling and a moiling world, gentlemen, it be-hooves men, as a tiger in a jungle, to move cautiously.

"The very foundations of this country were built by men of vision, integrity. Combined with this was that which is common in all men of wealth, a desire to help their fellows over the turbulent shoals of time. The more they can accumulate against the proverbial windy and rain swept day, the more of a legacy can they leave to those who follow in their footsteps, to whom it will have been given the edification of keeping alive the happy spirit of trade, of nonchalant barter, and trade in the vigorous marts of our unified nation. If by any chance any riches come through suggestion of mine, I pray that you shall not forget to thank the Great Founder of all wealth whose breath is mighty as thunder and whose touch is soft as the lilies growing by your charm-ing waysides."

He then answered all questions with advice to pur-chase heavily.

The Great Slavinsky had different methods of mysti-fying an audience. They varied sufficiently to deceive the most shrewd spectators. If such men were in the audience and doubted the Great Slavinsky, they were treated with that contempt with which the majority has always treated the minority since the beginning of time.

Often he would remove his turban and reappear upon the stage in full evening dress.

Instead of an ordinary crystal, he would use a ball of silver. This ball had a slit opening in the side which he kept toward him. The last half of questions had been copied on a long strip of paper which was wound on a roller inside the ball and which screwed about in the middle. A small wheel which the Great Slavinsky operated with the thumb of his left hand turned the roller inside. Thus were the questions of credulous humanity answered. It was his own device and he used it for fear the gentlemen might suspect the telephone system.

Often at the conclusion of his mind reading performance, the Great Slavinsky would place the wife of his chief assistant in a chair back of the footlights. He would then go over the bridge to the audience where he touched various objects of wearing apparel in the audience and would ask the blindfolded woman who sat in the chair to describe them.

The system was simple and yet it required great concentration and memory on the part of the woman. As the Great Slavinsky would talk swiftly at such time, it kept the audience in confusion. The woman, however, had to hit the target often enough to keep the audience in a high state of amazement at the infallible power of the human mind.

Touching a watch, a coin, and a scarf pin one after the other, the Great Slavinsky would ask, "What is this? Tell me this. Can you name this?"

"What" was the cue for all watches, "tell" for all coins, and the word, "can," for all scarf pins.

But the first cue word was not sufficient: for instance, the word "what" established that the object was a watch. It was followed by "is" which designated plainly to the woman that it was a gold watch. If the watch were silver, the question which the Great Slavinsky asked was, "What can this be?" The word "can" told the woman that the watch was silver.

After the woman had answered, "A gold watch," or "A silver watch," she was yet forced to tell whether or not the watch was a closed case or an open face. The Great Slavinsky, being kind, gave her the cue after a slight pause. "Well" he would say rather impatiently; that would tell her that the watch was an open face. "That is all," spoken abruptly, told her that the watch was a closed case.

In the instance of coins the variety of cues was much wider. There was a cue word for every possible country from which a coin might come, including ancient coins. The questions came rapidly in quick succession. After the woman had told from which nation and period the coin came, she would be forced to tell the denomination. He followed this with cues as she had in describing the watches. One cue told the date; one word conveyed the century in which the coin was made; other words gave the decade, others the exact year.

Getting the serial number of a watch was more difficult. Spectators demanded this often. These numbers often ran into six or seven figures.

The blindfolded woman had been trained to count with him in the same slow tempo. If a number were 987478, the first number would be conveyed to her by his first question. "Tell" meant the first number was nine and so on with variations. Whenever the Great Slavinsky interrupted with the word "quick" it was also a cue. "Hurry up" was another one, and built up a secret hope in the audience that the woman might fail.

The Great Slavinsky was never without able assistants in the audience who, with strong opera glasses, were trying to detect the secrets of the performance.

An assistant once prompted a yokel to shout at the Great Slavinsky while he was in profound meditation, "What is the color of this orange?"

A silence, doleful as doom, followed.

"Truth has ever been the flagellated victim of those who despise it. To sink to the level of moronic ineptitude is not the business of a philosopher. If there be any man among you who wish to know the color of an orange, pray take it to a grocer or a chemist. Such abtruse questions are not for me."

One trick was for the blindfolded woman to miss a cue. The Great Slavinsky would become angry and say sharply, "What's wrong? Are you going to slip?" She would retort, "If you keep still and let me think I will do better."

This would come at a time when people might begin to doubt.

The Great Slavinsky would say, "All right, I will remain silent. You may go ahead and think with what you have to think with."

He would then borrow a piece of paper money from a member of the audience who held a pair of opera glasses and was more interested than the others in detecting any possible fraud.

Dead silence would reign in the theater as Slavinsky would say, "Give me the number on the ten dollar bill which I have borrowed." She would then give the serial number which often ran into seven figures.

The man with the opera glasses would say, "That is right." His words would be followed with loud applause. The gentleman with the opera glasses would rub his right or left eye, either cheek, or scratch his head, or turn to whisper to the person on either side of him. He would convey to the watcher back of the drop, by cue, the desired information. The blindfolded woman heard the news and answered with triumphant conviction.

And so the farce went on. Men and women received answers that gave them a temporary solution of their problems and harmed them not at all; for the Great Slavinsky knew that his success as a faker depended absolutely in throwing more water on the always flourishing flower of hope.

*

THE Great Slavinsky had once been married.

He has long since disappeared behind the everlasting portals. One of the last of a magnificent and fascinating school that will soon be closed forever, this tale is told with ironical kindness by the lad whom he always addressed as "Bar Fly."

He had learned the business of magic with an old man who often entertained the inmates of asylums for the insane. It was considered helpful entertainment by those who had them in charge.

In one town a beautiful young woman approached him in the lobby of his hotel.

"Pardon me," she said demurely, "I must talk to you." She brushed a wave of auburn hair from her eyes.

In a more subdued tone she said, "My brother is the superintendent where you entertained — a week ago.

"While watching the audience as his guest, I was amazed at the alacrity with which they followed your every dextrous move."

Flattery was dear to the heart of the Great Slavinsky. From a beautiful woman — it was enchanting.

"Yes, yes," he said, looking about the lobby for possible listeners, "the test of a man's art is written in the applause and appreciation of his audience."

She murmured, "I should love to be your helper, to watch you scale the heights of renown, and remain a silent and happy onlooker."

The Great Slavinsky, taken unawares, said,

"But, my dear young lady — we who devote our lives to magic are ever the slaves of work."

The young woman looked appealingly at him, "But what would that matter with such a miracle working man? One would forget such things — in your presence," she said fervently.

The Great Slavinsky paused for breath. She went on —

"It is strange — my brother did not introduce us." She moved her body with unconscious sinuosity, and pouted for a second. "Brother has long wanted me to marry Dr. Walls — because they went to medical college together — and maybe because he's wealthy. But I've always told him that while father could and did arrange the terms of the will, in which he left me a few hundred thousand dollars more if I married the man who was my fit mate in Brother's opinion, at least he could not make me capitulate once my heart had chosen." She paused, "A half million is enough for any girl."

Immediately, the Great Slavinsky became concerned.

"But of course you are the ruler of your heart," he said.

"I was," she sighed, "until I saw you — and your performance." She sighed more deeply, and looked fondly at him, *"And then I knew."*

Gone was all the Great Slavinsky's magic. The petite face with the red tinged cheeks fascinated him. He was younger then, and hotel rooms were lonely. For not even a magician such as the Great Slavinsky could make so beautiful a young woman appear at the proper time.

They were married by the Justice of the Peace.

On the front page of the newspaper next day he read that a young lady had escaped from the insane aslyum at ———

He said nothing to his wife.

When the authorities came after the girl, the Great Slavinsky refused to give her up. He agreed to take care of her, and engaged a trained nurse.

Except for an exaggeration in speech, she was normal for two years. Then she cracked. And something cracked in the heart of the Great Slavinsky.

He may have been insane himself as other magicians thought. When they teased him of the affair he merely said, "Women are all crazy anyhow. I picked one that had beauty."

She told him something of the life of a demented young woman in a state insane aslyum.

The Great Slavinsky believed.

He had her placed in a private sanitarium, and went to see her, regardless of distance once a year.

She died after ten years of care, at the age of thirty-two.

The Great Slavinsky buried her under a willow tree near the river of her girlhood. He had a beautiful vari-colored portrait worked into a white marble monument.

Beneath were the words —

TRANSCENDENT THROUGH TIME

A SPIRIT OF IMMORTAL FLAME

THE

PURE WIFE

OF

THE GREAT SLAVINSKY

AN IRISH SHYLOCK

HIS FACE WAS DRAWN AND
of muscular bronze. Unobtrusive as a shadow he would
look about the saloon with the expression of one who
gazed on the last of living things.

His eyes were the saddest I have ever seen.

His hands were white in the palms. The fingers were
tapering and slender. Broken several times from bat-
tering an army of bruisers, there were heavy ridges
across the knuckles.

On the edge of the grave with consumption, he was
still a great pugilist.

He would enjoy humor which pertained to the ring.

His favorite tale was that of a young colored pugilist
who was taking a fearful drubbing. One eye was closed,

and all but a fraction of the other. His manager and chief second, not much older than himself, in an effort to encourage him between rounds, said,—

"You'ah a suah winnah. You suah is fightin' like a tigah."

The young Negro looked at his manager out of his fraction of an eye and said doubtfully,

"Ah'll bet you ain't nevah saw no tigah fight."

In training, and on the street, he wore a dark horizontally striped sweater with thin white lines. It gave his slender body the skeletonlike appearance of a witch doctor.

His features were more Semitic than Negroid. Unlike his breed, there was something detached about him, some quality which riper years have not helped me to define.

A fellow of more feeling than other leading pugilists, Joe Gans knew more of the fundamentals of his vicious craft than any other man of his time.

He could start a blow with lightning speed, and stop it within an inch of its objective.

If the art of pugilism can reach genius, Gans was so gifted. The elements were so blended in him — stamina, caution, cunning, swift and terrible execution — that it required a great pugilist to whip even his shadow.

He taught me the fundamentals of boxing.

Once in a long talk he said to me, "Watch a tigah — it's all tight befoah it springs — then it's loose — and it goes with all its body —"

Gans knew the science of hitting. When he landed a blow accurately, it was as if his opponent had been struck with a sledge weighing one hundred and thirty-three pounds.

He was a firm and a gentle person. His dignity was innate and far beyond his calling.

He had two vices according to Christian standards. He gambled incessantly, and gave all his money away. He was known to bet the last dollar in his pocket on where a fly would light.

When chided for giving too much money away, he would say, "It ain't mine."

He bet heavily on championship prize fights.

His system was simple. "Always bet on a champion till the last time. Afteh a man's good enough to lick everybody else, he's good enough to lick 'em for the next few years, maybe. Of course you've got to know when to get off of him, because everybody gets licked. But you neveh lose but once, and you win all the other times."

The climax of Gans' turbulent drama came in a fight with Battling Nelson for the Lightweight Championship of the World. The fight was held in a sun-scorched Nevada town.

His lungs were rotting in his steel body.

He had no fear of death. "It can't show me nothin' I ain't seen. I'm not goin' to let him sneak up on me nohow. I'm goin' to die right out in the road where the lightnin's streakin'. If Battlin' Nelson kin kill me — it's all okeh with me."

In the middle thirties, an advanced age for lightweight pugilists, the conditions imposed on him at this time were the most barbarous in the history of pugilism.

Needing money badly, as usual, he agreed to make one hundred and thirty-three pounds, the lightweight limit, at the ringside.

Nelson's manager demanded that he be weighed in at the ring in his street clothes instead of in fighting costume. This forced him to weigh one hundred and thirty pounds or less — his clothes weighing the balance. In desperation for money, Gans conceded the point, and made the weakening weight. He was also made to agree that if he were a fraction of a pound overweight he would forfeit five thousand dollars; and the same amount for each additional pound.

In order to make the weight, Gans was given nothing but beef tea for twenty-four hours preceding the fight.

In spite of such stipulations, the lung diseased bruiser was a ten to six favorite in the betting.

Fatigue had stretched his high cheek bones taut when he entered the ring. His eyes were heavy with languor.

A black right first sizzled upward in the second round. So hard was the blow that blood came from Nelson's ear. For seven rounds, Nelson laid no glove on Gans.

The crowd cheered madly. Nolan, Nelson's manager, rubbed his hooked nose in consternation. Gans glanced at him over Nelson's shoulder and smiled wanly.

Blinded by blood and confused by the Negro's boxing ability, Nelson charged desperately.

Black arms, with five ounce mallets of pain at the ends of them, rocked his head with deadly precision.

When the gong sounded, he staggered to Gans' corner.

The Negro turned him in the right direction and patted his shoulder.

In the seventh round when Nelson charged from his corner, he was knocked through the ropes.

Unable to pull himself back into the ring, Gans helped him to his feet.

A cheer followed.

Gans sneered slightly and stood for a second, without guarding until Nelson gained his equilibrium.

The Danish pugilist, seeing the advantage, suddenly hit him a vicious blow in the groin.

Gans ignored the foul blow.

The audience yelled, "Cur, crook, robber."

Gans' eyes were none too strong. They now squinted in the glare of the desert and sun.

He broke his hand in the fifteenth. To keep the audience from discovering the injury, he limped.

He told a second in his corner.

"My hand's gone. I can hold out for hours with one hand. You'd better stop my friends from betting any more money though."

He slid over the blood splotched canvas in the twenty-sixth and made Nelson miss every blow. He closed the

Dane's eyes, and pounded his mouth until his lips protruded large and red.

Fouled many times before the thirtieth round, he made no complaint.

Favoring the broken hand, he would step in close, and rip his blood and water soaked glove across Nelson's face, and pounded it beyond recognition.

Favoring the right hand, with body drawn taut, he blinked through his cocked fists, and lashed out with a left hook with such force that it twisted Nelson's mouth and made it drool blood.

The Dane retreated.

They circled the ring in roaring applause. In a neutral corner, Gans blocked a volley of punches with elbow, glove, and forearm. Men, old in the ways of the ring, gasped.

He then began his terrible one — two — one — two —, with Nelson's eyes as targets.

Nelson tried to block each devastating blow. His glove reached his battered eye a fraction of a second too late.

A dozen blows were thudded against his face in this manner.

"He's softenin' him up for the knock-out," a miner yelled.

In maniacal fury, Nelson charged.

Relentless as an executioner, his left foot far out, his body bent cable-like in the middle, Gans feinted the Dane into dropping his guard.

Again the terrible one — two procedure began — a right, a left, a right, a left, a right again that leaned on his jaw. Then three lefts that rattled like bullets on stone. Nelson's knees cracked together.

"There he goes," yelled some one.

The gong sounded.

The Dane's manager, with buzzard expression, glanced at the invincible Negro, whom all his trickery and Nelson's prowess could not vanquish.

The shadows of spectators were thrown across the ring by the swiftly sinking sun.

Nelson could vaguely see the dark specter in front of him with his rapidly closing eyes.

The fight was to go forty-five rounds. There were three more rounds to go, when Nelson, knowing he could not win, deliberately delivered a vicious blow in Gans' groin.

A look of astonishment came over the face of the Negro; then, convulsed with agony, he writhed on the floor.

The referee shouted to the battered Nelson. The words could not be heard above the roar of the crowd.

Nolan, thinking the referee had ruled in favor of Nelson, shouted with exultation.

Instead, fearful of mob vengeance, the referee accused Nelson of fouling, and named Gans the winner.

The Negro, unable to stand, was carried from the ring on a stretcher.

He recovered enough to walk next day.

"I wish you were a dark man, Mistah Nolan," he said to the manager as he held out his left hand. The right was in a bandage.

The Irishman hesitated for a moment. He took the proffered hand without meeting Gans' eye.

Hemorrhages in the head threatened the life of Nelson. He was in bed for days.

He was punch drunk ever afterward. It was claimed that the beating loosened his brain.

The citizens of Goldfield wanted to give a banquet in Gans' honor.

He declined with a wan smile.

THE ROPE THAT KILLS

THE GREAT SLAVINSKY WAS fond of Joe Gans. The two were often together.

Gans kept pace with the half trot of the Great Slavinsky's and did it as gracefully as Chlorine dancing.

The Negro held his elbows close to his sides when he walked. His hands were closed, pugilist fashion. His shoulders were drawn upward as if he were running. Unlike most successful pugilists, Gans wore no diamonds. "Can't keep 'em out of the pawn shop," was the reason he gave.

Gans generally had a slight trace of smile at the corners of his lips when with the Great Slavinsky.

When he was boxing a noted English pugilist, the Great Slavinsky remained with Paddy Croan to hear the result.

He had been drinking for hours at a table in the rear with the owner of a Kentucky distillery and Paddy. The distiller went away. Paddy and the Great Slavinsky stayed at the table.

"Do you think the boy'll win?" asked Paddy.

"Most assuredly, most assuredly," returned the Great Slavinsky.

"White's fast," said Paddy, "the best fighter out of England."

"It's only for ten rounds. No man on earth can whip Joe in that time, sick as he is."

The Great Slavinsky shook his head.

"That man is a mystery, an old soul if ever there was one. There is in him, by some mysterious decree, a quintessence of things, an accumulation of the silver and dross of centuries, spread forlornly and careless on the troubled highways of time, the dust from which has gathered in his lungs. He was born essentially impersonal, maybe of ancient Egyptians who sleep in the aeons of time but in whose brains and bodies flowed the hopes and dreams and the blinding pain of mankind. There is in him something of the tired old peasant with the winds of time in his heart and the dirt of the fields in his eyes.

"Joe had lived thousands of years before he was born. Through his brain had gone infinite and fantastic and frightful successions of reveries. The tragedies of millions of years had thrummed on the strings of his heart, the incarnation of vast hordes of men. Christ was such a man, Shakespeare was such, and my distinguished contemporary, Kellar, the Great Magician.

"Surely the eyes of Gans beheld Spartacus and six thousand rebellious and eternal slaves crucified on a Roman road. They couldn't have become so sad in his short life. He saw Toussaint L'Ouverture, the majestic black Booker Washington of his day, dying under the hand of the rapacious Napoleon in a French prison. Who knows — he may be the descendant of a daughter of Cleopatra's, willingly raped by a centurion with the face of an eagle on a windy Roman road where the grass was soft as the thighs of her beautiful mother. If nothing begins and nothing ends, Paddy — who are we to be definite about anything?

"No man is right. No man is wrong. All are ignorant. We know nothing. Why does a canary sing and an eagle screech? Would it not be better if it were the reverse? Then we'd have music in the mountains.

"Why does an Irishman like yourself hate facts? Why do you cringe from life? Why do you send a quart of whisky to a rascal about to perish? What difference does it make when he shuffles off this immoral coil? He's as everlasting as that which brought him here. Why do you have to get drunk, as do I? There's a reason for all these things and it will be found in the mazes of the mind. Why does it happen that people on one small island that is Ireland make the greatest drunkards? What seed put desire for drink in their brain? The Irish love illusions as a consumptive girl loves the feel of a man in her arms. Why does a just God allow a dying, lung diseased, girl to burn with passion? You are a stern man, Paddy, but you get away from yourself."

"Have another drink," said Paddy.

"Am I not right?"

"You are Slavinsky."

It was a creepy night outside. It was heavy with dismal fog which the lights turned yellow. The elevated trains could barely be seen a short distance away from Paddy's saloon. Fog horns on the lake and the roar of trains could be heard.

The saloon was well lit. There were many groups at the bar. Chlorine and Mink were the only women in the place. In no mood for anything else, they joined Paddy and the Great Slavinsky.

"Some straight brandy, Slim," Chlorine said to the bartender, "I'm a morgue inside — Give Mink the same."

Paddy rolled one thumb around the other.

Chlorine removed her gloves and rubbed the diamonds on her pink hands. Mink looked at them.

"God, they're beautiful," she said.

"The hands or the rings?" smiled Chlorine.

"Both," said Mink.

The bartender brought the whisky, whistling —

> *"Here's to the American Eagle —*
> *That flies far over the sea —*
> *A whisky glass and a woman's sass*
> *Made a horse's sass of me."*

Chlorine frowned.

"So you sent a quart to Jenkins — they're breaking his neck by now," the Great Slavinsky said to Croan. Croan nodded.

"I wonder what a hangman thinks about," said Chlorine.

"Did you ever know one?" the Great Slavinsky asked Paddy.

"Yes," replied Paddy.

"Where?"

"Everywhere. We're all hangmen — without ropes —" returned Paddy.

"One time in England I opened the closet door of my hotel and found it full of ropes."

Paddy Croan raised his eyebrows. Chlorine smiled.

"A hangman owned it. There was a pub in connection and the old devil used to wait on customers." The Great Slavinsky leaned back and rubbed his watches for a second.

"He did a big business for a while until he got into a quarrel with a yokel and yelled at him, 'I'll hang ye yet.'

"Sure enough the fellow committed murder and was hung by the old man. Then his trade dropped off as people thought he had an evil eye."

The Emperor of Magic gulped his drink. "I tremble when I think of that old monster. He was the living proof to me that God is blind. His back had such a bend below the neck a crow could lay eggs on it. His body caved in the front like a bend in the moon.

"His hands were always twisted as if he was climbing a rope.

"They had to smuggle him in and out of Ireland on hanging day.

"I was younger then, just getting a start in life — a mere pupil on fire and athirst at the great fountain of magic. There was only one hotel in the hamlet, and while the old devil repelled and fascinated me, I remained. I made capital of the incident, however, by having circulated about the place that upon the last day I would have old Billings tell in a trance, just what each murderer said before he popped his neck in the name of God and the law.

"Being curious to know why one man should kill another for pay, I asked him one rainy night how he happened to become a hangman.

" 'Times were hard,' said he, 'and I was a poor man.

" 'It's easy business, is hanging, and it has its bit of science too —' he insisted.

" 'One must judge the weight of a man about to die and test the rope that kills him according. The law says the man must hang by the neck till he's dead, and whether his neck strangles or breaks is of no great consequence. But I always prefer to break the man's neck — a little touch of mercy at the end is all that one can ask of God or hangman.

" 'After all, men don't tremble before they go to

sleep, and that's maybe all they do when they die. But none die easy, let me tell you that, just why, of course, neither God nor hangman knows.

" 'When I hung Barney Tucker, he says to me, "It's along with me I'd like to be takin' ye," says he — "I'd like to drag your heart out through your throat and let the wind blow it clean. But ah," says he, "the wind from off it would poison the snakes crawlin' over the meadow."

" ' "Never mind," I said to him. "Think of your God and not the heart He gave me."

" ' "I must think of one or the other," says he. "There's not room for both in my brain at this time."

" ' "But, after all," said I, "Barney, if it wasn't me, it would be a man with harder hands."

" ' "A hangman's hands are always hard," said he.

" ' "It was no mercy you had, Barney, on him you killed."

" ' "But," said he, "my blood was warm in the killing, and yours is cold."

" ' "I kill for money — you kill for hate —," said I — and I let him die slow like a dog with hot lime in its ear'."

The Great Slavinsky mixed another drink.

" 'Are you never haunted by the ghosts of the strangled men?' I asked him.

" 'Only once,' he answered me. 'I was coming home from Liverpool late in the night from a very successful hanging. The wind was roaring and the lightning flashing as I stepped into my house here. And there stood Barney Tucker, so close I could smell the scorched rope on his neck.

" 'Something knocked me down and I felt a hand going down my throat. It was cold as ice, and I could hear Barney saying, "Open your mouth wide so your teeth won't scratch your heart when I pull it out." Then I felt a cold breeze, and I didn't wake up until morning.

" 'But, of course,' said the old hangman, 'some go to their death quiet and refined and not like Barney Tucker.

" 'It was once my sad duty to hang a young woman who had killed a little baby, fearing it would starve.' "

Chlorine, with deep attention, watched the Great Slavinsky.

" 'She was round as an apple and her eyes were brown and soft and her face was pretty.

" 'The touch of her made, even then, my old blood warm. She trembled a little when she saw the gallows and stepped back as if she would not wish to be going further that day.

" 'So I said to her, gently as I could, "Come on, little girl, be brave. It will all be over soon in the name of God and the King. Either of them should know I'd rather love ye than hang ye." ' "

Chlorine closed her eyes while the Great Slavinsky went on,

" 'She looked at me for a second and stepped up quickly and was hanged without another word.' "

A gust of wind followed a group of people as they entered the saloon.

The Emperor of Magic looked at his watch, and then at Paddy.

"You can get drunk and forget every now and then, Paddy, but the curse is on a man like me who can do nothing but remember."

"You just think I can forget," snapped Paddy.

Chlorine touched her eyes with a tiny lace kerchief.

Mink sobbed several times.

MINK

MINK WAS NOT QUITE eighteen. She was slender, with brown hair, and eyes that always seemed ready to cry. Reared in an institution, she was seduced by her adopted father at thirteen.

Languid and yielding by nature, she easily attracted men. Unable to resist their touch, they always had their way with her.

She gave Chlorine another excuse for damning men.

"The cradle-robbing bastards," she often called them when she thought of the young girl.

Chlorine called her "Mink," on account of that animal's sexual proclivities.

Mink drifted, working now and then, half starved the rest of the time, until she was sixteen. A salesman then gave her fifty dollars a month and put her in a small apartment. He sold organs. She loved music. He gave her a second-hand organ. She spent hours in learning to play it.

It was not long before the man learned that several of his friends were intimate with Mink. He cast her adrift.

She begged to have the organ. He let it go with her.

Later, when the man's wife sued for divorce, she asked information of Mink and offered money.

Mink insisted she knew nothing of the man.

"Where did you get the organ?" the woman asked.

"Santa Claus," answered Mink.

When the man was divorced, he returned to Mink.

"Let's begin over again," he said.

"All right." Mink was radiant and happy.

She bought calico aprons to wear in the kitchen and little knickknacks for the apartment.

She begged for a baby. He would not let her have it. "One kid in the house is enough," he said.

The salesman made a trip for a few weeks. He returned and found that other men were seeing Mink.

"Why can't you be a good girl?" he asked.

"I don't know," she answered, "I try so hard."

He left her again. This time he took organ and all.

Mink drifted. Soon she found her way to Paddy Croan's.

As a dancing girl, she could not earn her room rent until Chlorine took her in charge. Each man used her body and left her more bedraggled and hopeless. Some paid her a trifle, the majority not at all.

Chlorine became interested in her by accident. Observing her lovely body and slip-shod appearance, she talked to her in an idle moment and became her friend.

All of Chlorine's watchfulness did not keep Mink in check. Her desire for men grew.

She came to the saloon one night with a woeful expression.

"You won't tell Chlorine if I tell you something, will you?"

"Not if you don't want me to," I answered.

"Cross your heart and hope to die?" she said.

"Yes."

"I had some bad luck —." She began to sob. Her face straightened. She rubbed her eyes. "It's been goin' on a month now and the thoughts of it nearly kill me — when Slavinsky told that story I wished I was that girl."

The tears came. "I gotta tell somebody."

"Is it a baby?" I asked.

"Don't you know why I wouldn't let you touch me for so long?"

"No — I just thought you didn't like me."

"It wasn't that, for I do." She flushed. "I think I got the old ral."

The news stunned me.

"The what — no you ain't — you're too young," I said quickly.

"Too young — hell — I'm beginning to break out —

it's the syphilis all right. I just couldn't pass it on to you. I'm losin' weight every day. Soon there won't be room enough on me to make the sign of the cross."

Her lovely body straightened. "I'm goin' to give it to every damn man I can. They gave it to me."

"My God, Mink,— you won't do that."

"The hell I won't — all but *you*."

"Who gave it to you?"

She smiled wanly.

"Do you know what fly lit on you a month ago?"

"But you've been bein' careful?"

"I wish to God I had."

"But Chlorine ought to know."

She grabbed my arm. "Don't tell her — for God's sake — I'd rather die. She's been too square."

That night we walked to the County Hospital.

I waited until Mink came out.

"They say it's all through me," she said.

I did not know what to say. The very name of the disease paralyzed me. I was very young.

"I'll just rot away." She shuddered, then sobbed.

"I sure bump into all the good luck, don't I?"

I found my voice, "It will be all right, Mink. A lot of people get cured of it."

"I never seen one. Look at old Madame Villy — big red eyes and hurts all over. I'd rather be dead and burnin' in hell. I'd at least be clean."

"But, Mink,— why did you take such chances?"

She laughed bitterly.

"Oh hell,— why is your hair red? I don't know why I'm made the way I am. I'm *Mink* —"; she said the word with scorn. "I need a man to bang hell out of me every time I look at another man." She sighed. "But it's too late now."

"But, Mink — you won't spread it — will you?"

She hesitated.

"Maybe not — I — I — want it more'n ever now — what can I do?" She became defiant. "Every man'll have to pay some way."

We entered Paddy Croan's and seated ourselves at a wine-stained table.

A few people were at the bar.

Mink was lost in deep thought.

"I'm tellin' you, Jim, nobody ever touched me them two years after I was raped by him. I didn't have no more home than a rabbit. He come to the Orphans' Home an' they called all us girls in from play and made us sit in our seats till he looked us all over — and he picked me. All the other girls were jealous because I was goin' to a nice home.

"Nobody knows what I went through the year I was with him and the two years after I left. I'll bet you I roomed at every house on the North side. I used to git so lonesome, I'd cry myself to sleep — and you know what that is."

"Yes," I nodded, "I know."

"The landladies never knew I was alive till the day the rent was due. I used to wrap bundles at the Boston

Store till my fingers got raw and I had to soak them in hot vaseline every night. I had to fight every man I met. I got so I could scream. I was human as they were. But I wanted to be good, and I was afraid of having a baby. I wanted one so much. I was so damned lonely — but what would I have done with a baby, I'd like to know.

"I used to steal panties and things from the Boston Store. I needed clothes so bad. Then one time when I stole two pairs of silk stockings and a lace hanky I got scared and never went back. I used to like vaudeville and I'd go to the Majestic every Sunday afternoon for twenty-five cents. After I left the Boston Store, I couldn't do that — then he came along — and I was hungry and lonesome and he took me like I was a piece of putty, only worse — for putty wouldn't have to worry every month like I did.

"When I learned he was married I didn't care — why should I? He was good to me. That was all I cared about. Then something happened to me. I was afraid to go out after one of his friends got me so easy it scared me.

"When he left me I nearly died. Nothing to go home to and less to live for. I tried and tried to explain things to him. I'd have died for him. He was all I had, damn the luck, and when he left me the organ, I used to cry myself to sleep with my head on it. If I just had it now I'd crawl to play it.

"They ain't nobody knows what it means to be a girl. You're licked the day you're born. Every girl should have a million dollars or die when she's a baby. The best they can ever git's the worst of it. If I was a man I could make girls do what I wanted. Now they make me. Every month I'm so sick I could go away and die — and then if I'm not sick I worry till I'm half dead because I ain't —"

A sob died in her throat.

"And when he took that organ — that was just *too much*. He didn't need to do that — no matter how bad I was. If he'd of just stayed I'd of given up the organ. I didn't want other men no more'n he wanted me to have them. I used to cry every time he went away, I was so lonesome. Then they'd call me up and promise to be good — but they never were. I'd stay a whole two weeks alone in the flat lookin' out at the lake till I begun to see things, and I burned up all over. One time I went down to Marshall Field's to do some shopping. I come home in the rush hour and a man stood close to me. I burned all that night."

As Mink leaned her head slightly to one side, her brown hair fell across her eyes. She did not brush it away for several minutes.

There was loud laughter at the bar.

"Did you ever notice how people are always movin' in roomin' houses? Nobody ever satisfied and it's no wonder. They're always lookin' for a place that's more like home."

She was silent for a second.

"Maybe if we moved away to some other world it'd be better."

"I'd hate to take the chance — it might be worse," I said.

"It couldn't," she returned. "It might be just as bad — it couldn't be worse."

Mink was soon drinking and dancing with a large man in a suit with green stripes and a red necktie. His eyes were deep in his head. His face was pasty, pale, and fat. He left the saloon with her.

*

She was found the next day with her head on the window-sill of her room, which looked over an alley. Evidently changing her mind, she tried to open the window to let the gas escape. She was too late.

Her hair fell in curls over her eyes. They were wide open.

A silver dollar was in her purse.

*

"Hadn't you better close the joint to-day, Paddy — it's the least we can do for the poor little devil." Chlorine waited for an answer. It came.

"What good'll that do? If I closed the place forever it wouldn't bring her back."

"You might show respect."

"For what — a dead trollop — and have the papers play it up that she had the syph —"

Chlorine took a deep breath. "I thought I'd met them all, Paddy — till I met you. You're just a proper son of a bitch."

"There's a lot of us," said Paddy.

He went on his periodical drunk that night.

Chlorine took charge of Mink's funeral. Her body was brought in a white and blue coffin, to Chlorine's apartment.

The lid was taken off.

Beautiful as a wax doll, she lay, partly on her side.

Chlorine looked at her and said to the undertaker, "That's all right. I hate to see dead people lying on their backs. It looks like some one had knocked them down." And then, touching the rose in Mink's hand, "No one ever had to knock the kid down."

A few people were invited from the saloon.

A singer, holding a book in her hand, said to Chlorine, "What will I sing?"

Chlorine tilted her head.

"It doesn't matter, one thing's as good as another." The woman sang,

> *"Out of the night that covers me,*
> *Black as the Pit from pole to pole,*
> *I thank whatever gods may be*
> *For my unconquerable soul.*
>
> *In the fell clutch of circumstance*
> *I have not winced nor cried aloud.*
> *Under the bludgeonings of chance*
> *My head is bloody, but unbowed.*

Beyond this place of wrath and tears
Looms but the Horror of the shade,
And yet the menace of the years
Finds and shall find me unafraid.

It matters not how strait the gate,
How charged with punishments the scroll,
I am the master of my fate:
I am the captain of my soul."

Chlorine kissed Mink's forehead and placed a little ivory crucifix on her breast.

"Tell Him I gave it to you." Her words trembled.

Pushing Mink's hair back, she turned to several girls who stood near.

"Will you girls go with her to the graveyard? I've had enough," she said. Then, forcing a smile,

"So long, Mink, don't lose the Cross."

PADDY CROAN WAS FOUND A week later. He had been beaten to death. His heavy buckthorn cane was at his side. It was split and bloody. The lead could be seen in the end.

His right hand was stretched fan-like from his nose. The murderer must have made him try to thumb it at the sky.

Neither his money nor his watch had been touched. The police told Chlorine the news.

"Dear — dear — everybody's dying," was her comment. "I wonder if he'll want the place closed while they plant him."

"It's a plain case of murder," said the policeman.

Chlorine shook her head, "That's quite a discovery —

I don't see how any one could have the heart to murder Paddy, he was such a sweet man."

The officer missed her meaning.

"Yes — I guess he was a good fellow."

"One guess is as good as another," returned Chlorine.

"Can you think of any one who would kill him?" asked the officer.

"Can you think of any one who wouldn't?" asked Chlorine.

"Was he your husband?"

"No — thank God — but what would that have to do with his murder?" Chlorine smiled. The officer rubbed the palm of a heavy hand over his badge.

"Do you know," said Chlorine, "it just occurred to me Paddy might have beaten himself to death. An Irishman will do that when he's drunk. I've seen him when he felt like that." She smiled demurely at the officer, "Are you Irish?"

The officer nodded his head, "An' proud of it."

"You should be — so am I." She looked enchantingly at the policeman. "Paddy was born to die in trouble. I always wondered why he wasn't sent to Heaven sooner. Up in Alaska he used to wear his finger-nails long. He would load them with the gold dust of the miners. He even made money that way. He might have met an old Alaska friend — or a whore from there he robbed. It's very cold up there, they say — and memories are a long time thawing out."

The saloon was closed.

BOOK TWO

ARRESTED

DETERMINED TO GET AWAY
from the road, I made many futile attempts. For weeks
I was in a kind of trance. The wanderlust is a fever that
burns deep into the soul.

Long before I had talked to Josiah Flynt, the king of
my world and the only real hobo who ever became articulate, a withered little cigarette fiend burned out with
the fever of the wanderlust, the hardships of which had
sapped his vitality.

His books are now forgotten, his name a hazy
memory. He died at thirty-eight, two decades ago.

He was the inventor of the word "graft" as used in
common speech to-day.

The nephew of Frances E. Willard, the temperance

fanatic, he dropped the name after going the way of thief and tramp.

Hoboes and road-kids, petty as the lice on their filthy clothes, hated him without understanding that a man of his mettle could never be exactly of them.

His mouth was small, his lips thin and tight. His hands were stained yellow with nicotine.

His eyes were too tired to be furtive. If human nature at its best is but a paltry affair, it is bound to be less where every man must be a rodent to survive. To trace the environmental and hereditary influences that make a hobo is not for this story. I deal with actualities. It is hard for a weak man to be honest. It is even harder for him to be sincere. Men who are too easily overwhelmed by circumstance are frayed reeds indeed upon which to lean on in a storm.

Flynt was more cunning than strong. His soul was shoddy. But it was a soul and not the life spark of a rat.

I sent a note to the hotel where he lay dying.

A bellboy took me to him. I was flustered in the presence of so great a man. He puffed one cigarette after another. As he puffed, a tennis ball could have lain in the hollow of his cheek.

He was gripped every now and then with a spasm of coughing.

He talked with an effort, but he was courteous even in dying. Bitterness puckered his face, and hatred surged in his heart.

"Get off the road, kid," he gasped. "They're all

snakes who crawl over it. It's not morals; it's nothing but protection. You want to live like a man and not a skunk."

He coughed violently. "I'm due for the last division soon," he gasped.

"I haven't got much, Kid, and I won't need it long — Here," he handed me a few dollars.

I left him staring at the ceiling.

He strengthened my resolve to leave the road; though I hated monotony even worse than I did the mongrels with whom I lived. I knew what I faced in leaving the road — a life of labor more dull than any I had known. It is only in romances that the fellow with potentialities is given understanding. In real life he flounders over his own sea of darkness until he reaches the shore, half drowned.

I would refrain from self-pity. It is not important that I have written.

I labored eventually until my heart pumped water. It was not easy. I will write a subjective book when I am eighty. I am still caught up with the flurry of living.

To get the mud out of my eyes I had to mix meditation with action. It is not always how far a man may go. He must be given some credit for having come from far down. If little of mental suffering is in my writing, the explanation is simple. In the world from which I came, if men knew they hurt you, they would hurt you again.

Cruel people in life are as thick as Jews in a Christian Science church.

The summer months found me in Cincinnati.

A covered wagon remained all night in an alley near Sixth and Sycamore streets. The floor was hard but clean. I used it as a bed for several weeks. A young Negro began to share it with me.

He annoyed me until I half throttled him. His screams attracted a passing policeman. I escaped but was forced to stay on the river front.

Three days later, I met the young Negro. Two other colored men were with him.

The fight began. I kicked the degenerate in the groin. He sank and lay still.

The other Negroes pounded my eyes black and blue; my nose was broken.

Hardly able to see, I stood against the wall of a building. Their blows came together. I ducked.

Their fists crashed against the wall. The hand of one dropped, limp. I went after him while the other pounded me on the back of the neck.

The wounded Negro rose and limped away.

Wise in the ways of such fighting, I backed against the wall again. When attacked, I ducked and fought back.

A crowd gathered. Some one yelled, "Cheese it, the cops."

The Negroes escaped. I was arrested.

Bleeding, I waited with the officers for the patrol wagon.

It was shaped like an omnibus, with no cover over it.

I rode, with a policeman sitting near me, to the jail.

A few small possessions were taken from me by the desk sergeant.

I was locked in the cell, my spirits trailing. I would go before Judge Lueders in the morning, a man whose name I dreaded. The sentence would at least be six months in the work house.

My beaten face throbbed. My body ached. I tried to sleep. Anticipated misery kept me awake. An hour or more passed.

The lights in the steel corridor went on. My cell door opened. My name was called.

Tommy Hester came with a policeman.

"I saw you by Sixth and Sycamore in the wagon," he said quietly. "I went over to Mike Mullen. He signed your bond."

I wept.

Hester said, "Brace up, Jim. Come with me."

It was night. Through wounded eyes I saw things dimly.

"Jim, you're on your honor now. Mike's on your bond. You appear before Judge Lueders in the morning."

"Will he have to pay, Tommy, if I duck? I hate to take six months at hard labor."

"He may not have to pay. It's a straw bond. But so many have been ducking — if you go — it'll make it harder for him next time to get some one else out."

Mike Mullen was the alderman of the ward. An

Irishman, brought up in a Reform School, a kitchen
flunky on an Ohio River steamboat, he became a policeman, and later, as the lieutenant of George B. Cox, the
second most powerful man in the city. Tommy Hester
was the "dummy" who "ran" against him.

"Here's fifty cents, Jim. Go down to the Standard and
get a bed and you'll have twenty-five cents for breakfast
in the morning. Meet me here at nine o'clock and at ten
we'll face the judge. Promise me you won't duck."

I promised.

I went to the Standard and got a bed in a little pine
room with a wire netting over it.

I decided, in spite of my promise, to get a freight out
of town early in the morning. Why should I serve six
months to make it easier for some other fellow? Besides,
Mike Mullen would not have to pay. It was a straw bond
— Mullen's word to pay one hundred and fifty dollars
if I vamoosed.

Troubled, I slept fitfully.

I awoke determined. Five jails in seven years was
enough. Once, I sat on the edge of the bed and started
to dress. Another mood came. I would face it out.

Until nine the next morning the battle went on in my
head and heart. I walked in the direction of the railroad
yards. In a dingy restaurant, I had breakfast.

I rose from a stool at the counter and watched an
engine switch freight cars.

I left the restaurant and went in the direction of
Tommy Hester in the mood of one who walked into a

jail. To this day, though glad I did it, I do not know why.

Hester was waiting.

"By God, Jim, you're game. It's not what you're facing. It's you. If you get six months I'll tell Mike Mullen."

"A hell of a lot of good that'll do, Tommy. Once I'm in the can, they'll all forget me."

"I didn't forget you, Jim."

"That's right. I'm sorry."

As we walked to the courtroom, people stared at my battered face.

Two detectives came to me. Years before they had accosted me as a vagrant in Fountain Square. I had several Holy Pictures on my person. Houlihan looked at them reverently and then at me.

"So long as ye carry thim on ye, me bye, ye kin niver go wrong." He handed them back, with a lecture. Several times he had come across me. I lied to him each time. I may have just tramped into the city, but there was always a factory in which I was working. Road-kids learn to save themselves the annoyances of jail if possible.

He asked me how I happened to be in the courtroom. I told him the truth.

"I slept in the wagon first and then I shared it with him. He was a fairy and I wouldn't come across. That's how it started. I may take a rap from the judge, but I'm right."

The detective heard me kindly.

"I've always believed ye, me bye. I believe ye now. But yere in a tough way. Ye know Judge Lueders."

He walked, with his partner, away. I could see them talking to some one near the judge.

"Telling my record, I'll bet."

I stood, with folded hands, before the judge. I had read of him for years and now I faced him. He looked into my battered eyes while the arresting officer made his charge.

"Your Honor," I pulled myself together. "I don't know how to tell my story. I didn't mean any wrong. The Niggers jumped on me." I looked in the direction of Houlihan.

The detective rose.

"Yere Honor, may I say a word for the bye? I know him. He's a good bye. No harm in him, Yere Honor. Raised at St. Joseph's."

He stepped near the judge's desk and talked to him.

"Case dismissed," said the judge.

I swallowed my heart and walked blindly toward Tommy Hester. Houlihan came and patted me on the back.

I grabbed his hand impulsively.

"There, there now — git yeresilf a job," he said.

I left the courtroom with Hester.

Tommy Hester took me to Moses and Scotty who lived under the bells of Saint Xavier's Church in an abandoned house, full of bedbugs and cockroaches.

Moses was a yegg with one arm and a laugh like a cackling hen. He was sallow, stooped, emaciated, and more than seventy years old. The owner of the building, a saloon keeper, knew Moses in a better day. He allowed him to occupy the house with Scotty, his friend, another old convict whom society had crushed. They were bitter against their conquerors. An old mattress upon which they slept was thrown in a corner.

The police did not molest Moses and his friend. They had the saloon keeper's word that all was well with the two old men.

The house, once a red brick, now turned almost black by smoke and time, had cracks an inch wide in the walls. The water spouts had long since fallen off. One piece still dangled from the roof. On windy nights it blew back and forth with a loud clatter. When heavy rains came, the roof leaked like a sieve. The sun shone through the cracks in the shingles and threw razorlike shadows on the floor and across the mattress.

Moses was not a man to ask questions. All his life a thief, he sank into senility with a cackle for a laugh. His arm had been shot away in a gun fight — four policemen against two yeggs in a small Middlewest bank.

It has been proven time and again that a yegg of the old school could shoot it out with a half dozen policemen. The newspapers after a night battle seldom reported a dead yegg. Always there was a dead policeman.

Moses and Scotty were of that breed.

They studied locations as engineers did maps. They knew the distance from one town to another and the roads which meandered across the locality in which they robbed. They knew the combinations of safes. In many instances they baffled the cunning of leading manufacturers and inventors. They could cook "soup" out of deadly explosives as deftly as an army cook did beans.

There was a once daring brain behind the cackle of old Moses. Moses and his partner turned.

They heard the cry, "Hands up." In the world of the yegg no man ever obeyed such an order. Old police officers told their men, "If you point a gun at a yegg you'll either kill or die."

Moses never used soup if he could help it. He would work an hour on the combination rather than use an explosive. He would always choose a stormy night for a robbery. Wind, rain, and storm drowned the noise of explosions and made police anxious to keep their skins dry.

Moses still stooped, his back to the police. The small bottle of soup was in his coat pocket. He rose in a flash, threw the bottle, and shot it out.

The fallen officer tried to crawl out of the débris. "For eighty dollars a month he wanted to die an' he did," cackled Moses. The second officer fell over him. A bullet caught Moses' left arm and drilled it through at the elbow.

"It never hurt," said Moses.

Another hunk of lead went through his partner's right lung.

"I could hear the wind go out of Bob's lung," Old Moses cackled.

Another bullet caught Bob.

"I knew I had to work fast — two more bullets left.

"I fell quick over Bob, came up, and the last town clown went down. I hated to shoot the last yap. He was game. But why didn't he let me alone? He didn't own the bank. People are always butting into things that don't concern 'em."

The newspaper reported that in a desperate battle with a half dozen yeggs, one officer was killed and two seriously wounded.

Moses got away with Bob, who died in a week.

Moses later served ten years for a crime he did not commit. He might easily have proven an alibi. "I was robbin' a bank in Kentucky that same night and I didn't even know the pete guys who turned that trick. And I did ten years." The ways of justice baffled Moses.

Moses wore the saloon keeper's old clothes. They hung loosely on his sparse body. The saloon keeper once bought him an artificial hand for Christmas. He pawned it and got drunk.

"How did you lose your hand?" a bar fly asked him.

"Wavin' a flag of truce in the Civil War," was the cackling answer.

Moses was so peaceful it was hard to realize that he had ever sauntered in the ways of doom.

Twice a day he went with a large basket to the saloon

of his friend. He returned each time with food enough to feed his three cronies.

In the old building was an accumulation of magazines and worm eaten books.

There was a walled brick court at the rear from which nothing could be seen but the sky and the tower of Saint Xavier's Church in which the bells hung.

For many days, until my face healed, I did not venture on the street. The evenings I spent with Moses and his friend in the court, the days in reading.

The clock in Saint Xavier's struck four times each hour — at the quarter twice, the half hour four times, and three quarters six, and on the even hour eight times. With a louder, more musical peal, it struck the hour.

As though projecting from an ancient feudal castle, the tower and the ringing bell became a part of me.

One midnight, the three of us were in the court. The clock struck, with heavy melody, twenty times. I watched the faces of the two life battered brigands as they listened. Through their own rays of smoke and the cloud streaked moonlight, something about them was different. They had stared into the barrels of guns. They were — undoubtedly — murderers. But here they sat, bony hands clutching pipes, and now and then looking up at the moon.

Scotty Whelan, older than Moses, but more firm in body and mind, had tan spots around his eyes and cheeks. Powder had once exploded too near.

Eyes black, shifty, narrow, a Quantrell guerilla in

the Civil War, he would seldom talk, even to Moses, never to strangers.

A week passed before he recognized me. There was little harm I could do him, even had I been one who would.

His hand was too unsteady to hold a gun. The knees of his once powerful body bent as he walked.

Habit was strong upon him.

"Listen, Scotty — the kid's *right people*. I know," Moses told him.

Scotty stared at Moses and asked,

"How?"

"Never mind. *I do*."

It is this valuable quality, to them in the underworld, that keeps the yegg alive. Less than any other class of human beings do they pick the wrong people in which to confide. They arrive at no conclusions by asking questions. Tongues were made to lie and hearts to deceive.

If a man is "wrong" it is known by something as subtle as space.

In the underworld, men are born *right* or *wrong*. Their conceptions of these terms are simple. One who does not betray is *right*. One who does is *wrong*.

Neither Moses nor Scotty ever judged men by any other standard.

The saloon keeper who helped Moses was of the underworld and "going straight." A gentleman of the underworld going straight is like a bishop who becomes a cardinal. His psychology is the same.

LADIES IN THE PARLOR

NEITHER MOSES NOR SCOTTY believed that I should work. Against their advice I got a job as dishwasher in the kitchen of Saint Xavier's college.

The wages were twenty dollars a month, my room and board. The room was on the fifth floor. The walls, once plastered white, were smeared with the blood of bedbugs long perished under the greasy hands of those who had preceded me.

For fifty years it had been occupied by scavengers like myself. It smelled of soap suds and refuse.

I worked from early morning until eight at night. On Feast Days, the work was harder and longer.

The priests came for coffee at four each afternoon.

Jesuits, and considered, I had heard it often, the smartest body of men in the world, they were excellent people. I asked them many questions and was answered kindly.

Father Francis J. Finn often came into the kitchen. He was handsome, his hair was partly gray at the temples, his nose aquiline, his eyes blue gray.

Little children followed him on the street.

I showed him my doggerel. He gave me a volume of Tennyson's poetry.

Every two weeks I received ten dollars and spent it with Moses and his friends. We cooked mulligans in the court and "rushed the growler," gallon buckets of beer until the money was gone.

One pay day I did not go near Moses and Scotty. Instead I went "down the line." Becoming careless with drink, I ignored the fifty cent girls and frequented only the dollar houses.

In one, the Madame called, "Ladies in the Parlor." A group of good-looking girls, about my own age, trooped into the front room.

Jessie was about eighteen. Slender and full bosomed, her body was so sinuous that the middle of it moved unconsciously as though she were doing a hip dance. Her nose was slightly beaked, her teeth even as little square stones in a row. Her eyes were restless and twinkling. Her hair was brown and wavy. Bold and demure, polite and aggressive, she became a whore at sixteen.

Beer at fifty cents a bottle was an item to be considered when one had less than ten dollars. But Jessie interested me. I bought four bottles.

She sat on my lap, and said,

"Come on upstairs."

"Nope"— I answered, teasing, "I got a girl. It's a sin when you pay for it."

"What's a sin?"

"Don't you know?'

I tried to explain.

"Is it plain to you now?"

"Plain as mud," she answered, "Come on upstairs."

She ran her hand through my hair; then stroked her breasts and sighed deeply. "It won't cost you nothing."

She drank her beer indifferently.

"Don't you like beer?" I asked.

"No — it's slop. All the heifers here drink it. I like whisky."

"Not for my money, kid."

"Come on — I got some up in my room."

She kissed me quickly and stood up. Her body moved alluringly.

We walked upstairs.

When the door closed, her arms went round me. She kissed me feverishly and said impulsively, "Wait."

She ran to the bureau, took some money from a drawer and left the room. She returned quickly, saying,

"I gave the landlady two and a half, her share for me staying all night with you. No one can bother us now till noon to-morrow."

"I've got to go to work at five."

"Oh, to hell with work. I'll *keep you.*"

After each crisis she would lie on the bed, silent and lovely as a sleeping child, her hair in waves on the pillow.

In a short time her fingers would steal softly over my body.

When at noon the next day we rose, she looked in the mirror and said, "I look like I been sent for and couldn't come."

She poured herself a glass of whisky.

"Wanta drink?" she asked.

"Yes."

We both drank the smooth bourbon.

"Have another."

"Yes."

"Where do you live?"

I gave her the address of Moses.

"I'll see you to-morrow. It's my day off."

She took another drink and shuddered, "What a life. To-day's pay day at the Binger Iron Works. I'll have to hang out with a dozen Greeks and bohunks."

"It must be tough."

"It sure is. But I don't blame the landlady. Money's money in a whore house. Girls don't come here to play with themselves."

She dressed quickly in pink laces and silks, and then slipped a dainty one piece dress over her head.

"Come on"— She took my hand. "You can have breakfast with me."

A group of girls were gathered about a large flaming red cloth covered table.

A dark woman of middle age, with earrings dangling, sat at the head. Her cheeks and lips were painted deep red.

The girls addressed her politely as Madame.

Madame Furey was maternal toward her girls. A strict disciplinarian, she was well liked even by the most irascible.

She took half of the girls' earnings and charged them ten dollars a week for board and laundry. Under these conditions Jessie earned about two hundred dollars a week.

Two of the girls had left that day. The Madame was downhearted.

"You can't trust a whore, you can't trust a whore," she said over and over. "I did everything for them girls. I wouldn't let 'em go to bed with drunken men, an' even paid Sue's doctor bill when she had the clap. Now when she gets to where she can make some money by takin' on some good spenders, she ups and leaves me." The other girls paid no attention to her chorus of woe.

"A whore had some honor when I was a girl. She wasn't around gettin' the clap or gettin' knocked up every time a man hung his pants in the same room with 'em. Now, my God, all they do is go back an' forth to the doctors. Between correctments an' knockin' babies, they ain't got no time to make money. I don't know why in the hell I wasn't a lady evangelist. There's more money in it, an' it's a damn sight safer sleepin' with deacons, an' you can have all the other men you want. So long as you're able to stand in the pulpit an hour on Sunday an' say 'Amen,' the money rolls in. Now look at me — I got thirty thousand dollars in this joint, an' I have to go to bed with the cop on the beat to keep him from raidin' me. I got a lot of oil paintings here that nobody ever looks at. Who the hell wants to look at oil paintings in a whore house? Their minds is on other things. Beds is all you need in a whore house, an' me like a damn fool fills my house with thirty thousand dollars' worth of junk."

The Madame reached for a slice of ham and slapped it on her plate.

"Twenty years ago, a whore was a whore and took her pay like any other self-respectin' woman. Now every town is full of charity girls, an' every fence corner along the road has one. I'll bet you if I had a spy glass in the moon I could count ten million girls every night givin' it away for nothin', an' me with thirty thousand dollars invested here, tryin' to compete against that. There's a sucker born every second, an' every other one's a whore. The rest is landladies tryin' to sell what most women give away on the ground an' on benches in the park, while we have decent beds and doctors to examine the girls."

"Madame," said a tall dark girl, "may I go home to Columbus over Sunday?"

Madame Furey exploded, "Good Lord, you hain't had a man all week, an' now you want to chase to Columbus. What the hell's there?"

"The Grand Gobblers' Convention."

"You won't get any money out of them. They're too damn old," snapped Madame Furey.

"You'd be surprised, Madame," laughed Jessie. "There's more'n one way to skin a cat."

"If it was an Eels' Convention you'd make some money," said another girl. "An Eel knows how to treat a woman like she was white."

"All of 'em give you as little as they can," answered Madame Furey. "You gotta take it away from all of 'em." She looked sternly at me, "How'd'you get in here?"

"He's my all night fellow," volunteered Jessie. "He paid his money in advance."

"I hope you didn't get cheated," sneered the tall girl who longed for Columbus.

"He went to bed with me, not you," flamed Jessie. "You whores should tend to your own business."

"Who're you, callin' me a whore — keep your names to yourself!" the tall girl shouted.

"Girls — girls," placated Madame Furey, "be good."

"She can't call me a whore an' get away with it — you're always takin' her part," the tall girl frowned.

"I don't take on dagoes like you do," Jessie shot at her.

"Girls, girls, be quiet," advised the landlady.

"Aren't they naughty girls?" she turned to me. I did not answer.

"You must quit this quarreling among yourselves. What in the world will people say?" Madame Furey rose from the table. The girls followed her.

I went into the parlor with Jessie.

"I'll see you to-morrow," she said. "Now you be there."

"All right," I agreed.

I did not return to work.

That night I told of my adventure to Moses and Scotty. "You been smokin' hop somewhere," Moses commented.

"Well, maybe I have."

"I know how it goes." Moses pulled at his empty sleeve. "I had a gal once — a banker's wife. Met her one night when I was workin' on a safe. She came in to draw her breath, and I explained why I was workin' with the safe. There was too much money in that section and I was takin' some of it away. I asked her as a favor to me not to speak of my presence to her husband.

" 'Of course not. Why should I speak of you to my husband? He shouldn't know everything. Besides, you have a perfect right to any money you obtain here. He takes it from others, you take it from him — so runs the unhappy world away!'

" 'But, Madame, you understand, I want to take you

to a hotel. You're a beautiful woman and you don't want to waste your life with a banker. Girls complain fearfully about bankers to me. They tell me their knees are made of silver and that other parts of them are cold as gold.'

" 'You don't know the half of it,' smiled the banker's wife. 'These many years I've been lookin' for a big man like you. I'm dreadfully unhappy. My husband don't understand me.' "

The two old brigands laughed, until Moses resumed,

" 'Pray tell me,' she says, 'I just know you are not a banker. You look too honest and refined. It's a shame you must work while dishonest men sleep.'

" 'Madame,' I said, 'I'm robbin' the bank.'

" 'Oh, shush,' she says playfully, rubbing her hip — 'you cannot make pretensions toward fooling me. I know all the directors of this bank and you are not one of them. Let us partake of midnight lunch together.' "

Again the old brigands laughed.

" 'I can tell a banker a mile off,' says she. 'They look like lawyers and pickpockets and you cannot presume to fool me. You are not one of them. Why do you treat me so?' she says, 'me, who has millions to give because I love you.' "

The old rascals laughed loud and long together.

When it ended, Moses looked humorously at me. "If you got a gal like that, I'm the guy that sewed the lace on Grover Cleveland's drawers."

"Well, I got her. Wait and see."

The next day a storm broke over the city. The lightning struck a church steeple, and knocked a Negro who was gilding the Cross into the Ohio River.

A deluge of rain followed the catastrophe. It clattered on the streets and against the roof of the ramshackle house in which we dwelt. It roared in rivulets on the roof. It rolled to the ground with the force of thousands of men emptying barrels of water from above.

We had several quarts of whisky in the front room. In spite of the warmth in the fluid, we were low in spirit and sad in heart. Moses was vindictive against life.

"What a long way I've come. I'm just smart enough to live on free lunch. That's all."

"But you only got one hand, Mose — that makes a difference. Now if you had two hands you could run a street car or somethin' —" Scotty's laugh was a sneer.

"Well, if I did — it'd be the Bankers' Special — but that's enough from you."

There was a pounding at the door. The ancient building shook. Scotty rose, sidled down the stairs in the manner of a man who went cautiously, gun in hand, to exchange bullets with another.

Above the rush of wind and water a man's voice asked if I lived at the house.

Scotty's answer could not be heard.

I went downstairs.

Jessie was paying the driver. She walked in and exclaimed, "My God, what a joint!"

Scotty frowned.

I introduced them. The stiffness left his hard body. He bowed politely.

"I'm pleased to meet you. Jim was speakin' of you to-day."

"Was it nice?"

"You bet. He likes you."

"That's good. I like him."

She followed us upstairs.

Her raincoat glistened. Water dripped from a small silk umbrella. "Is this whisky real?" she asked.

Moses stood erect.

"It is, Madame," he said.

"Madame — my God — am I that old?"

"No, Madame," answered Moses.

"Jessie," I said, "this is Moses, my good friend."

The old brigand rubbed the stub of his arm.

"Yes — we like the boy —"

"That's good. I'm glad I found him."

The bell at Saint Xavier's tolled the hour. We stood quite still and I listened.

When the reverberation had died away, Moses said,

"We own those bells — much as anybody. Will you have a drink?"

"Will I have a drink?" returned Jessie. "Just ask me."

She unbuttoned her glistening coat, threw it across an old chair, stood the umbrella at its side, and poured the whisky.

"Have a chaser?" asked Moses, half bewildered by her gusto.

"Not me — I take it straight. I like to feel it burning down my throat. And when it tingles up the back of my neck, then I know it's good whisky."

The two old brigands were pleased, and bashful.

Scotty rubbed his leathery hands.

The rain rattled against the dirty windows. Water fell on the mattress in the corner.

Jessie stood, her body undulating in a tight dress, her smile contagious as the plague, and looked about the room.

"Who bought the liquor?"

"The Kid —" Moses answered. "We rush the growler unless we find a live one." Moses poured more liquor for all.

Jessie looked at the picture on the bottle. It was that of a mule, carrying bottles of liquor.

Underneath the mule, forming a half circle were the words —"She was bred in old Kentucky."

She sang,

> *"That's where I was bred*
> *And lost my maidenhead*
> *At Fort Thomas to a soldier.*
> *He wasn't very much older."*

"Have you got a telephone here?"

"No, Madame," Moses answered.

The rain had subsided. Water still rolled weakly down the window.

"You should of been at the house last night, Kid. Some one asked a Greek if he was a Catholic and he says —'Jesus Christ, I ought to be. My father was a priest.' It made Madame Furey mad. She's a strict Catholic."

Jessie rolled a ten dollar bill and put it in a bottle half filled with whisky. "Fish that out," she laughed.

"That's easy," Moses cackled. "We'll drink the whisky and break the bottle."

Lifting her raincoat and umbrella, she walked to the door saying, "Come on, Kid."

Moses and Scotty looked at one another as we left.

"Good Lord," she said, "how do you stand it there? That place would give me the willies."

"I don't know. I just do."

"My mother lives in a joint like that. She won't live in any other kind of a place. And she's soused all the time. I can't stand it over an hour each week with her."

"Does she live here in Cincy?" I asked.

"Yes — over on Race Street." She looked at me quickly. "You know, Kid, I dreamt of you last night. Dreamt you were crying." She tapped the sidewalk with the end of her umbrella. "What was wrong?"

"Nothing. I wasn't crying that I know of."

"You surely was. I dreamt it."

A beggar woman held a handful of lead pencils toward us. Her red face was streaked with dirt. A frayed shawl was on her head.

Jessie gave her a dollar. The woman tried to make her take a lead pencil.

She motioned her away with, "I never write."

As we walked on, she muttered,

"If I ever get in that fix, I'll kill myself. I'd a thousand times rather be what I am — or dead."

The sun trailed miles of shadow across the Ohio River as we watched.

Jessie took my hand, "Come on, I'll show you somethin'." We looked through the Suspension Bridge which stretched, a mile long tunnel, over the Ohio into Kentucky. "I never get tired of looking at it. It's the only thing about the damn town I like," she said.

We turned into a clothing store.

A salesman approached. "My brother here wants a suit and some other things," Jessie smiled.

We went to a room on Twelfth Street which faced the Canal.

It was gaudily furnished. From the walls hung a half dozen pictures by Charles Dana Gibson.

One which Jessie liked was that of an old man and a little child. The youngster, telling the old man's fortune, was looking into his tired eyes and saying,

"You are about to go on a long, long journey."

"I keep this room ever since I went into a house. Mother don't know I got it, thank God. Neither does she know I'm in a house. She thinks I'm living with a jockey over in Latonia. She calls me bad enough names as it is." She whistled a tune,

*"If I only had just fifty million dollars —
And Hetty Green would come and be my wife —
With Pierpont Morgan waiting on the table —
Then I know that I'd be satisfied with life."*

"I don't give a damn about my mother. I'll tell the whole damned world that I'm a whore. If they don't like it they can sleep with their pants on. But if she knew where I was she'd be bummin' me for money day and night to buy whisky. She's the kind that can drink it in the morning before breakfast." She sighed,

"And so can I."

Jessie's mother was thirty years from the hills of Kentucky. She was hunchbacked and bowlegged. Her eyes turned upward in her head. Her husband took care of horses for an Express Company until he disputed the right of way with a Baltimore and Ohio train.

Jessie was fifteen then. Just out of a House of Correction, and carefree as a gypsy, she picked her career a year later with no more concern than if she had brought her mother a rose.

The old lady had one crow to pick with life. But two hundred miles from her native hills, she was unable to get liquor which she considered fit to drink. Bottles were hidden everywhere about her flat. Each night she drank a concoction of elderberry wine and whisky.

"It makes the bluejays sing in my ears until I go to sleep," she used to tell Jessie.

Jessie hated her mother. "I wish she was dead and in

hell every week. I could ring bells at her God damn funeral. Mother love makes my ears ache."

She was always cheerful until in the presence of her mother. Her body then became rigid, her face went stern.

When the old woman would try to touch the lovely girl, Jessie would shudder.

"Ashamed of your old mother," the old crone would say.

"You're right. Why in the hell shouldn't I be?"

A green scum was on the water of the canal which faced the old woman's house. Long legged bugs slid over the scum. Vari-colored insects, larger and swifter of flight than butterflies, and known by the children of Ohio as "snake-feeders" would buzz over the stagnant water.

Jessie's mother would sit in a pine rocking chair, a bottle on each side of her and stare, unseeing as death, at the narrow bed of water.

There was, in her dissipated face, a look of repose, something of decayed majesty. Her nose was larger than Jessie's, her face on a heavier scale. Wisps of gray hair hung from her temples. As the liquor took effect more and more, bringing with it the only thing it could bring except death, a paralyzing stupor, her chin shook constantly, her saliva-drooled mouth opened, her eyes closed. She would remain in that position until early morning, then straggle into an unmade bed with all her clothes on.

She only asked one thing of Jessie, besides liquor. To

be buried in her native hills. She would ask Jessie that boon each week. Jessie would reply, "Sure — the sooner the better — they can soak the ground around your grave and make whisky out of it."

"If they do, I'll drink it." The old lady would rub her shriveled breast with pride.

"It's time I'm going anyhow — my husband dead — my daughter a whore."

"She may be a whore, but she's not an old slut, Mother. She's got her father's drop of blood in her."

"Ay, her father that murdered a man by the moonlight when I was a girl."

"It's too God damned bad he didn't murder you."

"Yes — then I'd have given birth to no whore."

"Have it your own way — soak your hide all week. I'll be home then."

Jessie would slam the rickety door and go hastily down the dirty stairs. On the street she was a smiling happy girl again.

She knew many of the boys in the neighborhood. A half dozen of them had seduced her. "They can't push me over now for fun." She would laugh at herself, "Just to think — I used to be the neighborhood charity butterfly."

She was pleasant toward all the other girls in the house. In a quarrel she was as bitter against them as she was toward her mother. But her hatred of them was soon over. Toward her mother it was implacable.

One Wednesday evening the police raided a wine

room. I escaped. Jessie was arrested and sent to the Reform School on Colerain Avenue.

I had twenty dollars which she had given me that day. As I was not allowed to see her, I took her what presents I could buy and left them with the Superintendent.

After some days that gentleman suggested that I marry Jessie and thus obtain her freedom. There was no particular reason why I should not have done so. I made marital mistakes more sad later. It might have made a man of me. I refused to marry Jessie even to get her out of jail.

Released in a few weeks, the Superintendent told her of my disloyalty. We quarreled.

My home with the masterpieces of Charles Dana Gibson and the beribboned pillows was hard to leave. As for Jessie, wars had been waged for girls less lovely. The hurt was deep. I tried to explain why a marriage between us would have been impossible. She was no more interested in that blessed sacrament than myself. She did feel, however, that the loyal thing to have done was for me to have married her under the circumstances.

She handed me ten dollars, and flared, "Don't go away broke."

"I won't," I returned.

"You'll be back," she laughed. "They all crawl to me."

"Don't stand on your head till I do." I slammed the door.

I found Moses and Scotty under the Saint Xavier tower.

Seating myself on a chair, carved out of a rain barrel, I told them that I had ten dollars to spend on whisky and beer.

Moses had a bottle of gunshot whisky near him. He quickly pushed it aside and went for the gallon tin bucket that hung on a nail. "Gimme the money, Kid — Here, Scotty, it's your turn to go for the suds — bring some decent whisky too."

When Scotty left, Moses asked, "How's the little gal on George Street?"

I told him the sad story.

"Well — you can't hold them forever. When you lose one the only way to do is git another one. That helps you to forget. They're all alike in the dark anyhow."

Sick at heart, I did not answer.

"Why didn't you marry her?"

"That's what I'd like to know. Why the hell didn't I?"

"Sure —" drawled Moses. "Marry 'em all. A guy on the bum don't need to be afraid of getting married. It's when you got money that you wants to lay offa that stuff."

I took a heavy swig of the gunshot whisky. It rasped down my throat.

Scotty returned with beer and whisky while the bells of Saint Xavier's rang.

We drank heavily.

"You guys won't see me again after to-morrow, I'm

getting the hell away from all this forever," I blurted out.

"That's all right, Kid," Moses cackled. "I used to feel that way whenever I lost a split tail. But jist as I say, 'Git another one!' "

"No — but I'm leaving to-morrow."

"What — and leave that girl —" asked Scotty. "Don't be a fool."

"I'm not — she's left me."

"Tell her you're sorry," suggested Moses. "Women like that."

The lure of Jessie's body swept over me. Now, maudlin, I cried. Exasperated at seeing me weep, Moses said, "Well — you shoulda married her if you're so sorry — God dammit. Why the hell didn't you say somethin' to me?"

"I wish I had."

Moses staggered and rested the stub of his arm on my shoulder. "Jesus Christ, Kid — brace up. You ain't faced nothin' yet. Wait till you leave a dame in a court-room, one as purty as her. That's what stabs you under the heart. And you know that the dame'll be chasin' with another guy in a month—then you console yourself with thinkin' that if his Nibs knew it all he'd be sayin' —'An' hanged by the neck until dead'— and you go out of the courtroom to your cell with your chin rubbin' a hole in your breast."

He poked me with the stub of his arm.

"I tell you, Kid, you ain't seen nothin' yet. Wait till

you look at the Big House, six o'clock in the mornin' and you know you're goin' to be there no less 'an ten years even if you're good as a dead saint — and you gotta take everything to make it in ten. If you step out of line by accident a dumb guard says —'In line there, you son of a bitch or I'll lay your head open with a club —.' You wanta kill him — but you can't lose your credit marks — so you swallow hard and kick your pride in the pants an' go away marchin' like a wooden soldier. Wait, Kid, till you lie in the can till you kin count every streak of paint on the bars of your cell, till you count the minutes and the hours and the days till it seems like your heart's stopped beatin' and you're no longer where you are but somewheres else. And it's always at times like them that some dame gives you the go-by." Moses staggered away.

"You ain't seen nothin' yet — an' you cryin' because a skirt brushed you aside." He stamped his foot. "Jesus — you ought to be smart as a fly an' light on another skirt."

Scotty hiccoughed. "Mose is right, Kid. Wait till you crawl around your cell like a monkey to keep from goin' crazy. Why, hell, Kid, in a year you'll be glad this split tail left you. When you're old like me you'll be God damned sorry you ever mixed up with any of them. They all smell like fish and primp like parrots. You're a hell of a swell pimp, you are."

The bell at Saint Xavier's boomed the hour. Silence came for a minute.

"I guess I'll go after another can o' suds," said Scotty. "Sure," said Moses, "bring a couple handfuls of free lunch with you. I'm hungry."

Scotty returned with the grub. I refused to eat.

The bucket empty of beer, I stood, body wabbling.

"I'm going to leave you boys. Back on the road for me. I'm goin' till I find a little town, and I'm goin' to work. I'm goin' to git the hell away from all you bastards and hearin' about jails and whores —"

"Oh, to hell with that talk." Scotty jerked me backwards. I fell and lay still.

I awoke before dawn. Scotty was stretched by the rain-barrel chair. Moses was on the broken cement floor of the court.

I felt in my clothes for money and found none.

I rolled Moses over and took twenty-five cents from his vest pocket. My mind was on black coffee.

I looked at them for a moment, my head roaring with drunken pain, "I'm goin' to get the hell out of this." The clock struck again. I looked up. The sparrows were beginning to move in the eaves of Saint Xavier's.

A glint of light from the East slanted across the yellow crucifix above the clock. A spurt of wind whirled a cloud of dust along the lead gulley of the church roof.

I sat heavily on the rain-barrel chair. My temples ached as though they were being tapped constantly with tiny electric hammers. Over my eyes was a stinging pain.

My clothes were soiled and beer-stained, my hat was gone. I shook Scotty and asked him where it was.

"Go to sleep," he mumbled, "f — or — Ch — rist's sake."

I sat again on the rain-barrel chair and held my head.

Some one had told me to drink tomato juice after a debauch. I arose. "That's it — I'll go and get some tomato juice. Then I'll get the hell out." I started and got as far as Sixth Street. One foot dragging the other I managed to go forward. "I'll go and get some tomato juice."

I could hear the bells of Saint Xavier's ringing for the last time in my life as I turned into Drury's beanery.

THE WRONG DIRECTION

GETTING ON A FREIGHT without knowing where it was going, I awoke in Dayton, eighty miles from Saint Marys. My one resolve was not to go near that place. Would I return to Cincinnati or go north to Cleveland? While I debated, a freight started north. I climbed aboard.

In several hours it reached Lima, twenty-two miles from Saint Marys.

I walked into the office of a factory near the railroad and asked for work. The picture of a fish was on the wall. Beneath were the words,

"Any fish can float down stream, it takes a live one to swim up." I took the words seriously. I was just any fish. I had been floating down stream.

The man came, and refused me work.

My head ached. I longed for Jessie, and thought of Moses and Scotty.

Hatless, with a blazing head of long curly hair, I wandered about until I came to a jungle near a railroad crossing.

Five hoboes were gathered about a mulligan cooking in a large boiler. A saloon was a few hundred feet away.

They were rushing the growler. "Which way, 'bo?" one asked.

"Up from Cincy."

"Where before there?"

"Chi and the coast."

Two of the men were "snakes," railroad men hoboing about the country. They had money. Another was Windy Connor, a hobo of whom I had heard. He was small, red-faced, and Irish. His tongue seldom stopped.

"I'm choked, Windy," I said.

He handed me a two gallon growler, saying,

"Drink your head off."

I soon felt better, and slightly drunk.

A laborer waited for a freight train bound for Leipsic, and a stone quarry thirty miles away.

With food and drink aplenty, I decided to go with him.

"Better stay with us, Red. We got dough," yelled Windy Connor.

The train was running swiftly when it crossed the

Pennsylvania tracks. I caught it, looked back, and saw the laborer sprawling down the bank.

It reached Leipsic without stopping.

I looked over the dreary little town as the sun sank.

A man passed a combination saloon and restaurant. He wore a loud checked suit, and a red tie. Seven years on the road had taught me to read people. I was certain that he would be kind hearted. I told him a sad tale.

He took me into the saloon and bought me a drink.

"What do you follow, Kid?" he asked, handing me a dollar.

Observing the gold horseshoe hanging from his watch chain, I answered, "Been exercisin' at Latonia. I got drunk and lost my money."

"The hell you did."

"Yes — I want to make a stake. Heard there was a quarry here, hirin' men. It's hard work, but I'm not afraid of it."

"That's the way to talk."

"Has Jake been in?" he asked the bartender.

"Not this afternoon," was the answer.

"Well phone him — tell him about the boy here. Ask him if he'll put him on."

The bartender telephoned. "He says he needs men to unload some cars of crushed stone. Can you do that?"

"Sure," I answered. "Tell him I'll be glad to start in the morning."

The stranger gave me two silver dollars more.

"You'll need some overalls," he said.

I loitered the rest of the day about the saloon.

The owner of the stone quarry came later and arranged for my board and room at the place.

Early the next morning I had a hearty breakfast, took a packed lunch, and started for work.

The sun was already hot.

Heat rose from the steel rails.

I glanced at the crushed stone in the cars and walked on down the railroad to the hobo jungle.

It was completely deserted. Magazines and newspapers were strewn about.

Hanging my lunch on a tree to keep the ants from getting into it, I began to read.

By late afternoon, no train had come either way.

In desperation I decided to take a freight going in either direction.

At dusk, one came. Its headlight beamed in the direction of Lima.

Before long I was back with the hoboes in Lima.

"I told you," Windy Connor said in greeting, "never to travel with a hick. I knew you'd be back."

"Well, I bumped into a live one up there anyhow. I got a dollar left." I took the bucket and went for some beer. Some half warm food was still in the boiler.

Windy Connor had revived the fire under the boiler by the time I returned.

A railroad tie, heavy with the odor of creosote, stretched across two boxes.

A new moon hung above a water tank —
Windy Connor sang with heavy throat,

*"I'm goin' to live anyhow until I die —
I know this kind of livin' ain't very high —"*

I gave him money to fill the growler.
He went away, staggering and singing.
I watched the glistening piece of moon for a long time.
The noises of the night partly ceased.
Green valleys along the Columbia River passed before my eyes. *That was the country.* I would go there in the morning and settle down. The lure of the wanderlust, the mirage that beckoned, was far away.
The fire died to nothing.
I put my coat over my shoulders and slept on the railroad tie.
The sun was half way up the sky when I awoke. I looked about the jungle. It was deserted. There was nothing to eat. I walked to a nearby grocery and bought eggs, bacon, bread, and coffee with my remaining money. A skillet, made out of a tomato can, was in a pine box. With it, I prepared the breakfast.
I thought for a second of Windy. Such disappearances were usual on the road.
He returned with money. The day was getting warm.
"Let's have some beer," he suggested. "Where's the growler?"
"You took it with you last night," I told him.

"Oh, that's right — it's over to Pelkay's now."

He went for the bucket and returned with beer, and a quart of whisky.

That day we got drunk again.

Windy Connor wanted to go to Peoria. I went with him as far as Saint Marys and left him in a drunken sleep on the freight.

The lights of the main street were just being turned on. I walked from one end of it to the other several times and met no one whom I knew.

Then it dawned on me forcefully that I had returned to the place which I hated.

Everything looked different. I had left at fourteen knowing but little of life. I had returned, not yet twenty-one, but quite old.

A boy with whom I had heated links stood in front of Coffee's Saloon.

Years before he had given me his cast off clothing. He took me into the saloon in which I had my first drink with my grandfather. A few large glasses of beer and helpings of the free lunch and I had stepped over the chasm of seven years. It seemed as though I had not left the town. The young fellow heard me tell of my wanderings, and considered me a hero.

The chain factory had burned to the ground and was to be rebuilt.

He had served his time in a machine shop and was now a full fledged machinist. As we talked at the bar, I wondered if I had wasted my years.

Every boy was advised to "learn a trade." The hoboes who secured work easiest, had trades.

"Why don't you stick around, Jim?" the youth said. "When the chain shop's built up again, there'll be a lot of new fires and you, being a link heater, they might put you to makin' traces or cow ties."

The cheapest form of chains, all "learners" are given such pieces to weld.

He took me home with him to a small pine house that faced Rabbit Town. From the window of the little attic room I could see the house in which Edna had lived and whored.

He lit a kerosene lamp and placed it on a table.

"I'll wake you in the mornin', Jim. Ma'll have a good breakfast for us. I leave the house at six-thirty."

I blew the flame from the lamp and stared out of the window. Nothing could be seen by the gleam of red and green lights along the Lake Erie and Western railroad.

Down the yellow street which crossed the tracks had lived Pearl Wright. Still a child, she had killed herself.

I watched, with Old Hughie Tully, her funeral going down the miserable rain beaten street. There were four rigs, besides the hearse.

My old grandfather stood until the rigs had gone two blocks further. He shook his big head sadly, "Ah me," he said, "ah my." Then came a half smile, "The ind comes too soon fer us all — an' to die fer love of one bye — she may as well of loved a rain drop."

Old Hughie was also gone. My sister was in Chicago. Edna was — I wondered where.

Why did I happen to be in Saint Marys? I did not know.

In the morning I would pull out for Oregon without seeing any one. I was filled with hatred of the town and all its people. I was glad that I had not remained.

I was called to breakfast in the early morning. The house had the pleasant odor of food. The boy's mother and father were kind.

Mrs. Yeaver had never been out of Auglaize County. Her face was thin and red. There were gray hairs down each of her cheeks. "You must stay here a while with us," she said. "The little bed upstairs can be yours. Alvin has things for you to wear."

I did not answer right away.

"I knew your mother well," she said. "No finer woman than Biddy ever lived. She would do as much for Alvin."

"I think," I said at last, "I'd better be leaving. I hate the town and everything in it."

"But you mustn't," said Mrs. Yeaver, "people are not to blame. They just don't know."

"Will you promise me one thing, Jim?" Alvin asked.

"What?"

"That you'll be back for supper and stay to-night."

I did not answer.

"You can go over to Billy Joles — he's a straw boss at the chain shop. They're clearin' bricks away. You remember when he got started makin' cow ties. He'll give you a job, maybe."

"All right," I said.

Father and son left for work. I loitered for an hour with Mrs. Yeaver, and then walked toward the chain shop.

Men with teams were clearing away débris.

Billy Joles, about twenty-four, was directing them. Amazed to see me, he gave me work.

The pay was fifteen cents an hour, a dollar and a half a day, nine dollars a week. It all went over my head.

"Do you want to start now?" he asked.

"I'll wait until to-morrow morning, Billy," I replied.

People stared at me as, hatless, I wandered about the town.

I could hear the freight trains pulling in over the grade east of town. There was no one to whom I cared to talk. I wandered to the railroad yards and watched the trains go in and out. As the sun slanted down I went to Mrs. Yeaver's home.

In the morning I went to work.

The days passed drearily. My back ached, my hands became so sore I could not bend them. When the bricks were wheeled into an immense pile ready for use again, I was placed at a winding machine. All iron and steel wound into links must be heavily soaked with oil.

My clothes and skin became saturated. My body broke out and exuded oil and matter. Each night I dragged to the home of Mrs. Yeaver, vowing to be gone to Oregon in the morning. When the new day came, I dragged myself to work.

Six weeks passed at this labor.

My brain was completely stunned. When not too tired I would walk up and down Spring Street in the evening. My board cost four dollars a week, my laundry a dollar more.

The saloons trusted men. Burned out inside at the end of the day, I would owe my four dollars for liquor on each pay day.

I had no hopes, no ties. My intelligence rebelled at the thought of settling down to the life of an Alvin Yeaver. I felt that perhaps I was wrong in remaining.

In nearly every larger town across America there is something that resembles a library. In Saint Marys there was nothing. I was lost.

Each Sunday I would remain near the attic window with a large tablet and lead pencil.

At the end of the day, I tore up all I had written.

Three chainmakers whom I knew had gone to Racine. It was three hundred miles away. One cold Saturday afternoon I decided to go there.

I bade good-by to the Yeavers and caught a fast freight to Lima. From that town to Chicago it is two hundred and thirty miles. Hoboes seldom rode the Pennsylvania trains because of strict police vigilance. Learning early that people who lived in houses near railroad yards were more often generous than those further away for the reason that hoboes always let them alone, I decided to ride the Limited on the Pennsylvania road.

In five hours I reached Chicago. In three more I was in Racine, sixty miles west of Chicago.

I had beaten my way on three railroads over three hundred miles and had ridden into one large station in Chicago and stolen my way out of another. My destination was reached in fifteen hours.

CHAINMAKERS

CHAINMAKERS ARE THE GYP-
sies of manual labor. It is unusual to find one who has
not worked in a half dozen states. A man who has
learned his trade and has remained in one factory is
spoken of contemptuously as a "home guard." He might
be an excellent workman, but is never given complete
respect.

No man can become a first class chainmaker unless he
has had considerable experience with the fundamentals
of the trade as a youth.

Not even a scientific pugilist combines the speed of
eyes, hands, and feet as a chainmaker. At work, he ap-
proaches the poetry of motion.

There are about a dozen chain factories in America.
They supply most of the chain in the world.

Just as all railway engineers must first fire an engine, so must all good chainmakers start as link heaters.

The link heater begins in boyhood and works several years before being allowed to attempt making the cheapest grade of chain. Some boys have worked ten years as link heaters. Others, according to luck or favoritism, are given their chance much sooner.

I heated links for several periods of six months.

The link heater prepares the fire for the chainmaker at six each morning. For an hour the factory was full of the noises of children earning a living.

It was dark at this hour during the winter. The link heaters would dip pieces of waste in crude oil, and place them, lighted, on the furnace. The factory would soon be full of smoke, the odor of burning rags, and a dim, wavering, uncertain light.

When the engine started the blast at seven, we used the burning waste to light the furnaces.

Driven by the blast, red and blue blazes spurted out of the holes where the links would be heated.

The roar of the factory would start for the day.

When the furnace became warm, we would shape the hooks upon which we hung the links in the furnace.

This done, we would wait for the chainmakers, who came a half hour later.

The fires in the furnaces are made to burn strongly by a blast which is sent through a zinc pipe three feet and more in diameter, and which is directly beneath the roof. Smaller pipes lead downward from the larger pipe. One is attached to each furnace.

The noise of fire and blast can be heard for miles on quiet days.

The furnace is built out of fire brick in the form of a square stove.

Holes the size of the links to be welded into chain are cut in the top.

The link heater's job is to hang the open end of the link downward in the fire. Eight or ten, and sometimes a dozen links are thus hung. The chainmaker takes them from the fire with tongs and welds them into chain in endless rotation.

So quick does his eye become that he can detect the slightest variation in the color of each link. He seldom picks a link from the furnace that is not ready for welding.

The link must be exactly the right heat; otherwise the "shins," or ends, will project when the chain is tested. All chain must pull so many pounds, according to size, before it passes inspection and leaves the shop.

Coil chain is of four grades, common, two B, three B, and steel loding. Some men are never able to make any but common chain. Others can make steel loding as swiftly as less adept mechanics can the common grade.

The difference is in the workmanship applied to the chain, and the delicate adjustment of the dies upon which it is made.

A man who consistently makes good steel loding is considered a first class workman.

Block chain, that which runs over spools of pulleys, is also hard to make. The link must not vary a fraction of an inch, as each link must fit into a sprocket. A piece of steel loding or three B chain will pull ten times as many pounds as a piece of common chain the same size and material.

Drunkards are generally considered the best chainmakers. They are "free sweaters"— the alcohol keeping their pores open.

Short armed men are more often superior than those with long arms.

Some men become expert on one size of chain. Jim Welch, a drunken hobo, could make more half inch chain in a day than any three men. No other man ever remotely approached his speed.

He would work three days and get drunk the remainder. He was still more valuable to the firm than the slower workman, on account of his enormous output and the little fuel required in the making of it. Welch was welcome in any shop. If no furnace were available, one was made ready.

The floaters among chainmakers seldom paid debts to saloon or boarding house keepers. Often honest among themselves, they would say at the table of a boarding house if beets were upon it, "Pass the chainmakers." Thus warned, the landlady would go right on trusting.

If a chainmaker came into a town destitute, he was taken care of by others until he had a pay day.

If one refused to help another it was soon known in every shop in the country.

While working, a chainmaker stands with his left side nearest the fire. As a consequence, that side of his face is generally raw and red.

A chainmaker who works a "kicker" for many years, limps when he walks.

A kicker is a heavy hammer, not operated by factory power. Instead, a pedal is attached. The chainmaker kicks the pedal to bring the hammer down on the hot link.

The material for scarf link chain comes to the factory in the shape of hoops.

After being put in the winding room, crude oil and sawdust is thrown upon it.

The end of the "hoop" is put into a die, the shape of the link into which the raw material is to be made. A lever is pulled. The hoop is wound as one would a string around a stick until it is covered. When five feet long it is divided and taken to the link cutter.

He takes it, puts it between two heavy blades. The links fall in a box and are taken to the boy who heats that particular size of chain. The ends of the links must be scarfed according to the quality of chain made — on common chain, short, on better grades, longer.

Just as a man with too much imagination cannot be-

come a successful pugilist, neither can the same type be
a chainmaker of the first grade.

The sheer monotony of welding hundreds of links
each day in the same manner would madden the mind
that is too quick. This is particularly true of "scarf-
link" chainmakers. A scarf link is one already wound,
its edges scarfed, or cut, ready to be joined when heated
to another link — thus making the chain. Nearly all
chain made in America, from five-eighths of an inch in
size down, is scarf link.

Dolly chain, that which holds battleships at anchor,
is not made by oil or gas furnaces like the smaller
grades. This chain ranges in size from three-quarter inch
to four inches. The entire link is made from bars by the
chainmaker and his helpers. A few, a very few, mechanics can make all sizes of chain with equal facility.
The making of the two kinds of chain requires a vastly
different technique. A coke furnace is used to make
dolly chain.

If a strange chainmaker meets another and tells his
craft, the next question is, "Dolly or scarf?"

A man long in a chain shop can tell whether iron or
steel is rotten, hard, or soft.

I was a scarf link chainmaker.

The blast, which makes the blaze stiff enough to heat
the links swiftly, is regulated by a slide. Chainmakers
and link heaters often spend hours in delicately adjust-
ing the slide to get it at the proper angle. If it is out
of line the twentieth of an inch the links will heat too

swiftly or too slowly. The fire is regulated according to the speed of the chainmaker.

The link, grabbed out of the fire, dripping hot, is swiftly and skilfully attached to the cherry red chain lying on the anvil plate. With three rapid and accurate strokes of his hammer, the chainmaker shapes the link on the die.

The heavy trip-hammer descends swiftly, many times.

Between the blows of the trip-hammer, the chainmaker shapes the link with his hand hammer. He must be accurate in every movement. If he were a second late with the hand hammer, his tongs, the chains, the two hammers, and his hand would be mixed in a frightful welter. The hand hammer is used to smooth the link.

The holes in the furnace burn large through the day, owing to the constant rubbing of hot links. The link heater shapes them each morning with fire clay. So adept did many of the boys become with the clay that they often modeled figures of the chainmakers for whom they worked.

One lad modeled a horrible likeness of Old Man Krantz, the Prussian owner of the shop at Saint Marys in which I worked as a boy. His face was round, stern, heavily wrinkled, and unsmiling.

He walked through the factory smoking a rich cigar.

No one could have detected that he had spent his boyhood in a chain mill.

His clothes were rich, his shoes patent leather, his watch chain of heavy gold.

I worked for one of the fastest chainmakers in the world. So well did we work together that we anticipated each other's movements. I had to hang links as swiftly as he took them from the fire.

Old Man Krantz often watched us. The cigar was gripped tightly in his mouth. His face was stern as murder.

He glanced at an object near the gas pipe of the fire behind me. It was a pot bellied replica of himself in an attitude far from dignified. He shouted above the roar of the shop.

Lou Roberts, the foreman, came running. The purple old man pointed to his statue done in fire clay.

The foreman kicked it to pieces while the old man turned the fire off. The boy modeler was discharged. The next day he was back at work.

In a month he was given a "fire"— a forge upon which to make chain.

Seeing the boy's luck, many of us modeled statues of the old man. He paid no further attention.

The link heaters, though afraid of Old Man Krantz, liked him. When the Chain Trust was said to have slowly squeezed him to the wall, he had the sympathy of every boy. He was so stern we were afraid to express it to him.

We took a collection and bought him a gold watch for his seventieth birthday. No chainmaker was allowed to give money. Each boy added a dollar to the fund. Our wages were from forty to sixty cents a day.

I was one of the three boys chosen to present it to the old tyrant, who sat, looking like Bismarck, in a yellow oak chair as we entered.

"Mr. Krantz," I said, "we got something for you."

"What be it?"

The other boys pushed me toward him. With fear, I handed him the watch.

"T'ank you, boy," he grunted in broken English. "It's ver — very nice."

I saw his shoulders tremble.

Lou Roberts took us quickly from the office.

That Christmas each link heater was given a large turkey. As I had no home, I traded mine for four quarts of bourbon.

I absorbed many of the tricks of the trade as a lad, and only needed an opportunity to put them into practice. My youth and size prevented me getting a chance to make chain. I went on the road as a vagabond for seven years and returned to a chain factory as a day laborer. The pay was nine dollars a week. My board and other incidentals cost six. It was my only chance to get away from the road. Looking back over nearly two decades — I am proud of but one achievement — the unyielding determination with which I left the way of the vagabond. I had none of the usual illusions of youth. I knew that I would never become President of the United States. I came, on both sides, from drunken barbarians who groveled in superstition and were as illiterate as geese. All the vast realms of knowledge and beauty were closed to me. Nearly all my mother's brothers were half mad. Most of my father's people were witty Irish morons. My mother had moods which lasted for days. During this time she would wisely refrain from talking to husband or children.

I inherited her moods and silences along with the wild blood which flowed in two rivers of half insane Irish.

Thus equipped, after years as a hobo, I burned each worm eaten bridge behind me. I had, during the wandering years, been what is known in the decrepit fraternity, as a "library bum." I knew by heart the names of nearly every newspaper and magazine printed in English. Many pieces of Rabelaisian hobo doggerel, out of which the life has long since been squeezed, were written by me.

With the free and hard life behind me, my job was to stand at a forge in Wisconsin with a huge Dane and twist into rings the straight pieces of iron which he handed me. At the end of six months the foreman gave me a chance to make chain.

I worked eight weeks and went to Ohio, determined to get a job as a full fledged chainmaker.

I arrived in Kent, near Cleveland, one early June morning. It is situated on the banks of the Cuyahoga River. A fall of thirty feet in the river could be seen from the depot, from which, a mile away, could be heard the familiar roar of the chain shop. Down a street of symmetrical hard maple trees I walked toward the factory.

A pine building, covered with corrugated zinc, it was

three hundred feet long and a hundred wide. Openings, made of zinc-covered boards and operated by pulleys, were two feet apart the entire length of the shop. All of these were open. The fires could be seen blazing across a patch of woods, which came to within a hundred feet of the shop. The Wheeling and Lake Erie Railroad ran between.

Gossip travels quickly from one shop to another in the chain world. My career as a hobo was known in every shop. Many of the lads with whom I heated links were now chainmakers at work in Kent.

They hailed me as I asked for the foreman.

A stranger, first entering a chain shop, must yell to be heard above the roar. Chainmakers, to save their vocal cords, watch each other's lips.

I approached Jack Bracken, the good-looking young Irish foreman.

"What have you been making?" he asked.

"Three-eighths log chain in Racine."

I had heard of him. The term "mister" is not known in the chain world. "Can I talk to you, Jack?" He looked at me for a minute.

"Yes, come to my office." I followed him. Bracken had been a big league ball player. His ankle, weakened from kicking chain in the winter, had cracked.

He left the Cleveland American League team and became a factory foreman.

When I reached his office, I said, "I've been seven years hoboing around the country, Jack, and eight months in Racine among a lot of clannish Danes. I've only worked a fire two months, but I worked a long time in Saint Marys as a kid. I want to get away from the road."

Bracken had been a link-heater in Cleveland.

"All right, Red," he said.

He gave me three-eighths log chain to make. I could not find a link-heater; so I heated the links and made the chain.

During the hot summer months my clothing was streaked with the salt of perspiration; my shoes rotted.

Bracken soon gave me a better grade of chain to make than I was capable of making. When it failed to pass the test, he put me back on log chain. In a few weeks, he gave me another chance.

He was in charge of three hundred men, all of whom had grievances. He would watch me work and make suggestions. "I'll help you, Kid, so long as you try," he told me.

He had as little education as myself.

He could not master the habit of blushing when he talked.

He weighed nearly two hundred pounds, all muscle. His hair was jet black. He never laughed heartily. His voice was low. In the roar of the factory, he barely raised it enough to be heard.

When a general strike was held, the Chainmakers' Union was crushed, never again to function.

Only twenty-four men out of every hundred remained loyal to the Union. All returned to work, beaten.

So long does bitterness fill the hearts of men that those who remained loyal never again associated with the others.

The losers were the strongest men, the best mechanics. The foreman, Jack Bracken, had been one of the Union losers.

He later went to night school and became an oil salesman. Taciturn to the verge of silence, he blushed when he asked men to buy oil. Within a year large factories bought exclusively of him. He now earns seventy-five thousand a year.

Chainmakers, like all men who work in iron or steel, are (or sadly, were) beer drinkers. Burned out from the excessive heat, they would spend their evenings in a saloon.

The favorite bar in Kent was Jackman's. It was literally our club. Like more urbane men, we often abused its privileges.

Jackman could neither read nor write. He was ashamed of the misfortune. To make an impression, he would glance seriously at a newspaper while we watched him. He belonged to the Elks and the Eagles and wore an elk's tooth on a gold chain which stretched across a loud checked vest.

A little knob was on the end of his nose. His lips were thick. His eyes, half closed, were black, beady, and alert.

He caught conversation on current topics and, after glancing at the newspaper, would say, "I don't agree with Roosevelt on the Panama Canal enterprise. That will cost this country millions of dollars." In this way he would keep conversation going and the cash register busy.

He was never so happy as when David Ladd Rockwell came into the saloon. Rockwell later became the National Campaign Manager for William G. McAdoo and James Cox when they ran for the presidency of the nation.

He was then a young probate judge. A liberal spender, and a shrewd mixer in a saloon crowd, he had the gift of making all men believe they carried his weightiest secrets.

On all political questions Jackman would say, "As Dave Rockwell told me the other day,— and I hope I'm violatin' no confidence in repeating it." When he wished to make an unusual impression, he would preface his remark with, "As I told Dave Rockwell only yesterday."

Jackman had as bartender a heavy man who had once put his foot on the rough ladder of fame. He stood four rounds before Gus Ruhlin, the Akron Giant, who fought James J. Jeffries a twenty round draw.

Mike Kleikerman whipped many men who became boisterous in the saloon. He was a bland kindly German so long as he drank beer. Once he drank whisky he would look around for a war. He seldom had to leave the vicinity. Men developed manias to whip him.

"Let's go an' lick Mike Kleikerman," became the battle cry of many an inebriated chainmaker. Not having been beaten in years, he developed a swagger.

One night I suggested to Andy Porter that we go and whip Mike.

We staggered to Jackman's where men stood four deep at the bar.

Andy Porter was a "dolly man." He swung a five pound sledge daily with his right hand, while he held a heavy pair of tongs with his left. Four sledges weighing from ten to sixteen pounds hammered the link which he welded. He was dark, with thin lips and a wide mouth. A cruel precise man in a fight, he could crack a board with his fist.

We pushed men to right and left and took our places at the bar. Andy yelled, "Bring us liquor, you big bum, and bring it quick."

A current went through the saloon. Kleikerman stood petrified, a beer mallet in his hand. To help the situation, I said tersely, "Come on, you big flunky — you're only workin' here — mind your masters and bring us lager."

Gripping the mallet, Kleikerman rushed from behind the bar.

Andy Porter, five feet seven, and shoulders half as wide, moved backward to give Mike room to fall. He came rushing on and crashed the mallet downward. Andy pushed his arm out and caught the blow on the upper muscle. The mallet bounced as though Kleikerman had hit hard rubber. "Say your prayers, you big bully, I'm goin' to kill you," Andy shouted.

Unaware that he faced a man who could have broken Ruhlin's back, Kleikerman threw the mallet to the floor and swung a powerful right and left. Porter hunched his shoulders and stepped into the blows. Sickening thuds followed. Kleikerman tried in-fighting. He may as well have wrestled with a gorilla. He was knocked across the room. Blood spurted. Each terrible blow from Porter lifted him several inches and zigzagged him backward. He held desperately to Andy and tore his coat from his shoulders. It brought him no relief. To get away from the mauling pain, he stepped back and clubbed at Porter with his right. Porter held his left arm far out and drove his right fist straight from the shoulder. The blow struck the bone in Kleikerman's forearm. It fell, broken.

In another second Porter's right hand was again in position and slightly higher. It thumped against Kleikerman's jaw and knocked it out of place. Kleikerman grunted and crumpled.

The next day Porter paid a fine for disturbing the peace.

"I don't know what the hell peace was disturbed. They wasn't no fight."

A MAN WHO DID THE ACT

PORTER WAS THE GREATEST chainmaker on earth. He earned a large sum for a mechanic, about fifteen thousand dollars a year. His hands were calloused thick as leather. His face might have been shaped by one of his own sledges. The chin was square and lined with muscle. His neck was rope-gnarled and twenty-two inches around. Not aware of his own strength, he could twirl a two hundred pound man high above his head. His home life was simple and even had dignity.

Each week he would give half his wages to his wife. The other half, he spent, or gave away in the saloon. The money gone, he would return to work. Liquor did not faze him.

His wife was never heard to complain. Respectable,

and superior to her circle, she kept her home attractive. Out of the money which Andy gave her each week, she helped many hobo chainmakers and saved a small fortune.

Andy often bragged that she had been the only woman in his life. The daughter of an English chainmaker, she had known Andy since he was twelve years old.

As an artist, Andy was never surpassed. He had never read a book. His mind was strong and his apprehension so quick he got the ideas of most men in his world before they had framed their sentences. He had a habit of impatiently snapping in the middle of a sentence, "I git you."

He would stroke a link as a jockey would a horse. "I'd make chain fer nothin' 'afore I did anything else." When he saw a piece of chain anywhere, he would say, "I wonder what poor devil made that."

He could make any grade of chain, either scarf or dolly, and any size from three-sixteenths of an inch to four inches. His heavy hands handled the small tongs skillfully. On larger chain he had four helpers. Each man had his work allotted. His helper for two months, swinging, naked to the waist, a ten-pound sledge daily, I never tired of watching him work.

One helper would seize a steel bar four inches thick and forty long and place it in the fire. Another would dip a tin bucket in a tub of water and dash it against the iron door of the furnace. Another would operate the heavy door. The bar red hot, Andy would grasp it in the middle with a pair of tongs and place it in a machine which operated by hand, and from which projected a long iron bar as big around as the mast of a ship.

The four helpers would put their weight against the bar and push in a half circle. When it was bent in the shape of a U, Andy would put it back into the fire.

Another U ready, the end would be placed through the still hot link on the anvil. The helpers would pound the edges with the sharp ends of their sledges. This would "scarf" the link so that it could be welded. It was again placed in the fire. Stooping and projecting a knee, Porter would rest his left arm on it and place the link on the horn of the anvil. Then would begin the tremendous hammering of five sledges weighing from five to sixteen pounds. Each helper would swing a full circle with his sledge. The sledge would hit the exact spot at which it was aimed. One sledge followed the other swiftly, and nearly touched in making the circle. During this time Andy handled his five-pound sledge as deftly as a drummer would a stick. It moved in and out among the welter of heavier blows, while his immense body was crouched nearly double.

The link welded, Andy would throw the great chain on the anvil and hold the last link on its side. A man would select a "stud" from a pile and place it in the center of the link. Andy would pound the still hot iron until the stud was firm. The stud gave the link twice its strength.

This done, the operation would begin all over again.

Andy divided equally with his helpers. If he earned a hundred dollars in a day, they received half.

The spark would roll from his half nude muscular body. Chainmaker and helpers wore but shreds of clothing even in zero weather. Flurries of snow would fly about them when the doors near the fire were opened. After consuming large quantities of alcohol each night, they would sit half naked in a wintry blast, with a torn coat thrown loosely over their shoulders. I recall none who ever had a touch of pneumonia.

When Tom Grayson died, Andy Porter and several others, myself among them, promised his wife to sit the night through with him.

We brought a quantity of whisky with us. By three o'clock it was all gone.

Andy began to search the house, "It's just like old Tom Grayson not to have a drink in his shack. No wonder he died, prob'ly choked to death."

He came across some dark vinegar. "This may be it," he said hopefully.

"Yeah, that's it. I was with Tom when he bought it. Let me have a swig." I reached for the bottle.

Andy held it firmly.

"That's why you ain't rich, grabbin' fer things you don't git."

Fearful he would put his nose to the bottle, I reached again. He took a quick and heavy swig and threw the bottle through the window.

"Hey — do you wanta wake up Tom!" yelled another chainmaker, while Andy swore.

"What the hell's he got vinegar around for anyhow! He ain't a dago — Hey, Tom!" He stamped into the room of death. We followed him.

Tom's eyes were partly open.

Porter ran out of the room. "By God, he winked at me."

He walked a mile, got whisky, and returned, saying, "I'll betcha, by hell, when I die I'll have enough whisky to last you fellows all night."

Porter got his big chance at last.

The tale is well known in the chain world. He went to a Pennsylvania town and spread terror in the saloons. A chain manufacturer sent for him.

"Tell him to come to me — I'm drunk," Porter told the messenger.

The manufacturer found Porter seated at a table in the rear of a dingy saloon.

"Have a drink, Andy?"

"Certainly — straight brandy."

"I'll take the same," the manufacturer said to the bartender —"straight."

They drank the liquor.

"Now, Andy — listen good and hard. I'm going to make you a proposition." He motioned to the bartender. "Fill the glasses,— please." They drank.

"I want you to be the superintendent of my shop. I'll give you one per cent of the output besides your salary."

Andy thought a minute. "That's a good offer — what's wrong — strike or somethin'— you know me — I hate a scab's guts."

"Nothing wrong, Andy — we're getting into war — and there'll be millions of dollars' worth of chain to make. You understand now."

"I git you."

"I've only got one string on the offer."

"Ho, ho — thought somethin' wrong," sneered Andy.

"Nothing wrong —" said the manufacturer, "you don't have to sign a paper — nothing — just your hand on the deal."

"What is it?"

"That you don't take another drink so long as you work for me."

Andy grabbed his forehead, "My God — you ain't askin' much — I'd rather quit eatin'."

"Think it over, Andy — it'll make you rich."

"Whydyu come to me?"

Andy kept his eyes on the table, thinking. He stood up suddenly, "All right — here's my mitt on it — but I gotta ask one thing."

"What is it?"

"Your word to me that *I'm boss*. And when I say boss, I mean BOSS. I wouldn't hire a scab if his tongue was hangin' out a mile. I'll fight every man in the shop if I think he's wrong. If he's right, he won't have to fight."

"All right. Shake!"

Andy contrived a combination hammer and anvil upon

which chain up to the size of one inch could be made more quickly. Where three men worked at one forge before, one was now needed. The chainmaker required no helpers.

The helpers were given a chance to make chain, for which they had worked for years.

A belligerent, roaring man, Andy would scowl through the shop. His blasphemy could be heard above the noise of pounding sledges.

Liquor had been part of his life from early boyhood. To appease any desire which he might have for it, he kept either clenched in his fingers or between his teeth, an immense black cigar. A box of these was put in his office each day by the manufacturer.

Through Porter, the manufacturer was far better equipped to make chain on a large scale than any other competitor.

A government chain inspector, either careless or bull-dozed by Porter, sent eleven miles of two inch chain to Newport News. The Lloyd inspectors condemned it all. The mountain of chain was shipped back to Pennsylvania in dozens of gondolas.

The inspector was removed. I was ordered from Florida to take charge of the Pittsburgh Division.

I had lost track of Andy for several years.

"Meet the new inspector," a salesman called to Porter.

"Good God Almighty!" Andy broke his cigar.

Recovering from his surprise, he shouted, "So you're the new inspector from Florida — holy mackerel!"

"It didn't pay you to scare the inspector then — did it, Andy?"

"I guess not. But them damned theory guys don't know nothin'."

"Now, Andy, we both know what inspectors are. You see where I am. I've got to treat the chainmakers and you right — you're all my friends. I've got to be decent to the man who owns the plant. But I won't send chain out of a shop if it'll break and drown a lot of poor devils."

"Neither will I," returned Andy.

Between us there was deep affection.

We seldom spoke civilly to each other.

He looked at me now and bit his cigar, "We're goin' to have a lot of battles," he grunted. "If I kill you, I'll pay your funeral expenses."

"I'll do the same for you, Andy."

The shop was low and smoke filled. Each day the sun hung like a dying candle in the sky.

Money was as plentiful as dying soldiers in Europe. Chainmakers earned from twenty-five to one hundred dollars a day.

The chainmakers complained bitterly of the two shifts. The furnace had no chance to cool or be repaired. Pulleys and springs could not be adjusted.

A Grievance Committee went to Andy Porter.

"You guys must think I own the shop. Why don't you trust me to git things straight? You know damn well I won't sell you out."

"We ain't distrustin' you, Andy, you're gittin' your oats out of another stall now. When the owner cracks his whip, you run," the Chairman said.

"Who runs?" bellowed Andy. "I wouldn't run if lightnin' jabbed me in the rear. I ain't the runnin' kind, an' if you call me a oat-eater I'll make you swallow them words."

"You can't ride two horses, Andy."

"The devil I can't. I kin ride five so long's I don't try to do tricks. I ain't never done a crooked thing in my life, an' I'm too old to start now. There's a God up there even if we can't see Him, an', by God, I'm keepin' my slate clean."

"Will you be agin us when you talk to the owner to-day?"

"That's my business. You git so damned fresh, callin' me a oat-eater I won't answer you."

A chainmaker, with an honorable record, Porter stood on dangerous ground, the water coming from both sides.

Five hundred men waited. The shop was idle.

That afternoon Porter was heard to tell the owner — "I'm with the men. They're right this time. If they were wrong, I'd be against them. And if I was makin' chain, I'd brain the guy who went back to work until this trouble was over. You wouldn't like to sleep in a bed right after another guy gits out of it. Well, a chainmaker learns to love his hammer. He has pet names fer it. He don't want another man workin' it."

The owner, a kindly man, listened.

"You all know how I stand. This may mean my job — but that's all right. I couldn't get my shoulders in the door to-night if I didn't say what I'm sayin'. An' my wife 'ud know I'd killed a dog somewhere. My job don't mean nothin' when it comes to what ain't right."

The owner and Porter looked out at the waiting men.

"I can't tell 'em to do what I wouldn't do myself," Porter lit his cigar.

There was silence until he said, "In no time these guys, the best chainmakers in the world'll be trampin' to other shops. They know you. They know *me*. You'll never git back the loss."

"Tell them to come back to work, no more double shifts," said the owner.

Porter walked to the main entrance, and yelled, "All right, you crums, come an' start the fires."

The Chairman of the Grievance Committee said to Andy, "You're all right."

"Who the hell said so? You're jist a lot of trouble-makers, treatin' me this way."

The Chairman tried to shake hands.

"Git the hell away from me or I'll pound your head fer a link. I wish you'd just make chain 'stead o' thinkin' up ways to make a horse's neck outta me," he bellowed through the shop. "If it 'ud of been me you guys could pick manure with the chickens afore I'd put you back to work."

*

THE demand for chainmakers was so great that Porter would go to any length to keep a good man.

The heavy chain which I inspected was dragged about the floor by hooks in the hands of laborers. They fitted it into the testing machine and started the engine which put it under the same enormous strain a battleship would give it. If two links broke in ninety feet of chain, I was supposed to condemn the whole "shot." In time, Porter and I evolved a system whereby the chain was patched and made even stronger than before. One had to be careful, as too great a strain on the chain, though it might stand up under it at the time, would make it snap under a lighter strain later.

When Porter thought I was too severe, he would scream, "Good God Almighty, you gittin' crazy? You don't know a piece o' chain when you see it."

A tirade of abuse would follow.

When he had finished I would say, "Go on and bulldoze some one else, you big stiff. I suppose you'd like to get another eleven miles of chain back."

He would appeal to my sympathy.

"I'll have to fire that chainmaker if you turn his chain down that way — you don't want to see him on the bum, do you? Have a heart, for God's sake. I wish to hell we could git a decent inspector once."

The laborers who helped me often received fifty and more dollars a day. They were chainmakers. Something would be wrong with their forges, or, they might be waiting on coke or other materials.

To keep them from going to another shop, Porter would have their average wage figured over a period of three days. Whatever they had been able to earn in that time while making chain they were given as laborers until they could return to their forges.

If in doubt as to a link, I consulted my laboring helpers.

*

CHAINMAKERS have long memories. If a man committed the one mortal sin among them, that of going back to work before a strike is called off, or taking another man's job at such a time, it is known as "doing the act" and is never forgiven or forgotten. It was nothing unusual for Porter to say of a man, "He did the act back in '88."

An old man with stooped shoulders and hollow eyes tried to talk to Porter. I had known him when I heated links.

Andy glanced at him coldly and walked away.

Benedict Arnold, in the midst of Washington's army, could not have been more pathetic. No man in the shop talked to him. As a lad, he learned to make chain in Saint Marys. With a sick wife and three children, he refused to leave his forge when a strike was called.

He came over to me. "Hello, Jim, don't you know me?"

"Yes," I said, and shook hands.

"Can't you do somethin' for me? Andy kin forgive.

I'm damn near dead now. I'll be pushin' the clouds in a year. It ain't his money anyhow,— even if he does think I'm a snake."

I tried, as much as my prejudice would allow me, to see each spoke in the revolving wheel of labor.

"Come on," I said, "I'll take you to Andy.— Wait outside."

Still irritated from his encounter with the chainmaker, Andy sat at his desk and growled at me.

"Not me, Jim, not me — you can't talk to me about him. Purty soon I'll think you'd do the act yourself — askin' favors fer a scab. He'd cut his mother's throat on Sunday. Wasn't I workin' with him when he did the act?"

"His wife was sick, Andy."

"Mine's been sick too — that ain't no excuse. We'd of done somethin' fer her. You can't go on makin' excuses fer them rats; they'd gnaw your heart out the minute there was trouble."

I knew of Andy's deep fear of God and had seen him tremble at mention of His wrath.

"But, Andy, he's half dead. He's been square ever since that one time. You're not God, you know. What would God do? How long do you want to punish him?"

"From now on," gritted Andy —"they shoot 'em when there's war."

"But just the same, Andy — *you're not God.*"

"Who the hell said I was God?"

"But just the same, you're not God and you know it."

He snorted in disgust, "I may not be God — who the hell wants to be — with millions of men dyin' — but *I'm boss of this here shop.*"

"You may be boss of this shop, but *you're not God.*"

"To hell with God — what the devil's he got to do with it?"

"A lot — suppose he goes away and dies. You know — you believe in God and if He's the guy you think He is — He'll haunt you if old Ed croaks."

He chewed his cigar a minute.

"Well, if I do hire him, nobody'll talk to him."

"What the hell difference does that make? He'd be better off. I'll talk to him."

Andy snorted. "That won't help." He bit his cigar viciously and stared at me.

"Give him a fire, Andy — let him make half inch for a day. He can handle that — then he'll have an average of fifteen or twenty dollars if anything goes wrong; and he can help me drag chain around. After all, Andy — we ought to have a little pity — neither of us is God."

"Will you can that God talk?" he shouted.

"I don't like to ring Him in, Andy — but you *understand.* Maybe he got sorry for old Ed Burley and sent him to you as the one fellow who'd be decent. We're all makin' money, Andy — why not give old Ed a chance?"

"God never forgive the devil yit. When he does I'll put Burley on."

"Andy — for God's sake — have a heart — I

wouldn't be afraid to put the hiring of him up to vote if you want it."

"Who the hell wants it? — *I'm the boss of this shop.* I saw him do the act myself."

"You know me, Andy. I'd go to hell for you, and you would for me. I don't ask favors. Now do me a favor — put him on."

"All right then — damn it to hell — bring the scabby son of a —— in here."

I went for old Ed Burley.

He came before Porter with slow, limping step.

Porter, a snarl on his face, glanced quickly at the crumbling man.

"Ho, ho, ho — you didn't think this would happen, did you? I told you to leave your God-damn fire thirty years back — that you was doin' somethin' you couldn't never live down. Your sick wife divorced you and run off with a brakeman — now what the hell you got — God's a punishin' you."

I cut in,—"Maybe even God's got tired of punishin' him, Andy."

"Shut up — when I want your lip I'll ask for it."

"All right, Andy," I drawled, "but *you're not God.*"

"Holy God — shut up!" Andy yelled.

He turned to old Burley, "What you been doin'?"

"Nothin', Andy, I been sick."

"I'm mister to you — what you been sick about?"

"The con."

"Chainmakers' con — huh?"

"Yes."

"Where's your boy?"

"Over in France — dead."

Andy's mouth went shut.

"How long?"

"Three months now."

"Where's them two girls o' yours?"

"Workin'."

"Can't they keep you?"

"I wouldn't ast them."

"Sooner ask me, huh?"

"Only fer work,— nothin' else."

"You better not," grumbled Andy.

The old chainmaker ignored the words.

"You know, And —, since the boy died, my lungs hurt me more."

"That so?" Andy grunted.

"Yeah —" the old man's voice raised. "He was makin' three B over in Braddock before he left. He was a good boy."

"On the level too — wasn't he — never did the act?"

"Andy, for God's sake — have a heart," I snapped.

"Shut up, you red head! Who's doin' this?"

The old man's wrinkled hands clasped. His snagged teeth scraped together.

"You're right, And —, he never did the act, an' I wish to God I hadn't."

The words hit Porter. He tore the cigar from between his teeth, threw it in a corner, and stood erect.

"I'm sorry," he said, "but how the hell did I know?" He slapped the old man on the back and bent him nearly double.

"Wait outside, Ed, will you? I want to tell Jim something."

Ed Burley walked to the door.

Porter grunted twice. "Now here's what — I'm givin' him an average of twenty dollars a day, an' I'm puttin' him on helpin' you. You can do what you want to with him. If anybody says anything, I'll jist say you wanted him helpin' you because he knows about chain. Now go on back an' start raisin' hell with the factory agin by bein' a tough inspector."

I walked with Ed Burley to my office near the testing machine. "Say nothing about this to anybody, Ed, I'll turn you in at twenty a day as a chainmaker. Now watch things for me, won't you, Ed? You made chain before I was born."

Burley remained with me. In time, the chainmakers would nod to him casually. They did not condemn me for showing him kindness.

Porter never talked to him again.

*

WHEN the war ended, Porter started his own factory in the west. He took with him a group of chainmakers. Among them were none who "did the act."

One old fellow, through long gazing at a fire, was half blind.

Porter put him to work. His chain could pass neither test nor inspection. On Sunday or at night, either Porter or other chainmakers would remake his chain. The old man strutted, drank, and bragged of his ability.

"Do your eyes ever keep you from turning out good work?" I once asked him.

"Hell — no — a *good man* kin make chain in the dark."

He died in the belief that he was still a good man.

A BROKEN LEG

STALEY, HEAVILY MUSCLED, and about thirty was of the same snarling nature whether drunk or sober.

The chainmakers, always quarreling when drunk, forgave quickly when sober.

Staley never forgave and attacked without warning.

After a quarrel with Andy Porter, he nursed the grievance for months.

One night a group of chainmakers were in Jackman's.

Andy leaned his elbow on the bar and talked to me.

A heavy tumbler crashed against his jaw. He staggered, his jaw sagged, broken.

Staley stood about ten feet away, snarling. I rushed toward him.

"We'll fight till one of us drops."

Chainmakers gathered around. "Let's go in the back yard."

Men carried the groaning Andy.

The back yard was enclosed by a high board fence over which a strong light shone.

Andy was placed where he could get a good view.

"Do you want us to take you to a doctor?" Bud Powers asked him.

Porter groaned, pointed at me, and made motions with his fists.

"He wants to see the fight. Now don't get in his way," Bud shouted.

Up against a larger and more powerful man, I knew, as a road-kid, the brutal psychology of saloon fighting. That one should never let the other "get the first blow."

Staley threw his coat down. Kicking it out of the way, I threw my own in his face and followed it with a crash to the jaw.

I circled swiftly to get my back to the light. Once it shone in his eyes I threw both fists at his jaw. He shook his head and came forward, crouching. To blind him, I sent blows to his eyes. When I circled again his left eye was closed.

Staley's fists crashed against me, rapid as hail on a roof. A stinging right caught me. I went down.

I was up in a second, with a buzzing in my brain. I could hear Andy Porter making guttural noises.

Staley winced from a blow under the heart. I had

caught him off balance as he went backward from a punch. While he was still on his heels I flew in.

The blood streamed into my eyes. A pain roared in my right ear. The protruding tooth which the Navy doctor so long before had advised me to have pulled, was now stuck through my lower lip and drew my chin upward. I tore the lip from the tooth, and stepped backward to draw Staley forward.

He came in a second. I started a right from my toes. It landed under his heart. Then I threw my shoulder against his chin. His jaws clattered backward.

I rushed swiftly and stopped quickly. Prepared for an attack that did not come, he relaxed for a second. When he did, I charged.

We traded blows until one caught him under the heart. His knees buckled. I criss-crossed a right and left with all my power against his jaw.

He fell and buried his face in the deep dust.

His arms extended. He rolled on his back.

No man touched him.

When he came to, I said, "Lead him to me."

I said, "Now, Staley, I'm goin' to fight you every time I see you. And if I ever fight you again, I'll kill you. Do you hear?" I slapped his bleeding face.

He nodded, "Yes."

"If you ever come within fifty feet of me I'm goin' to fight you. You'll never break my jaw — do you hear?" I pushed him backward.

"Yes," he whimpered.

They took him away.

*

ANDY was carried into the saloon.

Kleikerman had apparently forgiven him for the beating. He spent a lot of money. His animus toward me remained.

He met me at the rear door.

"I was hopin' you'd git your damned head knocked off."

"You're not man enough to do it."

I grappled with Kleikerman. Men crowded around at the prospect of another fight.

Whether I was shoved or accidentally fell backward, I do not know. A dozen steps led downward from the door. Boards nailed across boards, there was a space between each step.

My leg caught between the steps and broke above the ankle.

The night marshal came. I stood on one leg and refused to go with him. Some of the men had taken Porter home and called a doctor. The others remained with me. They now pleaded with me to go along with the cop.

"Go and get Kleikerman. I'll hop after you — he started this."

The policeman started to pull me. "His leg's broke, you damn fool," Bud Powers shouted. After much pleading, I allowed my own gang to carry me to jail. The shoe was cut away. The ankle puffed to twice its normal size.

A chainmaker ran for Scott Rockwell, the lawyer.

He went my bail, saying, "He can't run away on one leg."

I was taken to my boarding house. A doctor came and put the leg in a brace.

The next day I was taken to a hospital in Cleveland.

I lay four days, my leg in the air, and no one to talk to.

I got up and dressed, took my one crutch and a suit case, and walked to the main door.

The head nurse met me, looked horrified and said, "The streets are full of ice. You'll break your other leg."

By street car and train I traveled the fifty miles to the boarding house.

For two months I remained indoors until it healed. Each day I sat in the lobby of the small hotel, my ankle propped high, my spirits low. The rumor spread about the small town that my leg had been broken in a house of prostitution.

The chainmakers were looked down upon by the citizens. That one of the roughest should have his leg broken in a bawdy house was a still greater affront to them.

I read the days away, and speculated much on my future.

There was in my nature much sediment that had to

go to the bottom. It dawned upon me I would never be a good chainmaker. I thought of chainmakers, all destitute in their old age. No matter how hard they worked or saved, few were ever but a few weeks ahead of the grocery bill and the rent. Porter was the one exception. I had no heart for manual labor. And yet, my energy was boundless. I recalled my grandfather's hatred of physical labor. He, too, had relentless energy, but was bright enough to realize that all his striving had left him crippled with rheumatism and a charge upon his daughter.

I thought of the prize ring as a way out. I had learned considerable about boxing from Gans. I thought of him and Chlorine.

Fifty yards away the Erie Railroad engines stopped.

Their whistles talked to me. One long sound, I knew the train was approaching the town. With two short sounds, the engineer answered signals. With four short, he called for a signal. A succession of short sounds — people to clear the tracks. One long and three short — the flagman must protect his train. I followed the movements of engines in the yard a quarter of a mile away.

Andy Porter's wife brought the money each week to pay for my board and room. Andy was taking nourishment through a straw. His jaw would soon be healed.

I had, during lulls in drinking and carousal, gone to the library in the evening where I read until closing time.

The girl in charge was different from any I had ever

known. She was the first person with whom I could talk of the books I had read. I told her of my long years of reading and of my efforts to write.

She lived a block from my boarding house.

A friendship had grown long before my accident.

She did not come near.

A PROPOSAL

ELVA'S COMPLEXION WAS olive, her eyes large, brown, and expressive, her hair very long and a brown-tinged auburn. Her lips were red and full. The upper lip was dented in the center and protruded slightly, making her mouth a cupid's bow.

She would rub her red and olive cheeks with delicate hands. She would then pull her upper lip with thumb and forefinger. When she had finished, the lip would remain puckered and give her the appearance of a hurt little girl getting ready to cry.

She resembled Chlorine so much they could have passed for sisters. Their movements were gracefully the same. Each had the same habit of suddenly dropping everything in the midst of conversation and staring at something not visible.

We were drawn to each other, evidently, by something beyond ourselves. I knew that she was a snob. She knew that I was a roughneck.

Her grandmother was a recluse on a half mile stretch of elevated ground along Lake Erie, an hour's ride from Cleveland.

The girl would watch gales sweep over the lake in winter. When it became calm in summer, she would take her books to a large rock at the lake's edge, and alternate between reading and dreaming. She would watch ships, gliding far out, over the blue water.

Ships held, from her childhood, a fascination for her. Each summer until she went to college, she sailed toy vessels on the lake.

Engaged at twenty to a wealthy young fellow worth millions, she delayed the wedding two years; then went to her grandmother.

The old recluse said —"All right — if you can live without him — I can."

"I want something, Grandmother, he cannot give me — to be free."

The old lady shook her precise head at her beautiful granddaughter,

"Poor child, that's another prison."

She went, with her books, to the rock of her childhood. That day, she did not read.

She had an independent income and wanted something to do. As she knew books, she became a librarian in the small town. She arrived a month before my freight stopped at the place.

She would not associate with the other girls in the town who were mostly the daughters of working class people.

Knowing the small salary she received and not of her independent income, they attributed her fine clothes to men who paid. She smiled at the gossip, shrugged her shapely shoulders, and said, "Oh well — one must consider the source."

It was exactly what she did not do.

Naturally aloof, she dreaded people, "They're so common." If she brought but little understanding to them, they gave her far less in return.

There was, in her every movement, something graceful. Her step was light. Her legs, perfectly modeled, were always in silk stockings.

Strongly sexed, vibrant and vital, she troubled me in heart and head.

Two phrases she used often were "a sense of delicacy," and "broadening one's horizon."

From a window of the library could be seen the silver and green Cuyahoga River rolling slowly.

The bridge which crossed Main Street was always of interest to her.

"It's like an old world etching," she said.

Facing always the softer winds of life, there was a storm within her.

She often wondered why working men did not read.

"They're too worn out at the end of the day," I told her.

The library consisted of one large room in one corner of which children read.

She was seldom busy during the day. Hours would pass in which no one came.

I wrote verses to a dead girl and showed them to her. "What was she like?"

I told her the story of Mink.

The flare of a street light shone over the darkening room and across her face. I saw that she was crying.

"Poor girl," she said, and touched her eyes with a small kerchief.

We talked of the future one afternoon.

"It will be interesting to know what becomes of you," she hesitated, "if you do not get killed in some saloon or the ring."

I told her I wanted to write.

"I think you will," she said calmly. "Your emotions are always churning — you must get them under control — you will need perspective — detachment." I had never heard the words used. I sensed their meaning, and remembered.

I was continually showing her sentimental verses. One concerned John Keats — It read,

> "Storm beaten soul that vainly clutched through life
>   At high ideal, how blissful it must seem
>   To leave the burden of the horrid strife
>   For one long dream."

She made the third line read,

"To leave the burden of stupendous strife."

It was sent to Ted Robinson who conducted a column in *The Cleveland Plain Dealer*. He published it.

We were the two proudest people in Ohio.

I began to write more verses.

"You will never be a poet," she said. "Your heart is too bitter."

I went to her that night at closing time and said,

"I want you to marry me."

She stood still for a second; then switching the lights off and shutting the heavy door, she put an arm about me.

I could feel the contour of her breast against my side. A delicate perfume was about her. No word was said by either for a long time. I held her body close, my hand resting on her lovely figure.

Her breath came quickly.

"I've never had anything in my life —. I've never wanted anything very bad before. I'll work hard," I pleaded.

Turning me about until her breasts pressed against me, she pushed my head back and ran her hand through my hair.

"I've thought about you a great deal," she said. "You worry me."

"But let's get married."

She caressed me without answering.

"You feel above me, don't you?"

"My grandmother — my — we are so far apart —"

I held her arms. "We wouldn't be if you weren't such a snob."

"Maybe so — I'm such a contradiction." She paused, "And so are you."

She loosened her arms. "Don't you see — you are so crude — so elemental — you would tear me to pieces in a few years."

"That's your way of getting out of it. You know you like me."

"Yes," she admitted, "more than that."

Clinging to me, "How can you change your life — how can I change mine?" she asked.

"Why is it necessary? You admit that I'm different, that every fellow you see is like every other fellow."

"I liked you from the first," she said, "you helped me so. You sneer at everything."

"Is that why you didn't come near when I had my leg broke?"

"I knew you would think of that. I was afraid to come if you must know — they have hurt me so much here."

I laughed.

"They hurt you just as much," she said,— "you make a bigger noise, that's all."

"But you're ashamed of me — you don't need any one like me in your life."

"I do. I do."

Her lips touched mine.

Her body relaxed.
Later, she sobbed, "You're a beast," and caressed me.
"But I asked you to marry me, remember."
"I did," she said.

A CHANGE OF LIFE

An ITEM IN A CLEVELAND newspaper prompted my decision. A boxing promoter in Lima was looking for opponents for Chicago Jack Tierney. Never having been in the ring, I would need evidence to show the promoter that I was worthy of a fight with a man like Tierney, who had won several fights in Lima.

An aged printer, Old Man Heck, was my friend. He was beyond seventy, with a crooked mouth, a clipped mustache, and a strong desire for liquor.

I told him that I must have several newspaper clippings, one — which had my fight record upon it.

He formed the type while I invented a record which read,

> *"KO Sweeney — Knockout   1 rd.*
> *Eddie Logan — Won   4 rds."*

In the imaginary record, which listed thirty-four opponents, I had not lost a fight.

I sent it to the Lima promoter and signed the letter Gustavus Heck, the *Kent Courier*, Kent, Ohio.

The promoter was told that I would draw a crowd of people from Saint Marys, which was not far from Lima.

A telegram from the promoter came to Gustavus Heck, offering transportation for three and a four hundred dollar guarantee.

At seventy-four, Old Man Heck was the manager of a bruiser. He entered upon his new work with solemn humor. He forbade me to drink beer.

"How about whisky?"

"Drink all you want. Whisky never yit kep' an Irishman from bein' a good fighter."

My fight with Tierney was for ten rounds. Danny McCall, an ex-pugilist chainmaker was engaged to box with me.

The night before the fight, I boxed fifty-one minutes with Danny who was twenty pounds heavier. We did not rest between rounds. Old Man Heck called a halt when I had worn Danny out.

The next morning we boarded the train for Lima.

The town was placarded with signs advertising the coming fight between Chicago Jack Tierney and Jimmy Tully.

Old Heck had a new suit, a plug of tobacco, and a vest pocket full of cigars.

On the train he said,—"You see — it's this way — fightin's simple. Danny here's a heavier man, and jist as fast as Tierney or Jim Corbett or anybody. If he can't even bother you in fifty-one minutes — that's seventeen rounds without a rest — why, you ain't got a damn thing to fear from Chicago Jack Tierney or anybody else. We'll own Lima after to-night. You wait an' see."

Heck took me to the promoter. Pleased with my appearance, he went with us to the newspaper office. On the way we passed Tierney's headquarters.

The promoter called Tierney.

I had heard from Gans, "Don't pay any attention to the fellow you fight — just act like he's not in the world."

I barely noticed Tierney.

As we walked along, Heck gesticulated, "This Tierney thinks my boy's jist crawled out of a corn shock and rubbed his eyes and come down here to fight to-night. He's wrong. There's goin' to be hell a poppin' in that ring to-night. When this boy o' mine gits to swingin' 'em, it's like pieces of lead hittin' the roof. He knocked Battling Juno out so long over in Altoona he had whiskers before he come to. Who'll we fight after we bury Tierney?"

"He's a tough boy," said the promoter, smiling.

"We don't care. So was Irish Johnny Rosenblum —

we like 'em tough. I'm takin' this boy to New York purty soon."

A Negro whom Tierney had knocked out, came to the hotel.

"Watch 'im when the gong sounds the first round," he told me.

Old Man Heck offered the Negro a cigar.

"If Tierney comes bouncin' out at this boy with his head down, he's liable to wake up over in Cleveland. Remember what you did to Battling Juno, Jimmy? You hit him so hard, they counted the referee out too. Why, he knocked a fellow out in the fourth row."

The Negro's eyes dilated.

I knew more of the rougher tricks of fighting than most pugilists. I had never been hurt by a blow. Gans had taught me how to "ride" men, to break their hearts with my weight, and how to "get under the eaves," as he used to say, and pound a man under the heart.

My chest measured forty-two inches, my neck seventeen. My eyes were protected by heavy ridges. I was not in the vernacular of the ring "an easy bleeder." My skin stretched tight and had long been seasoned by the roughest kind of winds and weathers.

Though I had never been in the ring before, I had fought men tougher than Tierney for nothing. That was my attitude.

Fearful of stage fright, Danny McCall told me not to look at the crowd.

I walked down the aisle when the semi-windup was

over, and looked neither to right nor left. I could hear the water bucket rattling on Danny's arm.

Tierney was already in the ring. He scraped the soles of his rubber shoes in a rosin box.

He was taller and as well muscled as myself. He shot a quick glance at me as I scrambled through the ropes, and then made way for me to rub my feet in the rosin.

His seconds inspected my bandaged hands before the gloves were laced on. Danny McCall looked at Tierney's.

A crowd from Saint Marys yelled my name. I did not look up.

Old Man Heck kept mumbling —"Where the hell's this guy's undertaker — they're never around when you need 'em. It'll be our luck to have to bury him."

Danny McCall tapped his shoulder and said —"Heck — tush —."

Silent, the old man patted my shoulder.

My heart beat fast.

Danny McCall rubbed my arms and whispered —

"Keep goin' forward, Kid, with your head down. Don't throw them till he leads, an' then never stop throwin' 'em. He can't hurt you if I couldn't: remember that — an' keep your left out."

The gong sounded.

Tierney was across the ring in a flash. His blows came rapid fire. With Danny's words fresh, I let go. Tierney swayed and grabbed a rope. Not caught by an old trick, I waited. He came forward again and threw blows at me. I crouched, head down, under the eaves, and began to pump blows. We mixed viciously at the gong. The audience screamed.

In the second, we both feinted and watched for openings. I could hear Tierney's feet shuffling swiftly over the canvas floor.

I missed a right that whizzed by the spot where Tierney's head had been a second before. He worked in close, and threw blows upward. I heard Tierney grunt. It gave me a cue. I tried to knock his heart out of his breast.

He broke ground.

I pounded his heart.

The referee, perspiring and puffing, his white shirt blood be-spattered, unloosened the tangle of Tierney's arms. I laid my entire weight on him.

For the next four rounds we volleyed rights and lefts to heads and bodies. I staggered from an over hand right and rattled the teeth in Tierney's jaw in return. I tried to get under the eaves. Tierney was wise. His rigid arms met my attack. Our gloves were now blood and water-soaked. My kidneys ached with pain.

At the end of the ninth, Tierney started a blow in my corner which he could not stop. The momentum of the spent effort threw him off balance. He was several precious seconds in getting to his corner.

The minute rest was soon over.

During the tenth, intent on winning, our heads crashed together.

Blood dripped from above our eyes. I did not dodge

low enough to escape an overhand right. It caught me
on top of the head and sent me backward.

To even the score, I waded in. I could hear, above the
clangor and noise of battle, Danny McCall shouting,
"Thataboy, Jimmy — throw 'em, throw 'em, God Almighty, throw 'em!"

The gong sounded. We did not hear it. The referee
tried to pry us apart.

Danny grabbed me.

"It's over, it's over, Jimmy," he shouted.

The referee called it a draw.

The newspapers gave it to me.

The Cincinnati *Enquirer* called it the fastest fight ever
seen in that section. A dozen engagements followed.

I lost a six round decision to Eddie Conway at Akron.

We were re-matched two months later, the fight to be
held on the last day of the Elks' Convention at Lima.

Johnny Kilbane, a future champion, was to box in
Findlay, a week before my fight with Conway in Lima.

The pugilist who was to box the semi-windup with
young McGovern did not show up. I was offered the
chance and hesitated for business reasons. If I lost to
McGovern, I would lose the match with Conway, which
called for much more money.

After a long talk, I agreed to go on if McGovern
would "go easy." He had no money. I wanted to help
him. I also wanted to save my match with Conway. "For
after all," I told him, "If I don't go on with you —

you'll get no money. There's no one your weight in town."

We entered the ring.

McGovern was the hardest and most scientific puncher I had met. He came out of his corner to "kill me," and did not.

He never let up the terrible bombardment. I returned to my corner, aware that I was in for a double-cross.

Danny McCall said, "Go out and fight until you either drop him, or he drops you. He'll knock your head through the ropes if you try to box him."

The gong sounded.

I met him in the center of the ring, and slugged.

The strain was so great I cried in my corner. Danny said, "You just hold your own — you've got to top him. He's out to get the Conway fight."

I rushed out in the third and slugged harder. He stood the pace and beat me to every punch. At the gong he had me staggering.

"I'd fight him more this round," advised Danny. "It's your heart or his."

I knocked him out in the next round.

Conway's manager approached me two hours before the fight.

"Make it a foot exhibition," he said, "and you boys can get a bigger purse in Cleveland."

I knew that if we were both on our feet at the end of the fight, Conway would get the decision. He had done it before.

I agreed.

His victory over me still rankled.

Other Conway followers talked to me. I agreed to everything.

When the gong sounded, I rushed out of my corner and knocked him down. He rose at the count of six. I had made up my mind to start the pace and not allow him to take it from me. I never backed up.

He had improved since beating me. In the third round my head was so clogged with blood I was hardly able to breathe. My second sucked it from my nose.

The fourth and fifth rounds were grueling and bloody. Men stood on their seats and screamed.

In the sixth, goaded to desperation by the killing pace, he made the mistake of standing toe to toe with me and slugging. In the other rounds he was jabbing and retreating. My right eye was closed. His left continually jarred it.

I redoubled my efforts. A right caught him on the jaw. So swiftly did he fall that when I threw my left in a follow-up he was on the floor.

The referee counted. He got up at eight. Fearful the round would end before I could connect again, I squared off as his knees wobbled. Another blow sent him through the ropes. He was back into the ring when he collapsed and was counted out.

In the morning a telegram from the library girl read,

"What is the use of whipping the whole world and ending up a bartender?"

An old fighter asked me for five dollars. His ears were

hunks of gristle. His eyes were pounded until they were half blind. His brain was loose in his head.

The thought of him made my victory hollow.

*

Within a short time I had but casual interest in pugilism. After months of practice I was becoming proficient in unconscious technique, without which no pugilist can go far.

I would carry a mood into the ring. A pugilist should be stolid.

Had I entered the ring a few years earlier, before a mental unrest took too complete possession of me, I might never have written. I lost two fights. They were with men I should easily have whipped. I had whipped McGovern decisively. He had whipped Battling Shultz, to whom I lost in Toledo.

I had beaten Sinclair twice in Akron. He had beaten McGlynn who had won over me in Cleveland.

At the ringside, Sinclair had said, "He's a cinch, Jim, he can't break an egg. You'll murder him."

I was taken to Cleveland in a special car.

From the window, I watched the dying red sun throw various colors through the clouds above.

On the night I fought Shultz, a pugilist in the semi-windup had his skull fractured. Booked in the main attraction, I stood in my dressing-room door waiting for my name to be called.

The dying pugilist was carried by. His mouth was wide open, his eyes glared.

The promoter followed him. Seeing my expression, he said to me, "He'll be all right, just out a little too long."

I had seen men die. I knew better.

On every exchange with Schultz I saw Curly Gerhart's dying face.

To make matters worse, the lights kept going off. We would stand in darkness. When they flashed on, we attacked each other.

Beaten, I took my money quickly and left on a midnight train.

HONEST MONEY WAS HARD to find.

I needed it badly.

A young fellow in Saint Marys was beginning to be known as a pugilist.

I had an idea and took it to Billy Grims. Once a near lightweight champion in the days of the Terrible Terry McGovern, Grims was also looking for money.

He was tall, lithe, crafty, with unusual intelligence for a pugilist.

A weakness for liquor, drugs and women had finally unbalanced a brain that the fists of McGovern had loosened.

He knew the ring and its vast dishonesty.

He went to Saint Marys and became Fosnight's manager.

As the only pugilist from Saint Marys to become known, I waited in Akron.

I was soon matched with Fosnight.

The match had excellent financial possibilities.

Fosnight was German. I was Irish. These people were about equally divided in several adjoining counties.

We found two men known as gamblers who were anxious to bet money on a dead sure thing.

First, they must bet fifteen hundred each for Billy Grims and I. We had no money.

This would protect them as we would not double-cross if it cost so much money.

The next business was to sky-rocket the odds against me. That was easy. I had been seen drunk in Lima. The news spread.

Fosnight, under the management of so great a boxing master as Grims was improving each day.

At a banquet given, strangely enough, in my honor, I told a tale which might have some bearing on the fight.

The Kaiser had sent an officer to New Bremen, near Saint Marys. His job was to recruit and drill two thousand Germans and return with them to the Fatherland.

They were drilled for months. The Kaiser had glowing reports of them.

Three special trains were ordered.

They marched resplendently to the railroad station.

Something unforeseen occurred. A drunken Irishman would not let them board the train.

There was much excitement in the town.

I entered the ring under a fearful strain. I must be knocked out, and make it possible for an awkward pugilist of little experience to accomplish.

As Grims crawled through the ropes with Fosnight he was given a great ovation.

Always bitter against the town, I smiled.

Grims and I raised the tempo of the farce. We quarreled over Fosnight's bandaged hands. I objected to Grims being in his corner. When the audience grew restive for battle, I gave in on all points.

The fight started.

After the first round, my heart went cold. Fosnight hardly knew how to put up his hands. He floundered on his feet with fear in his eyes. When I feinted at him, he would retreat.

The audience began to hoot.

I glanced at Grims. He rubbed his forehead — a signal to mix it. I hardly knew how to begin. The audience hooted louder.

If I failed to be knocked out, we would be flat broke.

The thought paralyzed me.

Pulling my punches, holding back the force of them within three inches of Fosnight, I waded in.

He tried to fight back. I managed to make him connect several times with my jaw.

I was getting ready to go down when suddenly Fosnight sprawled on the floor. His legs began to twitch. The referee began to count.

I had failed to pull a punch.

The audience was deadly still.

The referee reached the count of seven.

I began to move quickly in the hope of confusing the issue.

The timekeeper sat near Grims, who "accidentally" touched the bell, jumped into the ring and dragged Fosnight to his corner.

My second, not in on the secret, protested. I protested with him. The round was not up.

Soon I magnanimously agreed to go on with the fight. The audience cheered my sportsmanship. In the next round Fosnight was still dazed from the punch.

I dragged him about, wrestled with him, and appeared overanxious to finish the fight.

For three rounds he was dead on his feet. I had to "carry" him.

There was one more round to go. In desperation, I threw blows in close, which slanted, unseen, on his shoulders.

He fought back wildly. While the audience was screaming, I went down — and out.

Getting up, I attacked Grims. That gentleman fought me off valiantly.

All bets were paid.

So strange is glory. Fosnight is still known in that section as the man who whipped me.

As I apparently regained consciousness in the dressing room, a German put his head in the door and yelled — "Hey, Chimmie — you vasn't the fellow dat kep' dose Chermans off de train, vas you?" He hurried away.

*

In San Francisco were many pugilists looking for matches. Each man was given a tryout before judges.

With a new name, I was given a semi-windup with Eddie Doran.

My trainer, whose chief claim to glory was that he had been knocked out by Stanley Ketchel, kept repeating,

"Look out for his right."

It was in the fourth round — I learned later.

A right caught me. I was unconscious until the next afternoon.

All events which preceded the fight, and everything which happened in the ring has been in eclipse all these years. I do not even remember dressing for the fight.

My opponent, fearful I had been killed, called upon me while I was still unconscious. A kindly note scrawled with pencil begged my forgiveness.

Some minutes after I opened my eyes I vaguely grasped the situation. The note began, "You were knocked out last night —"

Still shaky, I went to the lobby, and from there to the street.

My intention was to go to a nearby restaurant.

The city whirled about me.

I hurried back to the lobby.

A bell boy took me to the restaurant.

My jaw was so sore, I could not eat. I took milk through a straw.

Returning to the lobby I sat motionless for hours. My head stung with pain.

Near me, people discussed the results of the fight.

"What happened to — ?" one asked.

"He was knocked out in the fourth round. It was a darb. He went up in the air and came down all at once. Another beating like that and he'll end up in the insane asylum."

I winced at the thought.

THE END

A SHARP PAIN ENCIRCLED my head. My thoughts went helter-skelter. I could recall vaguely the cheering of the audience the night before. The lights went on in the hotel lobby. I had been unconscious twenty hours.

I groped a long time as though my brain had been submerged in alcohol. . . . My thoughts became more ordered.

Joe Gans could tell me how to drive the pain away. He was dead — a lunger in Arizona.

Some one had said when the Great Negro lay dying, "Start counting ten over him; then he'll get up."

Either no one counted, or Gans was too far gone to hear.

The Great Slavinsky was in Australia.

Our trails had crossed in Omaha two months before.

He had not changed in the years that ran between.

"You will go on and on, my boy, the ultimate is in you. You are the beginning and the end. Countless generations of dead Irish will have uttreance again in you. You will be their eyes, their guide, their beacon light in aeons yet to be."

He had said about the same words to Joe Gans.

"Did you ever hear what became of Chlorine?" I asked.

"Yes, my boy — I am proud to say — Chlorine has found her end of the rainbow in the valley of beauty by the purple sea of joy."

"She's not dead, is she?" I asked quickly.

"No indeed," he answered, "Not Chlorine,— there will be an eclipse upon the day she dies — no, no, indeed."

"Well — where is she?"

"Chlorine is now a nun," he said. "She went into a convent — only three people know." I glanced away.

The Great Slavinsky touched my shoulder. "But she would tell you — yes, yes, my boy,— the transcendent mystery of human life"— He looked about for an audience as of old; then, hurried in a half trot, out of my life forever.

Jessie had written to me in care of a sporting editor of a Cleveland newspaper.

She asked for five dollars. I sent her the money and never heard from her again.

Elva was dead. Her telegram: "What is the use of whipping the whole world and ending up a bartender," I still remembered.

She had said I would never succeed in the ring, had talked of sensibilities.

But why had I been knocked out when I was so anxious to get another start?

The pain quit circling my head and lodged above my eyes.

I accidentally touched my jaw. It stung tears to my eyes.

I was through with the ring. That was certain.

My share of the purse had been enough. By being frugal, I could write for six months.

I reached in my pocket for the money.

It was gone.

THE BEGINNING

A RAIN, MIXED WITH FOG, came over San Francisco Bay. My eyes followed lanes of light through which the sea-gulls flew. One lit on my window sill and tried to look inside. I watched the daring white and black hobo of the sea until it disappeared in the rain drenched fog.

Then I gazed at the wall paper upon which small birds were flying. I seemed to hear their wings flutter in the silent room.

I desperately wanted a drink of bourbon. I did not have a dime. I thought for a moment. I was a guest in the hotel. I picked up the telephone receiver. "Will you send up a bottle of Pebbleford to 441?"

"Right away."

A bellboy placed the liquor on the table and busied himself until I could think of his tip.

"I will see you later, lad," I said, glancing at his number, "I have no change."

He bowed himself out.

A heavy swig numbed the pain in my jaw. My brain became more alert.

Once again I tried to remember what happened in the ring. Before me came the man I had fought the night before. A well known bruiser, his appearance was of other memories. Long arms, broad and heavy shoulders, his sharp jaws bulged under his ears. I recalled thinking the afternoon of the fight — that if I had to throw blows at his jaws with bare hands, my knuckles would be cut to shreds.

I could hear my chief second saying, "Look out for his right — my God — there's murder in it." I wondered if that did not have something to do with my defeat.

I emptied the bottle as the ghost of Old Hughie Tully came into the room. "I just finished it in time, Granddad," I said.

Strong as an ocean liner, he stood before me. His presence was very real.

How could I explain my defeat to him? He could not be made to believe there was a man my weight on earth who could whip me.

I rolled the empty bottle under the bureau.

The bellboy brought more liquor.

Old Hughie Tully, as if sensing that I wanted to be alone, went back to his grave.

The ache in my jaw began to throb again. I reached for the whisky.

"Who the hell took that money? That was a dirty trick — to damn near get my head knocked into the lap of a spectator and be unconscious for hours and wake up broke."

A pain stung in my side. "He must have nearly murdered me at infighting," I thought. "What a man he must be!" I jerked my head as though an overhand right were ripping to my jaw.

"Well, I would get him next time. I would keep in close and leave my jaw in the dressing room."

I set the bottle on the table, "Oh well, to the devil with him. I would have treated him the same. I will be riding high when he is a punch goofy bum."

I felt ashamed.

I was on a level with the other leather sluggers I knew. None was big enough to admit there might be a stronger animal in the world than himself. But they were at least simple. It was the managers for whom I had contempt — and those sly eels who fattened on the bruises and the blood of better and braver men. Now and then, out of the welter of distortions, a man like Gans arose who, within him, had a bigger streak than Christ, in that he took the bitter days without a parable or a whine.

Putty ears, broken noses, wheels rolling in their empty and roaring heads, I had pity, even while slashing my way among them. For I knew what it was to hear a fat porpoise, when I was weathering a gale that would make a Spartan sick, yell instructions to me — how to handle my fists — how to win the fight.

When the bees are in a man's bonnet, and stinging their way in and out of his ears, he is a very gallant gentleman or a damn fool to take jaw splitting jolts, any one of which might break the oaken door of an insane asylum and let him in. But he takes them — with no talk of how he was hurt when the last gong sounds. Even while riding the bubble of a little wave, I saw much to understand and admire in my fellow bruisers.

Simple as writers of romance, they bragged of their success in order to seduce women. With brains and ribs jarred loose, they took what money the promoters and managers gave them and shambled down the eternal road, a stolid, a hopeless, a game and a scar-faced crew.

Often the butt of jokes by sporting writers, who wish to allay the pain in the wombs of their particular whoredom by feeling superior to somebody, they grin like the gaudy gorillas they are, happy that such a vast person had noticed them.

But that was all shoved behind me — no more boasting to beruffled girls of what a man I was.

It was time to move on — and up.

With the faculty of tracing clearly the miserable and

muddy rivulets that made up my being, I was not without disdain and understanding of myself. The slightest wind of circumstance had kept me from being a highway robber. The two brightest children in the orphanage who had competed with me for six years — one was a bookkeeper, the other a kitchen drudge.

That was enough.

"We grow out of things —" I thought.

It was my turn.

Chlorine used to sing a song of mine —

> *"Time was made for slaves —*
> *And violets for old whores' graves —"*

But I would need time — and to work like a slave, if I ever intended to write.

Chlorine took an easy way out — got under a Catholic awning when it was raining.

I would travel a harder road. I could take no other.

Once again my resolve weakened.

I stared at the birds on the wall. More serious thoughts followed. I might drift as I had been for years. Who cared? Elva was dead.

The thought thrummed in my head. *I cared!*

I had walked the streets of the cities, and the railroads of the nation, thinking of things to write until my head ached.

Jack London's name was a by-word. He had been on the road but a few months. I had been seven years. Who said he could write better than me?

Old Ibsen's face came before me, stern as an executioner's. My memory, tenacious as grief, retained his words, "Never be so mad as to doubt yourself."

Now was the time to try.

It would soon be morning. The long rest in oblivion had made me wakeful.

I looked about the room.

My alligator skin handbag, remnant of a flush day, was in a corner. A tailored suit hung in the closet.

I could get neither of them out of the room.

"Oh well — the landlord could have them — an even trade for the liquor and the rent."

A half dozen expensive silk neckties were about.

"I couldn't get a dime apiece for them."

In a silver frame, vivid as a blaze, was a miniature of Elva.

"I might pawn the frame — Elva would understand."

The one morsel of beauty I owned — I gazed in the luminous eyes.

"She doesn't seem dead," I thought. "The one woman — with her in the world — I had not been alone. Suppose she did feel superior — maybe she was. She had her side of things. I shouldn't expect her to tangle with a cyclone. She did have faith — she too was young." For the first time it came — the impression I might have made on her. Why blame her for being what she was? I did not blame myself.

Warm with desire, I put the miniature in my pocket and picked up a new set of boxing gloves.

My heart jumped.

"I can get a couple of dollars for these — they cost twelve. I could easily walk out of the lobby with them."

I threw them across my arm and went to a pawn shop.

The Jew looked at them.

"A dollar and a half."

"All right."

He rolled the money to me.

"What'll you give me for this?"

I handed him the miniature.

"Three dollars," he looked at me, "as it is."

"But no one would know the girl."

"Somebody buy quicker — she's purty."

"But without the girl — the frame alone."

He inspected it again.

"A dollar and a half."

"Make it two bucks."

"All — right."

As I took the picture from the frame, he rolled the silver dollars to me.

He looked at me for a second.

"Didn't I see you in the ring at Dreamland Rink the other night?"

"Not me — Brother — that was some other fellow."

He stared as if I were lying.

Jingling the money, I walked down Market Street.

The ferry boat whistles made giant music on San Francisco Bay, while the clouds above, silent empires of shadow, moved slowly.

"Suppose I had won — with my heart in the game, I might have been a great fighter. What then?"

The lion might as easily roar in pride over its mane.

Father Finn had given me a volume of Tennyson's poems when I was a dishwasher at Saint Xavier's.

A verse ran in my head.

> *"I held it truth, with him who sings*
> *To one clear harp in divers tones —*
> *That men may rise on stepping-stones*
> *Of their dead selves to higher things."*

There was no dead self. I was still a part of everything I had been. I was no more ashamed of it than in the future I would be proud of that which I might become.

If in some far day, an old whore, blinking her eyes at the sun, could feel a bond between us — that would be something.

If some hobo, stuttering in senility, could say — "Thataboy, Kid — you ain't the kind to desert me," that also would be something.

If I made good, I would merely be one the lightning had struck.

The chance was worth taking.

I would never be happy at anything else.

I threw my shoulders back, "I'll write or starve."
The sky was still full of clouds.
There were none in my heart.
I had made the Great Decision.

*

IN ten years my first book was published.

THE END

JIM TULLY CHRONOLOGY: LIFE AND WORKS

1886: Born June 3, near St. Marys, in Auglaize County, Ohio, the son of ditch digger James Dennis Tully and Maria Bridget "Biddy" (née Lawler) Tully

1892: Mother dies May 1 at age 35

1892–98: Spends six years at St. Joseph's Orphan Asylum in Cincinnati

1898–1900: Works through record-cold winter during a year and a half at the farm of Solomon Boroff in Van Wert County, Ohio

1901–07: Travels the country as a road kid and a hobo

1907: Leaves the road in June, settling in Kent, Ohio

1907–10: Works as a chainmaker and boxes as a lightweight

1910: Goes to work for Davey Tree in Kent (first writing published in *Davey Tree Surgeon's Bulletin*)

Marries Florence Bushnell in Kent on October 14

1911: First professional print appearance, the poem "On Keats' Grave," published June 27 in the *Cleveland Plain Dealer*

Son, Thomas Alton, born on August 3

1912: Settles with family in Los Angeles

1914: Meets early literary idol Jack London

1917: Daughter, Trilby Jeanne, born on November 13

1921: Separates from first wife, Florence, in November

1922: First book, *Emmett Lawler*, published by Harcourt, Brace

1923: Divorced from Florence on October 28

1924: Second book, *Beggars of Life*, published by A&C Boni

1924–25: Works for Charlie Chaplin

1925: Marries Margaret R. "Marna" Meyers on January 24

Completes The Life of Thomas H. Ince (never published)

Maxwell Anderson's adaptation of *Beggars of Life*, *Outside Looking In*, opens in New York with young James Cagney as Tully

1926: Hollywood novel, *Jarnegan*, published by A&C Boni

Black Boy, play written with Frank Dazey, opens in New York with Paul Robeson in the starring role

1927: *Circus Parade* published by A&C Boni

Completes *Life of Charlie Chaplin* (never published)

Twenty Below, play written with Robert Nichols, published by Robert Holden & Company (London)

1928: *Shanty Irish* published by A&C Boni

Play version of *Jarnegan*, adapted by Charles Beahan and Garrett Fort, opens on Broadway

Director William Wellman's film version of *Beggars of Life*, starring Louise Brooks, Wallace Beery, and Richard Arlen

1929: With Marna, travels to Ireland, Great Britain, and France, meeting George Bernard Shaw, H.G. Wells, and James Joyce.

1930: *Shadows of Men* published by Doubleday, Doran & Co.

Beggars Abroad published by Doubleday, Doran & Co.

Divorced from second wife, Marna, on February 26

Knocks out John Gilbert during February fight at Hollywood's Brown Derby

Featured in the MGM film *Way for a Sailor*, co-starring with John Gilbert and Wallace Beery

1931: *Blood on the Moon* published by Coward-McCann, Inc.

1932: *Laughter in Hell* published by A&C Boni

Film version of *Laughter in Hell* with Pat O'Brien

Purchases three-and-a-half acres on a peninsula point on Toluca Lake and construction begins on a stone and red-brick home he will call Tall Timbers

1933: Marries third wife, Myrtle Zwetow, on June 26

1934: Travels to Mexico City to interview artist Diego Rivera

1935: *Ladies in the Parlor* published by Greenbrrg

Writer Langston Hughes and boxer Henry Armstrong are guests for lunch at Tall Timbers

Son, Alton, pleads guilty to attacking a sixteen-year-old girl and is sentenced to San Quentin for one to fifty years

1936: *The Bruiser* published by Greenberg

Purchases a one-hundred acre ranch, Faraway Farm, near Canoga Park

1940: Sells Tall Timbers and moves to Faraway Farm

Daughter, Trilby, marries airplane mechanic Raymond Beamon

1941: Alton paroled and released from San Quentin

Suffers a heart attack a few days after Christmas

1942: *Biddy Brogan's Boy* published by Scribner's

1943: *A Dozen and One* published by Murray & Gee

1947: Dies June 22 at Cedars of Lebanon hospital

BOOKS BY JIM TULLY

Emmett Lawler (1922) (New York: Harcourt, Brace and Company, Inc.)

Beggars of Life (1924) (New York: Albert & Charles Boni)

Jarnegan (1926) (New York: Albert & Charles Boni)

Circus Parade (1927) (New York: Albert & Charles Boni)

Twenty Below (1927) with Robert Nichols, play, (London: Robert Holden & Co. Ltd.)

Shanty Irish (1928) (New York: Albert & Charles Boni)

Shadows of Men (1930) (New York: Doubleday, Doran and Company)

Beggars Abroad (1930) (New York: Doubleday, Doran and Company)

Blood on the Moon (1931) (New York: Coward-McCann, Inc.)

Laughter in Hell (1932) (New York: Albert & Charles Boni)

Ladies in the Parlor (1935) (New York: Greenberg: Publisher)

The Bruiser (1936) (New York: Greenberg: Publisher)

Biddy Brogan's Boy (1942) (New York: Charles Scribner's Sons)

A Dozen and One (1943) (Hollywood: Murray & Gee, Inc.)

Reprints of *Beggars of Life, Circus Parade, Shanty Irish*, and *The Bruiser* available from Black Squirrel Books, an imprint of Kent State University Press.

Reprints of *Shadows of Men* and *Blood on the Moon* available from Commonwealth Book Company, St. Martin, Ohio.

MAJOR ADAPTATIONS OF BOOKS BY JIM TULLY

Outside Looking In by Maxwell Anderson (play version of *Beggars of Life*, produced in New York in 1925)

Jarnegan by Charles Beahan and Garrett Fort (play version of Tully's novel, produced in New York in 1928)

Beggars of Life by Benjamin Glazer (film version of Tully's book, directed by William Wellman and released by Paramount Pictures in 1928)

Laughter in Hell (film version of Tully's novel, starring Pat O'Brien and released by Universal Pictures in 1932)